THE WAY RAIN FALLS

THE WAY RAIN FALLS

MATHEW MICHAEL HODGES

Whisk(e)y Tit
NYC & VT

Published in the United States by Whisk(e)y Tit: www.whiskeytit.com. If you wish to use or reproduce all or part of this book for any means, please let the author and publisher know. You're pretty much required to, legally.

ISBN 978-1-952600-00-5

Cover painting by Jonathan Butterick.

First Whisk(e)y Tit paperback edition.

To my parents for their unending love and support and to Eleanor Clancy for tea, card games and listening.

ADVANCE PRAISE FOR *THE WAY RAIN FALLS*

The Way Rain Falls is a marvelous debut novel that impressively situates itself in the vein of a Rhode Island minded Salinger. With wit, and a dash of the understated poetic, Mathew Michael Hodges presents a world where a flawed character can become sublime.

– David Tomas Martinez, author of *Post Traumatic Hood Disorder*

The Way Rain Falls is a sizzling novel that never lets up. Hodges deftly explores the consequences of pursuing a first love at a hundred miles an hour. The weight of betrayal, the pulse of regret. His characters breathe alcohol and spit testosterone, often inhabiting an electrifying world of fists, brews, lust, and loud music. Jim, our protagonist, admirably pursues intimacy on the wings of faith as he tries to dispel the symmetry between himself and his son-of-a-bitch father. Teatimes with his mother are a charming reprieve from the chaos, signaling the undercurrents of hope that bleed through Jim's season of pain.

– Jonathan Starke, author of *You've Got Something Coming* and founding editor of *Palooka*

Jim "The Diff" Diffin is indifferent. To women, a career path, whatever (a word rife for the time period the novel is set in, often evoking the spirit of Douglas Copeland's Gen X-centric work). A languid lothario who grooves to Beastie Boys' "Girls" in between loosely pining for ones that don't really have an interest in him (he'll find another). The type of guy who rightly declares, "Fuck a real job." A sentiment befitting Jim's seemingly apathetic universe. Thanks to Hodges's deft prose, our antihero comes to life as a shining example of the last semi-pure human need: to love and be loved. The problem, as usual, is that when he actually gives someone a chance, it ends up feeling both unshakably unrequited... and synthetic. Struggling with the notion of being alone and continuing to "sow his oats" versus staying in a loveless (and, more to the point, sexless) relationship, Jim faces the same challenging decision we must all reconcile with at some point: Is it better to be alone than lonely with the one you love?

– Genna Rivieccio, Editor-in-Chief of *The Opiate* magazine

The Way Rains Falls presents Jim Diffin, a protagonist who is worried about becoming the genetic shadow of his father, and it follows him through his own self-identity and his follies of young love. It's a beautifully engaging book, offering nostalgic details of New England life and the brutal realities of growing up. I loved every page.

– Brendan Praniewicz, author of *Beat It*

In *The Way Rain Falls*, Mathew Michael Hodges gives the reader an unflinching, gritty, booze-fueled look at the adolescent American male in his natural habitat: clubs, house parties and bedrooms. Through this fast-paced narrative, Hodges allows us to explore the meaning of heartbreak, friendship, family and the quest to find meaning in it all. His characters are authentic voices that allow the reader to revisit a moment in time when all we wanted was to find out who we were and who was there to love us at the end.

– Joseph Kane, author of *Sarafish*

PART I

WINTER

"A man that is pressed to death, and might be eased by more weights, cannot lay those more weights upon himself: he can sin alone, and suffer alone, but not repent, not be absolved, without another."

— John Donne

1

When Jim Diffin arrived at St. Brendan's, he wondered if there was any point. He hadn't come for a full confession. He never did. A slight breeze picked up as he crossed the cracked pavement. This church in Riverside, Rhode Island might have been beautiful in some people's eyes; sixties space age had infected the architect's brain when he designed the building. Three blades of dull concrete thrust into the sky, holding several bells that rang and clattered in discord. Below the bell tower, curved the low, squat church itself. The fallout friendly elementary school built in the fifties hunkered nearly on top of it, looming several floors higher, a massive red brick embarrassment. Altogether the church grounds looked like a lame cousin to the beautiful cathedral in downcity Providence.

Every time he came here for absolution, for reconciliation, Jim committed what one might call lies of omission. Then again, there were some things he wasn't sure he felt ready to confess, and he saw no point in apologizing for something he knew he would do again.

Once inside the church, he slid the black, velveteen curtain aside, ducked into the confessional and sank onto the cold, wooden bench. The slot cracked open, half-revealing a priest. Jim blessed himself and began, "Bless me, father for I have sinned. It has been three months since my last confession..."

❧

A few nights ago—Valentine's Day. He drove his beat-up, four-cylinder, 1985 Dodge Omni: hurtling down the highway, steering wheel convulsing, car body trembling at speeds exceeding ninety miles per hour. He tried to live his life like this. Pursuing only happiness and pleasure. That's where women or girls usually fit in. He always believed monogamy was best left for marriage and that marriage was the end of the highway. Get what you can, while you can, until something better comes along.

In the last few years, he'd met mostly success along these lines, although he wasn't the most handsome man. If he let his dry, wiry hair grow, people called him brillo head. He tended to talk too much, too loudly and drink himself into an obnoxious oblivion. And if anybody cared to look closely, one ear sat higher on his head by a few fractions of an inch.

But something about him attracted women. Confidence seemed to rule his every action; it appeared he did whatever he liked, not fearing consequences or scorn. In a world filled with men creating new lines and new moves to "pick up chicks" he stood out by not trying so hard.

He had just been out with Susan Prima, a younger girl

he'd been dating for a few months. He got her home in time for her midnight curfew, before speeding off to his parents' house where he changed into club clothes: loose-fitting khakis, a black pair of shoes designed for skaters, an Irish Republic national team soccer jersey and his shiny, quasi-expensive watch. He said, "Good night!" to his parents and ran out the door before they could ask where he was going.

He drove out of suburban Riverside and onto the Veterans Memorial Parkway overlooking Narragansett Bay. Across the bay, the lights of Providence glittered. Only four buildings graced the city's humble skyline from here. The little capital would be going to sleep in a few hours, everything shut down not long after two a.m. He pushed down harder on the accelerator.

ঌ

Once in the downtown club, he bobbed his head and bounced his shoulders to the bass-heavy beats. The heat of the place made it feel like breathing through a thick blanket, and a tenuous mist hung from a recent fog-machine blast. He decided to take a leak and hope for cooler air in the bathroom. The d.j. spun White Zombie, and Jim mouthed the lyrics as he waded through gyrating bodies, searching for his friends.

He liked showing up like this. It made him feel like a loner, answering to nobody but himself, on his own schedule. He hadn't even made plans to meet up with his friends. They'd simply be here on any given Saturday night. Still, he worried a little that he'd show up solo, and they'd have left or decided not to come.

In the well-lit men's room, stickers of striving or long ago fed-up local bands papered the walls, urinals and stalls. He pissed, washed his hands and, with no paper towels left, dried them with toilet paper. Wiping fragments of the flimsy tissue from his hands, he drifted back into the pounding rhythm of the dance floor.

He wove a path through dancing couples, scantily clad sluts and hard-up jock types, catching more than a few dirty looks with each misstep. When he found himself near the door again, he stopped to look up at the stage, hoping to glimpse one of DeGawain's Hawaiian shirts or plaid numbers.

A sudden heavy force struck him from behind; he nearly fell on his face.

Somebody hung on his back, and he clung to the combatant's legs hoping to gain some advantage. Then he heard his friend Pow howl into his ear. He tossed the body off his back, turned around, socked him in the chest, then clasped his hand with a laugh.

"You scared the shit outta me, Pow," he shouted.

Thomas Powell went by Pow which was short for his last name and an appropriate nickname for him. From the usual look of Pow's eyes and his lackadaisical demeanor, he gave most people the first impression of always being stoned, though he never smoked. But he burned his energy in spurts that seemed reckless, giving the nickname "Pow" more currency, and those who met him in that state thought he was totally crazy; and maybe he was, a little—a seeming hedonist who wouldn't drink or do any drugs and was skeptical about the actual existence of anything.

Chris Cornell's voice, backed up by his Seattle grunge band Soundgarden, boomed over the crowd, singing about a black hole sun that would come and wash away the rain

Pow spread his arms wide, bent his knees and arched his back. "I'm sorry, man," he said with what sounded like the beginnings of a laugh in his voice. As always,

Pow wore a dingy old T-shirt and one of the two pairs of stained, blue jeans he owned, which were both several sizes too large. Recently, he'd started keeping his stringy, blonde hair in dozens of short braids with brightly colored elastics.

A slender-bodied, young blonde with high cheekbones and an enthusiastic grin hid behind him. Pow's smile faded and he said, "This is Helen. Helen, this is Diffin." Helen smiled and took his hand. Then she awkwardly attached herself to Pow's right biceps.

"Come on, homes, the crew is up on the balcony," Pow said and turned with Helen. Pow led them to the windows that overlooked Westminster St.

In the darkness of the balcony, near the foggy, expansive windows stood a solitary sofa where DeGawain slouched in his Salvation Army wardrobe—orange and blue Hawaiian shirt with brown cargo shorts, all part of his forced lack of style. He shopped almost exclusively at Salvation Army, looking for plaid, bowling, or Hawaiian shirts.

On either side of him sat two tired or bored, young bleached blondes. Jim slid onto the couch's worn arm and shook DeGawain's hand. Pow drifted off with Helen to the small dance space on the balcony.

Pow ground against Helen. Jim smiled. He never hung out with Pow back at Hendricken, their all-boys Catholic high school, mostly because Pow had always seemed like a stupid zombie, but he recently came off his meds for attention deficit disorder and immediately became "Pow," instead of Thomas Powell. This was the first time Jim had seen him with a girl.

DeGawain said something Jim couldn't quite hear above the crashing music. He leaned lower over the girl with the longer blonde hair and motioned for DeGawain to repeat himself. "I said, this is Diana..." DeGawain nodded toward the long-haired blonde. In the dark light, he could barely see the girl wearing a green, hooded sweatshirt and so he barely looked at her.

"And this is Nina," DeGawain shouted, his mouth close to Jim's earlobe; he winced and rubbed his ear, then DeGawain's lips said, "I'm sorry." He shook the girls' hands.

Suddenly, as though waking from a slumber, DeGawain jumped up and jerked his arm. DeGawain strode across the balcony floor, knocking into erratically grooving hips and shoulders. Jim snaked his way after him, and they stopped at the railing overlooking the dance floor.

"Did you smell some food or something, big guy?"

"Ha. Real funny. I'm looking for Panza. Last time I saw him, he had just about snagged a real whale."

"Huh?"

DeGawain had also been at Hendricken. He had been one of the "band-geeks." Jim didn't hang with him then, either. Marcus DeGawain, currently a culinary student at Johnson and Wales University, delivered pizzas. He loved ska and went out of his way to find the most talented, least popular bands to listen to. He also had the sort of posture one might expect from an erect rat. All the same, Jim loved hanging out with him. DeGawain was never self-conscious, never skirted away from a brawl to protect a friend and he was funny as hell.

"Look! There he is. Man, that's one fat chick. I think he might win this time."

"You guys still playing that old game?"

DeGawain didn't answer; he nodded his buzzed, bumpy, egg-shaped skull and exposed his crooked teeth in a wide grin. "You gonna get your groove on tonight or what, man? Running out of time here."

"Yeah. But ya know I need some good songs or at least one really good one before I can get out there."

"I hear that, but I'm going down to rub elbows with the masses and find myself the winning blimpy."

"You're crazy."

His bulky buddy jaunted down the steps, and Jim lost sight of him. He needed to get on the dance floor, too, but he wasn't quite feeling the energy. In the crowd below heads bobbed and arms swayed. From where he stood it seemed that hot ladies overran the dance floor. He needed a good song to start him up, turn him over and get him running in dance mode. The speakers blared The Mighty Mighty Bosstones singing about knocking on wood, and he caught a glimpse of DeGawain skanking it up—not quite his scene.

Then, it happened. It always happened. This time it carried light, bouncy sounds, similar to a xylophone; the d.j. had selected The Beastie Boys' "Girls." He was on the dance floor before the first lyrics came across the speakers. He danced with the unschooled, random, gusto rarely seen on Lupo's dance floor—most people either danced well and confidently or merely bounced as inconspicuously as possible. His head rolled, his hips pumped, his feet shuffled and slid, his arms went wherever they needed to go for balance, and the whole time his lips formed the words of every lyric. When the song finally ended, he looked cursorily around to make sure he hadn't made too much of a spectacle. Nobody gawked at him, so he felt he hadn't gaffed, but he had found his rhythm for the night.

After that he lost himself in the beats of each song. But even as sweat ran in rivulets down his ribs and face with the exertion of dancing, it occurred to him how much easier it would be to really cut loose if he'd had a few drinks first. Nevertheless, he scanned the crowd for a girl. With so many to choose from and with so many looking like total sluts, he wasn't sure where to start. He moved in on a short-haired brunette whose toned, flat belly seemed to slither ever so sensuously with the beat of "The Humpty Dance" thundering across the dance floor.

"How's it going?" he asked with a wide-eyed smile.

"Not bad!" the girl shouted, leaning toward him.

"What's your name?"

"Alexandra! And you?"

"Jim! So, who are you here with?"

"My girlfriends, Theresa and Erin."

"That's cool. Where are you from?"

"Rehoboth. How 'bout you?"

He slid in closer to answer. "East Providence. Do you go to school around here?"

"Nah, I dropped out."

"Where did you go?"

"LaSalle."

A high school drop-out—bright one. He no longer cared to know any more about her.

"Wanna dance?" he asked. She nodded.

He grabbed her waist and pulled her close. Within seconds she was practically riding his leg and, after a minute, she literally humped it. At this point he slid his hands to her ass; she didn't resist, in fact she smiled. He held the back of her head as he pulled her in for a nice deep kiss. She tasted like a sweaty ashtray, but again he didn't care. Lathered in sweat, she rode his leg, and he bumped it up and down with the beat. Alexandra caressed his sides, and he ventured to grab her chest. She leaned back as he held her semi-firm C cups, and before he thought about it, he had his tongue on her belly. She didn't flinch, instead she remained leaned back as he tongued her pierced, sweat-salted belly button.

When a slower song came on, he asked, "Do you wanna sit down for a minute?"

"Yeah, I could use some water and a seat."

He went to the large, orange water cooler the bartenders had put out on the bar, got two waters, and they sat on one of the couches lining the back wall. They exchanged phone numbers, then groped each other mercilessly, kissing and hardly coming up for air until the music stopped, and a booming voice came over the speakers, "Closing time! Everybody out!" Alexandra and he separated to find their respective friends, but promised to call one another.

He found DeGawain, Pow and the girls standing outside the club. A horse-mounted officer shouted at everyone to keep it moving, but nobody seemed to have seen Panza recently.

"Do you think he actually went home with his fatty?" Jim asked.

DeGawain shrugged. "I don't think so. But you never know."

Some kind of commotion caught his eye around the entrance to the alley at the end of the building. The thick crowd blocked any clear view, but the shouting and shoving hinted at a brewing fight. He wandered away from his friends without a word and quickly clove through the crowd. As he neared the circle, Panza backed into the alley, hands raised as if in protest. The large girl Panza had been grinding in the club shouted something from behind three punk-rock guys. While still within three steps of the group, he could only watch as a skin-head stepped up and cold-cocked Panza.

He rushed ahead, throwing elbows into random people in his way and dove-tackled the skin-head. The bony, leather covered frame beneath him took the brunt of the fall to the pavement, but soon his ears, neck and ribs were pounded from above. He kept the skin-head beneath him, throwing rabbit punches into his sides and savagely head-butting his bald-scalp. He didn't even notice when the assault from above had ceased and didn't realize that the hands pulling him off the punk were Pow's. He bit the arms trying to pull him off, then he almost took a swing at the guy until he recognized the braids flapping on Pow's head.

"Sorry, Pow," he said, laughing.

Pow shrugged with a half-smile of understanding. The skin-head scrambled off, cursing them as he ran to find his friends who had fled as soon as Pow and DeGawain showed up.

Panza sat on the cold, wet ground, one hand over his face. Jim stepped over and gave Panza a hand up. Panza didn't say anything, but his face communicated wonder; it seemed to have never occurred to him that he could be upsetting anybody with his little "blimpy" competition, or that anyone could ever want to hurt him. Panza had always been the clown, had always gotten away with saying and doing things.

DeGawain looked at Panza's face and rubbed his hands together. "All right, who's down for drinking tonight at Panza's?" DeGawain asked, knowing that Mr. and Mrs. Panza had been gone for a week on vacation and weren't expected back for a few more days.

Panza smiled. Jim said, of course. Pow and the girls backed out.

"Well then, time for the real drinkers to put on their drinking shoes and get rambling," DeGawain said.

Once the three of them arrived at the house, they wasted no time cracking open a bottle of Myer's dark rum and throwing back shots. DeGawain and Panza chased their shots with Coke. Jim chased his with Myer's. The booze flowed at the breakneck rate that only underage drinkers, trying to prove themselves to each other and get their livers ready for future, legal drinking can appreciate.

After they'd lost count of their drink tallies, drinking games came into play. Panza found some cards, and a few rounds of "asshole" turned into many more. The next thing anybody realized was the sunrise. With the sun lightening up the playing table, Panza slipped into his room; DeGawain found a couch, and Jim settled into an armchair with dirty clothes on it. That ended the long "night," but "morning" came three hours later with Jim heaving in the bathroom and Panza soon having sympathetic symptoms into the sink. The noise awoke DeGawain, who Jim could see standing in the dining room with a perfect view of both sufferers, chuckling, probably from pride in himself for not being sick and at the disgrace of his friends.

❧

The hard wood of the confessional soon warmed beneath his jean-covered back-side. After explaining that it had been three months since his last confession, he did his best to rattle off "An Act of Contrition:" "O my God, I am sorry for having offended you and I hate all my sins, because I dread the loss of heaven and the pains of hell. But most of all because I have offended you, my God, who are all good and deserving of all my love. I resolve with the help of your grace, to confess my sins, to do penance and to amend my life. Amen."

The priest, who had waited patiently for him to recite the words, now shifted his weight. "What would you like to confess, my son?"

Many things leaped into his mind. He knew that his life should be amended, but he had no intention of confessing without a real repentance. So, he breathed deeply and confessed to the one thing he really wished he hadn't done.

"I struck someone, father."

"What did this person do that you felt the need to strike them?" the priest asked curiously.

"He cold-co—he punched my friend in the face, father."

"You were protecting or avenging this friend?"

He never liked when the priests had interesting questions to ask; he wanted to confess, get his penance and leave. "I think maybe a bit of both, father. I saw him do it, and it made me really angry, but I also wanted to stop him from hitting my friend again. Plus, he had two friends with him."

"Who won the fight?"

He rolled his eyes, felt guilty about it and hoped the priest couldn't see him better than he could see the priest through the screen. "We did, father."

"Well, my son. Jesus doesn't want us to stand idly by and watch the people we care about suffer. What you did was a selfless act, my son."

He shifted awkwardly on the wooden seat from what he took as a compliment.

"But even so, it was partially motivated by anger, and so I will assign you penance and absolve you of your sins."

❧

A lonely silence filled the house when he got home. He missed going to confession as a child and telling the priest how he'd yelled at his mother or hit his brother and then leaving with the knowledge that he'd made a full confession, that if he died at that moment, he would go straight to heaven. The powerful peace of mind that it lends even a child now eluded him every time he went to confession. He was a sinner, but he figured he could at least work on the things he really did feel bad about and maybe he'd get himself into purgatory with his partial confessions.

Inside his parents' darkened bedroom, his mother lay on her back, clutching her rosary beads below her breasts. After yanking the door closed again, Jim retreated up the narrow hall to the linoleum-floored kitchen. Moving the bills and other assorted junk mail on the table, he made space for two seats. He put the fire on beneath the kettle, pulled two mugs out from the brown, particle-board cupboard and set a tea bag in each one. His mother emerged from the hallway, squinting against the light.

He sat down to tea with her.

"So, where did you go?" she asked.

"Nowhere," he shrugged. "Sorry to interrupt you like that, ma."

She shrugged, too and waved away his comment as she raised the hot cup to her lips. "So, what's new with you, James?"

"Not much." He hadn't meant to say that. He waited a moment before broaching the topic. "The other night Susan bought me tickets to a Broadway play up in Boston. Valentine's Day present."

"What did you get her?"

"Nothing." He paused for a moment then added, "Well, I did take her out to dinner."

"Wow, big spender," she said with her overstated irony. "You know that was really nice of her. You might get her a little more than a dinner for that." She got up and breezed into the kitchen. She never could sit still; she probably had adult A.D.D.

"Yeah, she's really nice," he said, sipping his tea.

She clanked a dish down and placed herself between the dining room and the kitchen, looking at him. "But you don't really like her much, do you?"

"Nah. It makes me feel really bad, too. I mean, this girl is the nicest girl I've ever dated and nothing, no feelings, no emotions, just blah. She's fun and cool and smart and generous, but I can't fall for her." He rubbed his forehead. "I think I'm incapable of love."

"You don't want to fall in love, do you?"

"I don't know. I guess I feel like even if I don't want to love her I should because she's so great. Ya know?"

"She's not the right girl, James. When you meet her, you'll know." She swooped back into the kitchen; the sound of dishes and silverware clinking and clanking into order reverberated from the kitchen.

She had an awful way with clichés. He felt no better.

"Well, I did meet a new girl last night," he said, remembering Alexandra, the sexy high school drop-out. Probably he wouldn't like her any more than Susan. He still hadn't decided if he'd even call her. "Is it wrong of me to date a new girl before Susan and I go to this play?"

"What? You're not married, are you? Don't worry about it, play the field, have fun while you're young." Again with the helpful clichés.

He felt emotionless, hollow, but at least things were looking up. He'd met a new girl, and his mother had given him her blessings to double-dip.

2

Jim typed in the password, hit enter and waited while the modem rapidly dialed the seven digits and responded with a busy signal. The modem tried to hook-up with his internet server again as he got up to fetch a soda and some chips; it always took forever to log on.

It was Monday of the following week, and he didn't have class all day, so he'd slept until noon. It was around five p.m. as he passed the living room where his father sat watching his big screen television. The kitchen beyond had a small island in the middle, which barely left room for the refrigerator and the oven to open. His mother finished pouring a soda into his father's tall glass and put the drink down saying, "So, what're you up to?"

"Nothing much, ma. About to sign on-line, check my email and stuff."

"Doing email, huh? Well, you better be getting straight A's then."

He shrugged as he opened the cupboards and

snatched a bag of chips. His mother delivered the soda, and Jim poured himself a glass, too. As he walked back past the living room, he heard his father grumble, "What'd he say he was up to?"

"Email, honey," his mother responded.

He heard his father's displeased grunt, then returned to the den and his computer. When he sat down in his chair, he found he'd been logged on while he was away and that DeGawain was signed on, screen name Skaman78. He sent an instant message, and a new window opened.

> Diff07: 'sup, fat man?
> Skaman78: Not much u?
> Diff07: nothing.   my parents are illin' that I don't study enough. I can't stand living here for much longer
> Skaman78: I hear that. But I can't fuckin' afford an apartment.
> Diff07: yeah, but if one of us got one, then nobody else would need one. We could all chill together.
> Diff07: I mean you could come over here, but my parents'd be breathing down our necks.
> Skaman78: word. Listen, you know what i've been thinking we should do?
> Diff07: what?
> Skaman78: we should start meetin' up for lunch someplace and shit. I don't do shit most of the day, and neither do you, right?
> Diff07: well, after last semester's performance my parents are making me go part-time to make the g.p.a. go up. So, to answer the question, no I don't do shit most of the day.
> Skaman78: what r u doing tomorrow afternoon?

Diff07: dude, that's like the one day I actually have class. well, one of two.
Skaman78: when's good?
Diff07: Wednesday I got work and then class again on Thursday. Call it Friday?
Skaman78: a'ight dude. Where and what time?
Diff07: anyfuckin' time, anyfuckin' place
Skaman78: how about noon at the Arcade downtown?
Diff07: shit, sounds like a plan
Skaman78: nice. a'ight I gotta bounce now. see you Friday.
Diff07: peace, kid.

He closed the dialogue window and checked his buddy list. Nobody he really knew on-line, just people he'd met on-line. He didn't feel like talking to any of them. He thought he'd write some email to his brother to waste time. His older brother William was a senior at Northwestern in Chicago. William hated being called Will, Willie, Bill, Billy or any other abbreviation imaginable. So, of course, their mom and dad liked calling him Willie and Bill respectively. Neither of them could win with their parents. He liked being called Jim, but his mother loved the name James and so did his dad. Years ago, he and William had given up the battle with their parents to be called what they wanted.

He typed away, bitched about the parents for a paragraph then typed about his success with Susan on Valentine's Day, how she wasn't mad about not getting any tangible present and how, after her curfew, he went out and had a little adventure meeting a promising new girl. Alexandra might be a waste of time, but he might get some. He and William had told each other their tales of conquest with the opposite sex and sent each other stories of drunken adventure since Jim started college the year before. He signed the email: peace, bro. Then, he clicked the send icon.

His soda glass sat on the desk next to him, empty. He'd had enough chips and didn't feel like signing off-line yet. A cup of coffee was the thing. He got up leaving his dirty glass on the desk, but bringing the bag of chips with him to brew some coffee.

As he passed the living room his mother called out, "James!"

He veered into the room with its dark green leather couches, worn, old, brown carpet and tightly drawn, vinyl-lined drapes. The single bright spot in the room was the glowing television which had his father's brooding brow entranced.

"Jim, we're wondering how your grades are doing. We haven't seen you doing any homework. You slept all day, probably hung over on Sunday and then spent the whole night watching TV. And then slept the day away again today!" his mother said. "We really do expect A's if you're sitting around this much."

"Well," he said, shifting his weight to one side. "I don't have much to do. I've got a paper due tomorrow. But I'm gonna do that once I get home from work tonight."

"Tomorrow? It's due tomorrow?" She pressed her palm to her forehead. "And have you done any work on this paper yet?" she asked.

His father turned down the television.

"No," he said, thrusting his hands in his pockets. "It's no big deal. I can bang it out tonight."

"Another all-nighter?" she asked with her head tilted and her eyes widened. She seemed to want him to speak up, but he half-shrugged a form of assent.

"Well, you better be banging out A papers." She cast a glance at his father. "You can't keep burning the candle at both ends like this. What time did you get home Saturday night anyhow? Or did you come rolling in Sunday morning?"

He stood in the middle of the living room, his palms sweating, trying to remember..

"Honey," his dad said curtly, pleadingly. The one thing his dad was good for, protecting some of his private life.

"Your mother's right, Jim," he said, looking away from the television. "You damn well better come home with A's. We won't have another semester like last year. You do that shit and you're done. On your own, you hear me?"

He was never sure if questions like that demanded a reply. Reply and his dad might yell at him for interrupting, don't reply and he'd bite Jim's head off for a response. This time Jim grimaced and nodded.

"Well, do you hear me?" his dad's voice rose along with his posture.

"Yeah," he answered.

"Yeah?" his dad questioned, mockingly.

He clenched the rolled-up portion of the chips bag, which crinkled in protest.

"Yes, sir," he spoke with a moment of eye-contact.

"Well, you better stop wasting time with that on-line business," he said, easing back into the couch cushion. "We didn't buy it for you to loaf around on. It's a research tool. You're supposed to be doing research with it."

"I do, though," he pleaded.

His dad smacked the couch cushion with his remote. "Don't talk back to me, damn it."

He stood there in the darkened silence, broken only by the television, waiting to be dismissed.

"Now get outta here. Do something useful," his father said with a wave of his hand and a readjusting of his couch-potato posture.

Jim drifted out of the living room toward the kitchen where he threw down the chips, angrily separated a coffee filter and scooped some ground coffee. As he readied the coffee, his heart pounded with angry adrenaline. Every time, it got harder for him to keep from blowing up at his father.

He could hardly look the man in the eye. Sometimes his father's eyes were cool blue pools of corny jokes and simple favors, but lately he knew them as a cold blue. The color of shadowed glaciers, yet with an intensity behind them that seemed to burn. And his mother. She never came to his defense. Even on matters they had privately discussed and agreed upon. She would never contradict that man. It seemed to him that the coffee percolated sympathetically with the same gurgling heat he felt in his heart. To calm himself, he crept past the living room and back to the den. When he sat down and bumped the mouse, the screensaver blinked away, revealing an instant message dialogue box.

> Helen939: Is this Jim?
> Helen939: Jim, this is Helen from Lupo's r u there?

Not knowing how long ago the message had been sent, but with a thrill of excitement, he added the name to his buddy list and learned that she was still logged on. The anger washed away by the thrill of flirtation; he typed rapidly.

> Diff07: Helen, Jim here. Was making coffee.
> I'm back. u there?

A long pause filled him with a moment of anticlimactic let down. He knew Helen was supposedly Pow's girl, and he was proud of Pow for getting with such a hottie, but he couldn't help himself. Even though she probably got his screen name from Pow, maybe even sat beside Pow as she typed.

> Helen939: Hey, how's the coffee?
> Diff07: still brewin' I think. What's new with u?
> Helen939: nothing. What'd you do after the club last week?
> Diff07: not much. Went to Panza's and drank till the sun came up
> Helen939: hahahahaha. u r crazy.
> Diff07: maybe
> Helen939: so, what did you think of Diana?
> Diff07: Who?
> Helen939: The long blonde-haired girl. She was with her sister with short hair, Nina
> Diff07: Didn't look at her, y?
> Helen939: She was lookin' at u though
> Diff07: oh, really? And what did she think?

Suddenly, he felt a bit let down. Helen hadn't contacted him for her benefit, but for her friend's. As suddenly as that realization hit him another followed. This girl, Diana, apparently wanted him. He couldn't recall her face. Not a good sign, but any decent-looking girl always became more attractive when she wanted you.

> Helen939: she thinks you're hot

And there it was. This was worth looking into.

> Diff07: oh really?
> Helen939: She thinks you look like that guy Marc from Blink182
> Diff07: Who the fuck's Blink182?
> Helen939: This little punk band from San Diego she's really into. she really likes u. thinks you're funny, too.
> Diff07: how'd she have time to decide that?
> Helen939: I dunno. she just did. so, what do think?
> Diff07: Well... I'm game.
> Helen939: you should email her. She's goddess339
> Diff07: ok. I think I will.
> Helen939: good. I gotta go now. Bye
> Diff07: a'ight. peace, kid.

He watched her name disappear from his buddy list, then he added goddess339. She wasn't on-line either. He sat back and smiled. Then his dad stepped into the room, sighed and sat down next to him at his larger desk.

"Still on-line, huh?"

"Yup," he answered.

"Your mother and I aren't kidding, you know."

"I know."

Silence fell like a heavy sound of its own on his ears and slid down his back and shoulders. He could hear his dad getting angry.

"You know, but you don't care, do you?"

"I care, dad. I'm almost done," he said feeling like he needed to reply to that insult.

"You're always almost something. Always on your schedule, your time. You don't care what anybody else wants or needs."

The computer said, good-bye as he logged off, and he shut down the system.

"Nothing to say to that, huh?" his dad asked.

"Dad, I don't know what to say. I don't think that's how it is, though."

"No, you just don't think at all."

With a sigh, he stood up, flipped off the power switch on his computer and stepped toward the door.

"You going to walk away from me while I'm talking to you now? Huh?" his dad spoke with a deep menacing tone.

"I gotta go to work," he sighed as he left the room.

He sped further down the hall to his bedroom, grabbed his bag and headed back up the hallway, past the living room and gripped the door handle to leave the house.

"Jim? Leaving already?" his mother called.

"Gotta go to work, mom. Later."

"What about this coffee?" he heard his mother say as he swung the door shut behind him.

3

"Hey, fucker. Last time I saw you, you were bowed down to the porcelain god with the reverence and devotion of a true heathen." The first words out of DeGawain's mouth as he stood on the steps of the arcade, Weybossett side—the February air chilling his words into a fog.

The arcade was one of the nation's oldest malls. Located in downtown Providence, it rose three floors, with balconies overlooking the cramped, downtown streets and wide, stone stairway entrances on both Westminster and Weybossett Streets. Johnson and Wales University had bought the mall and converted it into a food court.

"Heathen, eh? If you'd felt my agony, you'd have put me into the category of the Beatitudes. Happy are those who live in pain, for they shall find comfort, or some crap," he said as he firmly grasped DeGawain's hand.

"Whatever, Diffin."

"Man, I'm serious. Do you know what it's like to wretch for over an hour on an empty stomach?"

"Dude, we're here to eat, and I'm not about to let you ruin my appetite." DeGawain waved him through the double doors into the arcade.

"Right, like anything I say could ruin your appetite. If that were the case, you'd always have me around. You could call it the Diffin diet," he said, then burst into maniacal laughter.

DeGawain giggled his little girl giggle and said, "You've got a point there, guy."

They discussed food options before splitting up. He headed to a deli and DeGawain to a pizzeria. The usual monotony had dominated the previous weekdays—classes, homework, avoiding parents, work, more classes, more homework. Friday was like a guest he'd been expecting to arrive, but who showed up three hours late—leaving him exasperated, yet relieved.

His sandwich was ready first, so he signaled for DeGawain to meet him up on the second-floor balcony. He sat down, took his first bite and thought what a great idea meeting here had been. All types of people wandered up and down the aisles and stairs; the old warped floors like tiny swells, the whole place exuded antiquity rejuvenated by fresh businesses and new customers with him and DeGawain sitting in the public privacy of it, free from parental harangues and incidental eavesdropping.

"So," DeGawain said, startling him. "I haven't talked to you or seen you on-line since like Monday, guy. How've you been? What's new with 'The Diff?'" he asked, easing into his seat.

"Same old shit, man. Well, the fucking parents really piss me off. I've been thinking how nice it is to be out of their reign for a little while. I need to get the fuck out."

DeGawain expressed his doubts about whether he could even afford his own place. He explained to

DeGawain that he'd spend less money on going out, since he mostly went out to get away from his parents' house. Besides that, everyone would have an open invitation to chill at his place. He'd even give his boys their own set of keys.

"Well, you gotta get yourself a real job then, guy. No more of this lifeguard bull, sittin' on your ass, working ten damn hours a week. Hell, I go to classes, work forty hours a week and still live at home." DeGawain rammed half his pizza slice into his mouth.

"Fuck a real job," Jim said, watching the lunch crowd shoulder and elbow along the narrow walkway.

"Then you're stuck at home, guy," DeGawain mumbled through half-eaten pizza.

"Yeah," Jim said, catching a whiff of coffee from the nearby donut shop. "Looks like we'll have to keep on partying. Too bad huh?"

DeGawain furrowed his brows sullenly. "Yeah. Sucks to be us, huh? Somebody's gotta do it though, I guess," he smiled.

"Yeah, no shit," he said. A very short, black skirt containing a tight, pert ass strode past them. "Hey, look at that ass."

They watched as the girl disappeared into the crowd.

"Man, you could see her panty-line," DeGawain sighed.

"I know," he said, sipping his soda. "That shit was almost a thong, too."

"Nice." DeGawain said, dragging out the soft 'c'. "I need a girl, damn it."

"Headaches, man, headaches," he proclaimed. "Or at least mine is becoming that right now." Recently, Susan had been acting aloof at work. He thought it might have something to do with Valentine's Day. But when he asked her what'd been bothering her, she'd said, "You know what you did."

"Uh oh. Tell the doctor what's ailing your relationship," DeGawain said with a ridiculous air.

Jim chuckled lightly.

"Oh, you didn't know I was a relationship doctor? I am. I can't do shit to help myself out, but that's the irony in it. Ya see? I help people sort their shit out all the time. So, what is it?"

One thing Jim found really funny about DeGawain was that he really thought he knew a lot, or at least he consistently acted like he did. Jim decided to humor the big guy and told him what had happened between him and Susan.

"Come on, guy," DeGawain said. "You don't need a doctor to tell you that putting your neck in a noose and kicking out your stool will end shit." He jabbed more pizza down his throat and continued to talk. "Buy her some goddamned flowers, write her an apology about the V-day travesty, go to that Broadway play and move on."

"So, you think that's what she's mad at me for?" he asked.

"What the fuck else did you do?" DeGawain said, swallowing some of his over-stuffed mouthful.

"Well," Jim said, picking at his sandwich. "She did give me that, 'you know what you did,' crap."

"Yeah," DeGawain said, dropping his pizza to sip his extra-large soda. "That's no good, but I think you're in a jam of your own creation, guy."

"What d'ya mean?"

"You're thinking about this too much."

"Think so?"

"Of course," DeGawain said flatly. "Another problem

diagnosed and treated by the doctor. I gotta tell ya Diffin, you amaze me."

"How so?"

"How the fuck do you get any girls? I can't get chicks and I know what's up. What's your secret?"

"No secret," Jim said. "I talk to them. I don't do pick-up lines. I say, 'Hi, how are you?' Then maybe, 'Who are you here with?' Can't forget, 'What's your name?' 'Where do you go to school?' I fuckin' talk to them, man. There's no equation, no secret communication code to crack. The biggest secret to me is that all this hype about the gender gap is exaggerated bullshit."

"I don't know about that, guy." DeGawain wadded grease from his meaty hands with a stack of napkins. "I've known some strange fucking chicks."

"I've known some strange fuckin' guys, too. Haven't you? Girls are just people. There's no 'chicks dig this and that.' There's like no universally attractive trait to women. Some girls like scruffy hockey player types and others like pretty boys. Some like lean guys and others like jacked guys."

DeGawain crushed his paper plate with his napkins. "I'm none of those, may I remind you."

"I'm trying to make a general point. There's girls who like the big teddy bear DeGawain body type, too. You need to find them and show them how damn charming you can be."

"I can charm the shit out of people, can't I?" DeGawain said with lackluster confidence.

He laughed and rested his chin on his fist. "I don't know. Women aren't strange, alien creatures." Jim munched on his sandwich, wondering if he should even discuss his other concern with DeGawain. "Dude, you know what, though?"

DeGawain slurped his soda and shrugged.

"I may talk shit, but Susan really is a great girl. The thing is, I know I could never love her."

"Why the fuck does that matter?"

"I don't know," he said, running his hand through his hair, which badly needed a cut. "I've dated a bunch of girls and I'm starting to feel like I'm not emotionally capable of love."

"Why do you even want to love a girl? You're 'The Diff' for fuck's sake. You ain't got time for love. You're the fuck and run type, aren't you?"

He bit at the nail on his index finger. Everyone assumed from the amount of girls that he dated and from the times he'd gone home with girls that "The Diff" was some kind of ladies' man, always getting ass. But that really wasn't him. It'd always been easier to let them think what they wanted than to explain the truth. He did date a lot of girls, even went home with girls from parties or clubs, but he remained a virgin. Truth was, the girls who took him home wound up too timid, perhaps virgins themselves, and the most that ever happened was some reciprocated oral sex, sometimes simultaneously—good ol' 69. Of course, that was still better than what his friends were getting; so that was one more reason not to contradict them.

"I don't know, kid. I sometimes think about falling in love though. I mean, isn't that a sign of a sociopath? To be incapable of love? What if I'm some kind of fucked up freak?"

DeGawain almost spit soda in his face. "Diffin, trust me. You're not a sociopath. You're a young guy, sowing his oats. Trust me, you don't want to meet the right girl right now anyway. You still gotta get your own damn life together, figure your shit out."

DeGawain had a point. He still wasn't sure he had the

right major in school and, even if it was what he wanted, he hadn't figured out how to make a career out of it.

"Forget about it, Diffin. Eat your sandwich." DeGawain slurped on the last ounce of his soda, then seemed to brighten suddenly. "Did you happen to notice that girl Diana the other night? Fuckin' hottie, huh?"

"Well..."

"What did you think of her, seriously?"

"Okay. Here's the thing. I can't really conjure up an image of her right now. I think I was paying too much attention to Helen to be honest."

"Well, I met Helen, Nina and Diana 'cause Diana works with me at the pizza place," DeGawain explained.

He thought he understood immediately. Diana had asked DeGawain to find out what he thought of her. She really wanted him.

"I think she likes me," DeGawain said.

His expression changed instantly from joyful expectation to shock without DeGawain noticing.

"I want her so bad and this time I think I have a good chance," DeGawain said, leaning back in his chair. "I'm gonna play it safe though. Don't wanna come on too strong. Right now, I feel like we're good friends and I wouldn't wanna screw that up quite yet, ya know?"

"Yeah. I hear ya. Asking girls out who are friends can really strain the friendship," he advised as objectively as he could, but still feeling a bit shocked and thinking whether or not to tell DeGawain about Helen's instant messages.

"She's so flirty with me, ya know. We share jokes, and she'll like tickle me and rub my head. Stuff like that," DeGawain explained with enough enthusiasm to break Jim's resolve to tell him. DeGawain asked, "So, what d'ya think I should do? Wait on her or ask her out?"

He wanted to tell him, to spare him the further trouble of flirting, but he couldn't find the words. "I don't know, man. Maybe you should play it day to day. You're sure she's not seeing anybody? That could screw it up right there. She'd know you liked her and would feel weird about flirting with you 'cause of her boyfriend."

"Yeah, but I already found out about that. She told me about breaking up with her last boyfriend. She talks to me about all kinds of shit. She's not a girly-girl either. She tells dirty jokes and burps and shit. She's so mad cool, definitely a DeGawain-type girl."

"I don't know, man. I told you I don't even know how I do it. Seems to me, every situation has its own unique dynamic with unique problems to overcome every time. But, uh, keep me posted."

"Totally."

"And good luck with her, too," he said with complete sincerity.

The rest of lunch they talked about future party plans while he felt detached from a bizarre sense of innocent guilt.

4

The night's last few shoppers trudged out of the grocery store loaded down with food. A boy ran across the empty lot, pushing three carts locked into one another, no doubt eager to end his shift and go home. Jim slammed the Omni into park. He snatched the directions from the seat beside him and read them one last time. He'd taken the right exit. As for the rest, he must have gone wrong somewhere. The route cut through Pawtucket and Central Falls to get to Cumberland, not far from Mendon Road. He'd jokingly said he wouldn't be on time, so when he arrived punctually, he would look even better. Getting lost hadn't been part of the plan.

Fast food wrappers and a C+ essay covered the bulky car phone on the passenger floor. He swatted the junk aside and snatched it. The antennae fell off as it always seemed to, and he fished through the flotsam to find it. The power cord also tended not to stay in the cigarette lighter. He turned down the music. He plugged in the power cord, holding it there, then dialed the number, hit send, positioned the phone between his shoulder and ear, finally securing the antennae into place. The phone rang.

"Hello?" It was Diana.

He explained what had happened as best as he could. Of course, the grocery store was a major chain, so that didn't help; and he didn't know the name of the road where he'd turned off, so he wasn't sure how any of this would work out. He babbled on anyway, and eventually she giggled and said, "I think I know where you are. I'll be right there." She could have told him how to get to her house, but she'd hung up too fast. He turned the music back up and struggled to get comfortable.

He hadn't purposefully gone behind DeGawain's back to get the date with Diana. He never did email her like Helen had suggested. She'd emailed him. All he did was respond politely, and they'd struck up a regular correspondence. She explained to him that she thought DeGawain was great, hilarious, but not the kind of guy she would think of "in that way." He didn't know how to tell his boy about it, and—he figured—there really wasn't anything to tell him yet. This was nothing but a first date; it could easily go nowhere.

Three songs later, Diana's Chrysler LeBaron pulled into the lot. He opened his door, but she pulled up beside him, rolled down her window and said, "Follow me, fuck-nuts." She smiled, rolled up her window and pulled away. This, for a moment, left him nonplussed, but he quickly recovered, laughing. A funny chick with attitude might be a nice change. He'd totally forgotten that she'd had bangs, and she was even prettier than he'd remembered.

He followed her through what were basically New England ghettos; the houses would be nice if their owners could afford to maintain them: tightly packed, filthy Victorians with rotting wood, crooked, rusty fences and tall cement stoops or wide, front porches on each floor; all of them broken down into apartments.

Diana's house was the same; it had more in common with the Central Falls neighborhoods they'd driven through than with the more affluent town of Cumberland where the post office and politicians claimed it belonged.

Diana climbed out of her car and met him beside the Omni. "Sorry I'm late," he said. She'd dressed plainly enough, but she still looked hot. Tight blue jeans hugged and flattered her round butt, and a tight t-shirt made her pert B-cups seem bigger.

"It's okay. You said you wouldn't be on time," she answered with a snicker. "Come on in for a sec. Meet my mom."

Meet her mom?

Diana, as if she could hear his thoughts, paused on the walkway between the front bushes. "Unless you don't want to. I mean, is that like, too fast, or whatever? I mean, it's no big deal or anything. I just thought..."

He laughed. "No. It's fine. No big deal, right?"

"Yeah, totally." She skipped ahead up the cement front walk. "She wants to see that you're not some kind of thug or something. I think."

The big, brown house had a wide, high stoop with two doors, one for each apartment. Diana opened the door on the left. Inside, a short, narrow hallway led into a living room. The back of the couch faced out and stood a few feet from the wall, creating a walkway straight into the kitchen where it smelled like recently cooked pasta.

A tall, thin woman in her mid-to-late thirties with curly, brown hair, a blousy white shirt and tight, faded blue jeans glided across the kitchen. He took her slender hand and shook it.

"So, you must be Jim." She had dark brown eyes and straight, white teeth.

"Yup," he said, then realized he probably should have said, "yes" or maybe even "yes, ma'am," "yes, Mrs. Huntington" (was she still Mrs. Huntington, or had she changed it after the divorce?) or something better than the barely literate, yup.

"Well, very nice to meet you," she said. "What are you two planning on tonight?"

"Mom," Diana complained in a drawn-out voice.

"Sorry, don't mean to pry."

"I think we're going to catch a movie," he said, smiling.

Nina burst into the kitchen wearing cartoon pajama bottoms and her hoodie; her bedroom door was apparently right off the kitchen. "What movie?" she asked.

"Ugh," Diana sighed, taking his hand. She led him back into the living room and through a doorway of hanging beads. They stepped into a room that looked like the inside of a giant watermelon. He squinted against the color. The pink room had been painted complete with black seeds and green trim around the baseboards, door frame and closet.

"Wow," he said.

Diana closed the door, noticed his awe at the room. "I did this years and years ago," she explained, walking toward her bed. "I used to be a total girly-girl." She snickered at herself while searching a shelf lined with records and CDs.

Jim considered how long-ago years and years could've been, Diana being sixteen as it was. "Yeah, right," he said.

Diana looked up from the shelf confused, almost hurt. Jim sputtered. "I mean—"

"You're easy to fuck with," she said, laughing. "Here," she said, handing him a record in its sleeve, a Siamese cat on the cover. "This is Blink 182."

He looked at the cat curiously. Then he remembered. The band she loved, the one whose bassist or something she thought looked like him—the whole reason she'd been interested in him in the first place. Well, that and how fun he was, of course.

She flipped the record over in his hands. "This is Marc," she said, pointing to a guy making a crazy face. "Well, this isn't the best picture. Trust me though, you look a lot like him."

The resemblance didn't easily present itself as he stared into the face on the cardboard.

"Well, whatever works for you," he said, handing her the record and pushing her back onto the bed with a laugh.

"Hey, careful," she said, sitting up to place the record back on the shelf. "You could have wrecked it."

Outside, Diana offered to drive, and he figured that'd be easier since she knew exactly how to get where they were going. Besides, the girl should have her way, at least on the first date. She unlocked and even opened the door for him. He paused before getting in, wondering if he should wait for her to open her door or not before he got in. She walked around the rear of the car and popped the door open. He sank inside.

The car started without a grumble; the digital displays on the dash cast a gentle green glow on Diana's face. The speedometer, odometer, even the fuel gauge were all digital; the latter even displaying how many miles until the next fill-up.

"Nice car," he said.

"It's all right. At least it's mine," she said, pulling away from the curb. "Actually, it's always needing work."

"Oh, that sucks; so, it's always in the shop, huh?"

Diana stopped the car at a yellow light. "No. I fix pretty much everything myself."

He pictured her with grease on her cheek, a wrench in her hand, the car on lifts in front of her house...

"Where do you do all of that?" he asked.

"At home," she said. The route she drove to get to the theaters took them down Mendon road. They would drive right past the pizza place where she worked with DeGawain. Would the big guy be working today, delivering pizzas in and around the neighborhoods they drove through even now?

He kept the conversation going naturally. "Really? Nothing major though, right?" They cruised past the pizza place, no pick-up truck, but DeGawain could still be out on a delivery somewhere.

"Well, no. I don't replace the engine or transmission or anything like that. But I did fix the speedometer last weekend and I'll be changing the oil tomorrow if it gets as warm as it's supposed to."

He pictured her underneath the car, oil still smeared on her cheek. The image strangely aroused him. He would never put that much effort into a car. She told him she did it primarily to save money. Thirty, forty dollars every three thousand miles does add up, but it was still better than climbing under the car, especially in winter. Although dating a thrifty girl would be nice. The girls he dated always liked to spend money, go shopping, buy superfluities. He would jokingly quote Thoreau, "Simplify, simplify!" Most girls didn't find it funny.

Later, in the warmth of the movie theater lobby, they

stood to one side of the ticket line. Nothing started for at least another hour.

He thought about the advice his brother had given him when he started dating in high school: "Most guys want to take a girl to the movies on a first date. That's a total no-no. You want to take a girl somewhere you can talk to her, get to know her, have her get to know you. Mini-golfing, a dinner date, bowling, even a picnic if you want to be cheap, anything but the movies."

He'd done a lot of things to be like his big brother: joined Boy Scouts, played soccer and swam competitively, yet he didn't follow William with his dating tactics. He'd come to his own conclusion about first dates. Why waste the energy to find someplace to have a good conversation? Why not make it up as you go, until you really liked the girl, then impress her with a fun, interesting date?

With this in mind, he said, "Oh well. Wanna grab some coffee or something until a movie starts?" Diana agreed, and they picked a movie to return for.

Fortunately, a donut shop sat on every other block all over the state. They only needed to drive across the street. Inside, the warm, familiar, heavy donut smell set him immediately at ease. His parents' house was downwind, less than a block from a donut shop, same chain even, and whenever they cooked a batch, the aroma filled the neighborhood.

He bought them each a small coffee (regular for him, extra-extra for her), and they sat down at a corner table under fluorescent lighting. He moved the styrofoam cup across the bright orange table-top and searched for some good questions. To make first dates less tense, he always pretended to conduct an interview. He'd ask good questions, never interrupt and try to think of follow-up questions while listening.

"So. What do you do for fun?" he asked. Not a great start, but it was vague enough and, another important point, wasn't a yes or no question.

She squinted into the distance. Then she broke into a huge smile, perfect white upper teeth partially concealing miserably crooked lowers, a glow to her cheek. "Horseback riding."

Her hips pumped rhythmically, back, forth, back, forth—he had never ridden a horse, but somehow figured her riding could've developed some strong muscles that might make her very good in bed.

"You don't think that's—like—totally weird or dorkish do you?" she asked.

"No," he said soberly. "Actually, it sounds cool. Maybe you could teach me to ride sometime." He'd always thought it would be good if he could learn something new, a skill, talent or anything from each girl he dated. So far, he'd never really come up with anything. Horseback riding would be a great start. "So, where do you keep the horse?"

"My aunt has a ranch in Cumberland not too far from my house. I can totally take you by there sometime." She fiddled with the plastic lid on her cup. "You could probably ride Bullit; that's my horse, and maybe Nina would let me ride hers."

He told Diana he would love that. She added that she competed. Red coat, riding crop, black cap and high, black boots... While he imagined her in the outfit, she explained, as if reading his mind again, that she didn't do what she called "that gay English kind." She rode in Western competitions, which were less stiff and more fun. He wanted to go watch her ride, but when he flashed the huge grin that often made people think he was being insincere, she grew shy.

Deciding to let it go, he asked, "So, is that how you met Helen?"

She laughed leaning back, then sat straight in all seriousness. "Helen. No way—she's too cool for horses. She's always trying to get me to slack on my horse chores, like combing and exercising them."

"That's fucked up." Headlights flashed into the tall store-front window as a pick-up truck pulled in. The lights shut off, and he waited to see who would step out. It was the same make, model and color as DeGawain's truck. Had he found out? What if he'd decided to grab a donut snack between deliveries?

"Yeah, well that's Helen." She took her first sip of coffee. "She drives me crazy sometimes."

He tried not to seem distracted and asked, "Really? How so?" A skinny, balding man stepped out of the truck, and he sighed, sipped his coffee and turned his full attention back to Diana, who'd been talking the whole time.

"...moved here this year from The Cape, and I, like, totally went out of my way to befriend her because—ya know—she had no friends being the new girl and all." Diana hooked a few strands of her long blonde hair behind her ear which had a half-dozen piercings. "But now it's like she's taken over, and people don't even notice me anymore."

Valentine's Day came back to him. He'd met Diana that night, but Helen had really stuck in his mind even though she was clearly with Pow. Helen had more of a model's frame, thin and elongated. Not that Diana was big. She had a more athletic frame and was wearing her hoodie that night, while Helen wore a skin-tight t-shirt.

"It's because she's so loud," he said, smiling reassuringly.

"Yeah—well, I don't care. We have a wicked lot of fun together."

"That's what really matters," he said. "My big brother taught me that. My parents said, 'Don't be like William, always out to have nothing but fun.' And that's what made me realize how good an idea it was. Any time a parent tells you not to do something, it's usually what you want to do."

Diana giggled. "Yeah, my mom doesn't really tell me what to do. She really trusts Nina and me to do the right thing."

"So, she's not too strict then?"

"Hell no. I don't even have a curfew," she said with a quick shake of her head to readjust her bangs. "Of course, if I'm going to be out all night, I call to let her know. That's common courtesy."

A good point. He always thought of that as more of an obligation.

"Of course," he said, smiling like a goof.

"So, you have one brother then?"

"Yup. Just William."

"How come you call him William?" she asked, exaggerating the name.

"It's what he likes being called. Like I prefer Jim. Weird thing is that I always introduce myself as Jim, but nobody really calls me that. My parents call me James and my friends call me—"

"The Diff," she broke in, giggling.

"Yeah, or Diffin." He felt his ears redden and warm —a reaction usually caused by anger or embarrassment. It embarrassed him a bit to be called "The Diff." It sounded stupid, and he didn't want Diana to think he liked it.

"But you guys call each other by last names. Except Pow, but that's short for Powell, isn't it?"

"Yeah. I think that comes from Hendricken where it seemed like everybody was John, Jim or Jack. So, we used last names."

"Oh yeah, you crazy Catholic Micks," she said flirtatiously.

He smiled, his ears really burning now. Her smile hadn't faded. "What about you? Your last name's Huntington, right? That English?"

"I think. I don't know. I'm kind of a mutt," she said, popping the lid off of her coffee.

"Oh, and you're—what—Protestant then?" he asked without thinking. He realized he only asked that because later his mother would want to know.

"Nah." She shrugged. "We're really not very religious."

"Well, whatever. It's no big deal. Just curious," he said. He hoped he hadn't ruined what seemed like a good date with less than romantic denominational concerns.

"So," she said. "Have you known those guys forever?"

"What guys?"

"You know. Your 'boys,'" she said like she was making fun again.

"Oh, no. I've only really known them since high school, but we really didn't even hang out then. We got close working at Camp Waetabee for the past few summers. You live and work with someone, you get really close."

She leaned in and slid her coffee cup aside. "So, what exactly does that mean, being 'boys'?"

He sat back and thought for a moment. He wasn't entirely sure she wasn't making fun of him, but he'd decided not to try being somebody else on a first date.

So, he explained in sputters and false starts how the three of them, DeGawain, Pow and he had realized they had a common disdain for inhibitions in general. That they were each other's "boys" meant looking out for one another, taking a beating for somebody if it would lessen their beating, sharing whatever could be shared, forgiving whatever could be forgiven. They believed theirs was a true fraternity, stripped of Greek letters, initiation rights and fake friendships.

"So, is this like an exclusive deal? Or could there be more boys added later?" she asked, smoothing her hair behind her ear again.

"Exclusive?" He shook his head with a smile. He still didn't know if she was fucking with him or not. "DeGawain and Pow are my boys and I'm theirs, but it's not like we're some secret group." Then, remembering DeGawain, he felt guilty. He was having a good time chatting with Diana. Damn it, he'd see her again if she was willing. DeGawain couldn't stay mad at him. They were boys after all.

"What about Troy and Panza? They're not your boys, too?"

"Nah. Panza is mostly DeGawain's friend and Troy, mostly Pow's. They might be their boys, but I hardly know 'em." It struck him that he had been talking about himself too much.

"So, anyways..." he tried.

She smiled. "Anyways..."

"I don't know," he said, then suggested they head out so they'd have time to get popcorn and soda. As they stood to leave, he nodded at her pierced eyebrow and nose ring and asked if they had hurt. She told him, not really, and he asked if she had any others, which made him immediately hope she didn't think he was being lewd. She laughed, cupping her mouth and told him about her belly button ring, which did, in fact, hurt. He brought up tattoos, and they shared the same feeling about them: what could be good enough to be imprinted forever?

Stepping outside, they noticed that everything had been covered with a fresh, pristine, layer of snow. Flurries dashed through the parking lot lights. They shared a smile. A brief, comfortable silence followed as they crossed the beautiful lot to her car. But soon he felt compelled to ask more questions.

"Do you do any other sports besides horseback riding?"

"Not really. Helen's trying to get me to run track," she said. "What sports do you do?" she asked, quickly turning the tables.

"I used to run track back in junior high. I also used to play soccer," he said, then finished his coffee. "I swam in high school and then my freshman year at R.I.C., but with my bad g.p.a. to bring up, I haven't had time this year. Hopefully, I'll be able to swim again next year."

They stopped by the passenger door. She leaned in close to him. "Why did you quit soccer and track?" Then, she unlocked his door and headed around the back of the car.

"Bum knee. Well, Osgood-Schlatter's disease, actually."

"Oz-good what?" she asked, stopping by the trunk and raising her eyebrows. Snow clung to her bangs.

"It's nothing but an inflammation in the knee or some kind of tendon separation or something. I had to quit soccer straight off, but track was different." He stopped, hoping she wouldn't want to know any more.

"How was track different," she asked, as they got in.

Jim told her how in junior high he hadn't been very popular for some reason. It might've been his thick glasses, that he'd been a pretty big punk in elementary school or even that he'd been accidentally placed in all lower classes his first year, which made him seem like a complete super-smart dork to the tough kids. He paused. "It's kind of a long story."

Diana turned the key, switched on the heat, raised her arm with the green watch band and checked it. "We have time, Jim."

"All right, so my knee had been bothering me for a while. I basically had to limp-run," he said, trying to imitate from his seat the awkward motion with a grunt and a laugh. "Anyway, my mom finally made a doctor appointment for one day after practice. That afternoon, when everyone had started doing the warm-down, I told the coach I had to head out. And he was all, 'all right get going.'" He lowered his voice, trying to sound dense. "So, I limped all the way back to the school and uh... By the time I got to the gym, a bunch of kids ran past me. They had finished their warm down and got back before me and my pathetic limpin' ass. That's when they surrounded me and well... They jumped me, beat the crap outta me."

"No. Where was the coach?" she asked, as they stopped at a red light. "Weren't there any other teachers?"

"This was after school. Coach was still with the rest of the team warming down. Anyways, what really sucks is that one of the kids had been in Cub Scouts with me since I was four or five. My mom had been our den mother. I mean, the other two kids... I expected it from. But the one kid... That made it hurt more, honestly."

Diana put her warm, soft hand on his, which made him feel pitied. He knew she didn't mean it that way, but it made him laugh and he took his hand away. "No, no. I'm not telling the story for pity," he said, laughing.

"But anyway, you can see why I couldn't quit. They would've thought they'd intimidated me."

"But you did quit, right?" she asked.

"Hell no. I quit running. I had to. I stayed on the team by changing to field events. I threw shot and disc. To be honest I hated it, but I felt like it was something I had to do."

"I can understand that. It's respectable." She gave him a wry smile. "That wasn't such a long story, though, Jim."

"Sorry. I'll do better next time," he said, smiling back. In the theater parking lot, he kept thinking he saw DeGawain's truck. Each time it turned out to be a different make, wrong color or had Mass. plates. He couldn't shake the feeling that DeGawain was going to find out and overreact.

They watched Great Expectations with Ethan Hawke. In the seats, he wrapped his arm around her. She took his hand in the parking lot, and, as he walked her to her door, she gave him a long, deep kiss. He asked her awkwardly, "Can we do this again sometime?"

She laughed in his face before saying, "Of course, fuck-nuts." Then she ran inside, turning before she closed the door to whisper, "Goodnight."

5

The sky hung low and gray as he crossed Pow's front lawn. It looked like a blizzard was coming. The picture window framed Mrs. Powell, who resembled a cartoon owl. She wore wide, round-rimmed glasses, had large eyes, a small beakish nose and a short, squat stature. Her words came slowly, articulated with a high pitch and tempered with a tone of joy. She welcomed her son's visitors not only as if they were her guests, but as if she was truly happy that Pow had friends. So, when the door opened, he graciously met Mrs. Powell's outstretched arms in an awkward embrace. He quickly excused himself and retreated downstairs to Pow's room, leaving Mrs. Powell alone with the television.

Pow's room was really a corner of a basement which was otherwise used for storage. He maneuvered past bikes and boxes cluttering the dark corners around the stairs and made for the back corner lit with the soft, multi-color glow of Christmas lights. The "room" was squared off by two couches and a small butterfly curl machine.

"'Sup, Diffin, you fuckin' showed up, huh, bitch?'" Pow said, feigning a punk tone and adding a gangsta-lean.

"Word up, kid. Don't make me hafta regulate up in here," he countered.

Pow shuffled over to the corner of the room and tumbled onto his bed.

He took off his coat and asked, "Yo, Pow, all I gotta know is... is there crashability here or what?"

"Crashability, well that depends on whether or not you can snag a couch," Pow said honestly. "Some other heads are cruising over right now."

"All I'm sayin' is that I don't wanna have to drive home in this shit if it gets ugly."

"Yo, I'm sure we'll figure something out, homes."

"Word," he said as he dropped into a couch.

Pow propped himself up on a stack of pillows and pinched a braid between his fingers. "So, your dad's being a dick again, huh?"

He nodded.

Pow had experienced his father's moods on a few occasions. The first time Pow saw it was when Pow had come over to pick him up. On their way out the door, his mom had come home from the market. The two of them unloaded bags of food with his parents. When they had finished, Pow closed the trunk as his dad approached for another load. The amount of force Pow had used to close the trunk upset his dad who tried to calmly and jovially explain to Pow what he had done wrong. What came out was some bourgie explanation about how the car wasn't a "clunker" and required a minimal amount of force to handle. Clearly the car meant too much to the old man; also, the implication seemed to be that Pow's parents must own a "clunker" and because of that he must be somehow inferior.

Earlier that day, his dad had misunderstood what had, admittedly, been a heated discussion between his mom and him. His dad yelled at him for being disrespectful, and his mom didn't say anything to disagree. From then on, all day, his father stormed around in a foul mood, muttering things about respect and ingratitude. Jim felt fortunate to have a car and called Pow.

He didn't want to think about his dad anymore, and he sunk snugly into the musty, trash-picked couch. All of Pow's furniture had been rescued from a curb somewhere. Something about people throwing away perfectly good things simply because they had new ones amazed Pow, and he furnished his room with the things discarded by those who must be overly fond of newness.

Jim couldn't really blame people for wanting new things. Pow easily contented himself with the bare necessities, and Jim wished he could be as satisfied. Not that he would want a new couch because the old one had grown worn, but there were some things, even the sight of them grew old—like girls. Like Susan.

"Hey, Pow. Did I tell you I broke up with Susan?"

Pow sat up, but kept twisting the braid he'd been playing with. "No, homes. You didn't. Did you ever go to that play?"

"Yeah. It was awesome. Something called 'When the Lights Go Out,' or 'After the Lights Go Out,' or something. Anyway, Marissa Tomei played a blind chick that some robbers thought they'd take advantage of. But when they came around, the blind chick scuffled with them and turned out the lights..."

"Oh, and it was like, just because she was blind didn't mean she couldn't see?" Pow said, not releasing the braid.

"Yeah, she housed 'em," he said. The play had been fun, but he had felt awful the whole time, knowing he'd be dumping Susan as soon as he could. "Anyway, not long afterwards, I told Susan that we should see other people."

Pow leaned back down on his pillows. "How'd she take that?"

"Not very well. Apparently, she was way into me. I told her it had been a quarter of a year and that seemed like too long for me, not being a commitment guy and all."

"That's harsh, homes," Pow said, starting to laugh. "You really said that shit?"

Jim hadn't thought of it as harsh, but honest, maybe overly honest. No. If he'd been overly honest, he would've told her about Diana and how great she was—somehow though, that sounded even more harsh. He nodded. "Yeah, that's what I said. I told her one day at work. I waited 'til her shift was over and she was putting her shoes on."

Pow roared with laughter now. Jim hadn't meant to be cold to Susan and he wasn't trying to be funny now, but Pow's reaction was infectious. He chuckled.

Pow calmed down and nodded. "Helen tells me that you went out with Diana recently. That's why neither of you were out at the club. That true?"

He smiled. "Diana's awesome. To tell you the truth, I didn't really even notice her. But then Helen told me she was interested in me, and emails followed... I went with it and I'm glad I did, too." He really couldn't wait to see her again, either. She wasn't like any girl he'd ever dated. It seemed crazy to him, but a few days after their first date he already missed her. "Pow, you mind if I call Diana and ask her if she wants to come chill, too?"

"Nah, homes. Go ahead."

Jim slid over to the other couch where the phone sat on Pow's night stand. The phone rang three times, and then she picked up. She seemed excited to hear his voice. The fact that a snow storm had been predicted to drop six to eight inches didn't deter her; she'd be right down. He hung up and told Pow the good news. Pow teased him for seeming so excited.

"I think she might be the one, Pow," he said in defense.

"The one that what?" Pow said, skeptically.

"You know. 'The one.' She's really great."

"Who the fuck are you kiddin'?" Pow asked, beginning to chuckle. "You're 'The Diff.' The only 'one' you want to find is any 'one' who lets you toss your cock inside."

"We'll see," he said, once again not correcting his false image.

Pow suggested that he call DeGawain, too, while he sat by the phone. It sounded good to him. DeGawain seemed vaguely interested.

"Who's going to be there?" DeGawain asked.

"A bunch of Pow's friends, kids from high school, Troy; nobody you hung out with back then," he said, knowing he wasn't being very convincing. "But Diana's going to be here," he added to tempt him.

DeGawain took a moment to think and then got all weird. "Nah, guy. You know what? I'm just getting out of work, and it's already snowing up here. I should probably go home and get some rest."

Jim tried to convince him to change his mind, but DeGawain could be intractable at times, so he gave up after a few attempts. He asked Pow if he'd want to call Helen, but he shook his head and got very quiet. Not long afterward, a ruckus rumbled down the stairs, and a group of guys streamed into Pow's room, falling on couches.

He knew Troy from club nights and recognized the

other guys as Mike Dean, Brian and Nick. They gigglingly related a story about a girl named Tracy; (whether her last name was Gigglefinger or Dookenheimer, they couldn't decide). This girl had been over at Brian's house and had been on the point of blowing them all when her mother called to say she needed to come home. Jim told the guys he thought they were full of it, and as Pow started relating some of Tracy's well-known whore-exploits to convince him that not only was it likely to be true, but that he'd probably like her, a creak on the stairway tensed Pow up and silenced him. Mrs. Powell meandered into the room.

"I brought you some soda and chips. I'm goin' to go to bed soon, so if you need anythin' befaw then, let me know. Okay, boys?" she asked.

"Sure, Mrs. Powell."

"Thanks, Mrs. Powell."

"Yeah, thank you very much, Mrs. Powell."

"Goodnight, Mrs. Powell."

He held his breath along with everybody else as they waited for Pow's mom to clear the basement. Then they busted out laughing.

"Do you think she heard anything?" Troy asked, as the laughter subsided.

"I don't know, homes. I hope not, though," Pow answered.

Moments later, another set of feet came down the steps. They sat still, holding conversation until they knew who was coming.

Diana pulled a winter cap off and shook her long blonde hair. "What the fuck's wrong with you guys? Sitting here staring at each other in silence, when it's fuckin' snowing out!" Her cheeks blushed more than normal from having come in from the cold. "I got a great idea for some real fun, too!" she said, threading between the couches and dropping into his lap.

Five minutes later, bundled up and haloed with puffs of white breath, he stood with Diana and the five other boys by Mike Dean's Chevy Beretta. Pow tied a bowline around the bumper while Troy tied a granny knot to a saucer sled. The street was slowly accumulating a blanket of crystalline, powdery snow.

Dean slapped his thickly gloved hands together a few times and asked with a puff of steamy breath, "Who's first?"

Diana jumped onto the saucer and clutched the rope. "It was my fuckin' idea. Who do you think's first?" she said.

Dean dropped himself behind the steering wheel. Diana screamed like a drunk spring-breaker as snow kicked up from Dean's tires and splashed into her face. The guys had been very receptive to Diana's idea; it seems they'd done it before tons of times. They called it ghetto-gliding. Diana called it street sledding. He called it crazy.

The car rolled off and turned lazily around the corner. He hoped she'd be all right.

"Funny how he's only going like fifteen miles an hour..." Brian said.

"Yeah, it seems so slow in the car..." Troy added.

"But motha fucka is that shit fast when you're tied back there!" Pow concluded. Jim worried about what might happen if Dean needed to stop quickly or if a snowplow somehow hit her as they went around a corner.

He laughed, trying to act casual as the group stamped their feet or jumped in place to keep warm. Ten minutes later, Troy enthusiastically slid away on the sled, and Diana rushed around Pow's front yard giggling from a slight adrenaline rush. She came over and wrapped her arms around him, kissed him on the cheek and said, "Why don't you go next, fucknuts?"

"I don't know," Jim said. A voice in his head that sounded like his dad very much disapproved of this, but he didn't want to disappoint Diana. He didn't want his reputation to suffer, either. This ghetto-gliding reminded him of George Orwell's elephant. And like Orwell had to kill the elephant even though he didn't want to, Jim—looking into Diana's bright, brown eyes—knew he'd probably have to suck it up and risk his life to keep up his rep. When the car came back, he threw up his arms.

"Oh, fuck it," he said, jumping onto the sled. The warm exhaust sputtered in his face as he grasped the frozen rope. The car pulled away from the curb, and he could feel the snow-laden street swish by beneath him. They had been right, too; he knew he was going maybe fifteen miles per hour, but that speed sitting on the ground seemed incredibly fast. As they rounded the first corner, the sled swept out toward the opposite side of the road. One thing he wished he was sure of, was he doing this to impress a girl? Or was he doing this to impress his friends? And either way, was he really being himself? If only the flowing adrenaline and snow kicking up in his face would override his cognitive mind.

When he glided back into the curb, he felt like a pansy. Sure, it had been fun, but he'd only done it because everyone else, especially Diana, had expected him to. And even though he had done it, he had remained nervous the entire time, afraid, even. None of it seemed in line with who he thought he was. Fortunately, he didn't have time to dwell on it; as soon as he stood off the sled, Diana threw her arms around him.

Pow and Brian took their turns, and the cold bit into Jim's nose, ears, fingertips and toes. Pow drove Dean's car, so Dean could have a turn, and Troy rode in the passenger seat to keep warm. By the time they returned, Diana had instigated a snowball fight. It was him and Diana verses Nick and Brian. She threw like a girl, but still managed to have killer aim. As soon as they came around the block, Dean, Troy and Pow joined in the chaos, and the shouting brought Mrs. Powell outside.

"Now you boys try and keep it down, please. Pow, I really need some sleep. Ya fatha will be home soon, and if you guys are still creatin' all this ruckus, he won't be happy. I promise you that." Bundled against the cold, Mrs. Powell wagged her finger, then stepped back inside.

"A'ight, we need to cool out a bit," Pow observed. "But I still need to take another ride on that shit."

"So, let's get this shit goin'," Dean said with a laugh. Brian climbed into the passenger seat, leaving the rest of them to shiver on the lawn. Until Diana slid alongside Jim and squeezed him tight.

"You'll keep me warm," she said.

Nick dropped into the snow and rolled up a snowball. "Yo, let's make a snowman!" he said.

"You kiddin' me?" Jim asked.

"That's kinda wack, man." Troy agreed.

"Yo, it'll keep us warm," Nick argued.

"I haven't made a snowman since I was like twelve." Jim laughed.

"Exactly, it'll be like being a kid again," Nick said, as he rolled the snowball across the snow.

"Nick, you're always acting like you're a kid again. In fact, you're not a kid again, you've never stopped being a kid," Troy said.

Nick rolled the growing snowball in a new direction.

"Besides, man, this snow isn't wet enough to make a really good one," Jim said. "It won't stick right."

Nick patted his ball in progress and glanced up. "I guess you're right, but it's getting pretty cold out, y'know?"

"And now you're all wet, you jackass," Troy said, and they laughed.

Nick rose, and they circled together with their backs to the wind. They turned around when they heard a car rolling up slowly from behind. Dean pulled the Beretta into the curb a little too fast, and Pow, on the sled, hit the snow-covered curb and caught air. Pow released the rope and flew headlong, crashing into Troy's legs, sending them both tumbling.

"Holy shit!" Dean screamed as he jumped out of his car. "You guys all right?"

Brian hopped out, laughing. Troy and Pow pulled themselves from each other and climbed to their feet. When everybody was calm again, Pow said, "I have a wicked good idea!"

"Pow, you don't wanna try to do that shit again, do you?" Dean asked.

"Nah, I thought this up while I was glidin'." Pow brushed some snow off his black fleece and said, "Let's grill burgahs!"

"Grillin'?" he asked. "Isn't it a bit cold, Pow?"

"Nah, check it. While we grill, the hot coals under the burgers will warm our frozen asses."

"Yeah, that's a great idea!" Nick agreed.

"Better'n hot chocolate," Pow said with a grin.

Soon they huddled around a small hibachi grill that rested on the Powell's front steps, passing condiments and talking excitedly about the club, parties and trash picking. Rounds of ghetto-gliding continued into the night until the group had grilled and eaten all the burgers in the house.

With the burger supply exhausted, cold setting in hard and the plows making it to the side streets, they retired into the house. When Mr. Powell came home from working at a local convenience store, he must've thought it strange to find seven pairs of socks, jeans, gloves, hats and similar accessories resting on the radiators all over his living room. By that time Brian, Nick and Dean had gone home in some of Pow's clothes. Diana, wearing some of Pow's sweats, nestled in Jim's arms on one of the couches. Troy crashed on the other one.

Bleary-eyed, Jim woke up the next morning. Diana still snuggled him; Troy was gone, and Pow snored in his bed. He jostled himself a bit, and she woke up, rubbing her face. When she finished, she smiled at him and gave him a big, deep kiss. They made out for a while on the couch, but Pow's rumbling snores didn't set a very good mood. After a particularly long, loud snore, they broke out laughing.

He got up and smacked Pow gently on the cheek.

"Wha—Wha—What the fuck?" Pow said, sitting up, ready to brawl.

"Yo, kid, we're goin' home," he said. "Thanks for lettin' us crash."

"Damn, what time is it?" Pow asked, seeming not to have heard him.

Jim checked his black-banded digital watch and answered, "Noon."

Pow scratched his scalp. "Troy still here?"

"Looks like he jetted."

"Damn, homes, he's always doin' that," Pow said and rolled over to go back to sleep.

He and Diana weren't sure if the Powells would

approve of having had a girl spend the night with a boy under their roof. They tip-toed around upstairs, collecting their clothes and taking turns changing quietly in the bathroom. Outside, they kissed briefly in the cold, moist air.

"I had a lot of fun with you," she said.

"Me too," he said. "We'll have to hang out some more."

"Definitely," she said, then kissed him and got into her car. He closed the door for her and walked to the Omni.

6

Her flesh against his flesh, her warmth pressing against him, her hands moving through his hair. A buzzing whirred above his head. Diana's legs straddled his knee while she stood over him, clippers in hand. His hair had been getting powerfully curly, bushy, large. Now dark snowflakes of hair drifted around his face and fell on his shoulders, into his chest hair, on his thighs and still farther down.

He sat in his plaid boxers on a hard, wooden chair in the dining room where his mother used to cut his hair as a young boy. His parents were at work. He'd finished finals, and Diana's school year was winding down, but summer had come so early that it seemed spring had been skipped. Diana offered to give him a much needed, extra short, summer haircut. It was already months ago, in late March, when Diana rolled up in front of his house with her little sister Nina and Helen, so that they all could go to the beach for the first time that year.

Helen and Nina had strolled down the beach together,

leaving him alone with Diana. Puffy clouds passed over, waves crashed loud and long, and a salty breeze swept over them. They'd been dating by then for about a month; they lay on a blanket together, nestled in next to each other, kissed and talked.

Now she sliced hair from above his left temple with a confident buzz, the inside of her thigh, bared by her short-shorts, stuck to the inside of his. His hands stayed at his sides and he imagined for a moment that she was giving him a lap dance, but then she poked him with the black, plastic clipper extension, and again the hair tumbled down around him, a rain of ash surrounding his chair.

She had made him fall for her fast.

Jim started dating her with very low expectations. Diana would be nothing but another girl he dated, another girl he would make out with and attempt to disrobe, to kiss, to lick and suck on and hopefully to fuck until she got too demanding of him; he would get uncomfortable, find another girl and start again.

He'd seen her every weekend since March—parties, clubs, dates, all late nights and good fun. "I like you," she told him. "Really?" he answered rhetorically. "You're fun," she said. Yes; Jim liked being fun.

In the last week of Lent, he and Diana had gone on a long date, a full day with each other. They ate lunch, wandered the mall and then cooked deviled eggs together at Diana's house. She needed to make them for a family Easter gathering, and he tried to help. After the eggs, he took her back to the mall where she'd fallen in love with a little, white rabbit. He bought it for her as an Easter present, and she named it Jack.

Jim never had that talk with DeGawain about her. Instead, he figured DeGawain would understand that Diana had chosen him and that it had been out of his control to change. Jim assumed his friend understood; DeGawain seemed to take it in stride, never said anything at parties, always remained the big, dancing fool, laughing it up, chugging brews and enjoying life. Things were great.

Until last weekend. Jim took Diana out to dinner. Everything seemed normal, an average night together. After dinner, he took her up to Veterans Memorial Parkway in his Omni where he had taken many girls to make out and fondle in the back seat with a panoramic view of the capital city across the Narragansett Bay. Jim expected nothing sexual. Diana was a virgin and had plans to stay that way until she found true love; a disappointment, he'd lost many young ladies' phone numbers for less. But something about Diana had made him forget about trying to get laid. He really liked being with her, spending time with her, talking.

It was that night in the Omni, lying on the tiny back seat together, her head on his shoulder, he whispered, "I love you."

Diana sat up and turned in the dark, "What did you say?"

He stammered, "I, uh, I said, I said, I love you."

"Why did you say that?"

He had never said the "L" word before, he knew of guys who would say it to get their dicks wet, but he always saw that as cheating. He wanted to get laid, of course, but he never wanted to give a girl the wrong idea. He planned on telling her for at least a week. He discussed it with Pow and his mother. He told them he knew he was screwed but that he couldn't help it. He told her he loved her...

"Because I do," he said, sitting up and touching her warm thigh.

"But I thought you never say that. That's like your

thing. You don't say that." Her face scrunched up in disbelief.

"Yeah, I know." Jim didn't understand why she seemed upset; he got a bit defensive, "I've never said that, because I've never felt it."

There was an awkward silence.

Now Jim watched his hair drift aimlessly down before his eyes. He didn't remember anything else about that night. He knew he'd gone to dinner with her, he'd gone to that spot on the Parkway, sat in the back seat, said those words, and most importantly Diana had not said them back, had maybe even gotten a bit freaked out by them. But what time he got her home or what time he got home or anything else about the night he knew nothing.

Her fingers brushed over his ear, his scalp, his neck, all over him; her naked thighs rubbed against his naked thighs. His head felt cool and light, a good summer haircut, his wild hair gone. He looked into Diana's big, brown eyes and smiled up at her. She smiled down on him.

PART II

SUMMER

"Not till we are lost, in other words, not till we have lost the world, do we begin to find ourselves, and realize where we are and the infinite extent of our relations."
  –Henry David Thoreau

7

"I love you."

"I know you do."

The familiar exchange played out in his head. The sun beat down on his bare shoulders and back. It roasted his scalp and tanned skin. He pushed his sunglasses up on his small nose and pulled down on the brim of his floppy, orange lifeguard hat. He bent over a rake and dragged it across the hot summer sand in the well-practiced slouch of one whose eyes usually study the ground. He felt cooked and dry. The sun was unusually hot this morning, and he was particularly hung over.

Above him, to his left, a hawk coasted on air currents before diving into the woods on one of the pond's distant banks. A small splash a few hundred yards out caused a wide sphere of far-reaching circles, breaking the placidity of the pond. Other than that temporary break, the water was a dark mirror, reflecting placidly the morning's cloudless sky. Birds sang with furious joy all around the beach.

"I love you."

"I know you do."

Normally this exchange wouldn't trouble him. He'd acted it out enough times in the past. But before, with other girls, he'd utter the latter phrase or something similar. But not with this new girl. With Diana Huntington the familiar dynamic had swung around on him.

"I love you."

"I know you do."

He couldn't stop hearing it. His head hurt, and his mouth tasted thick and stale, like dried bile. She said she'd visit this weekend, but she hadn't shown up last night, so his friends got him drinking. Now he raked the beach at nine a.m. on Saturday morning, hoping she'd come tonight.

For the past three summers he'd worked at Camp Waetabee on the Rhode Island/Connecticut border, first as a dishwasher, then the last few years as a lifeguard. Camp Waetabee was a privately-owned campground for families who still roughed it. It had twelve-hundred acres of forest land and a lake they called a pond even though it was a quarter-mile wide. The lifeguards lived on the edge of the pond where a cabin had been built overlooking the man-made beach.

The Vice Principal of Hendricken Catholic High School for Boys, who had managed the camp for decades, got him the job at DeGawain's recommendation. DeGawain still worked at the camp, but now instead of washing dishes, he ran the kitchen. Camp Waetabee knew that not every family's definition of roughing it included cooking over an open fire, so they offered three meals a day at the camp mess hall where the staff ate.

He raked the beach and could hear himself say those

dangerous three words and could hear Diana not repeating them. In the past when a girl fell in love with him, he ended it. Not that commitment scared him. But he knew he couldn't love those girls and he knew also that it'd be unfair to drag out an emotionally lopsided relationship. But when it came to him, he couldn't give up hope. Diana could fall in love with him any day, any week; it could happen, and he didn't want to lose his chance by quitting. He was completely committed to his feelings and to his girl.

"Hey, Jim!"

He looked up toward the cabin, the only building on the beach.

"You daydreaming or raking out there?" David Gräbe, the lifeguard captain shouted.

He looked around and realized he'd been raking the same spot for quite some time. "Sorry, Gräbe!" He went back to work and found himself next to chair number four, filling in a hole dug by some camper's kid.

Three other lifeguards raked different sections of the beach. He'd known most of the other guards from high school or previous summers; some he'd never seen before, but they were really cool guys in their own way. They'd been helping him cope with his Diana problem, especially his boys Pow and DeGawain. Neither one of them had ever had much luck with the ladies, yet they always listened to his girl problems.

"I love you."

"I know you do."

He was nearly done raking his section of the long empty beach when he discovered a small sand castle near chair three. A primitive-looking job, like a motte-bailey arrangement, some kid had done little more than pile up a hill and mold something of a squarish structure on top. He imagined it being populated with tiny sand soldiers and wondered what they'd think of his rake coming down upon them. Would they think it was a judgment from God or would they imagine some other...?

"Jim!"

He jumped when he heard Gräbe shouting at him again. Gräbe was always a cool captain, but this morning the bosses were hanging around, so he needed to act tough. Gräbe was annoyed because, with the supervisors there, he would miss his morning nap. Jim snapped out of his sand castle musings and pushed the metal rake's tongs through the sand pile, the castle structure tumbling. With a few swift movements the area was flattened as though nothing had ever been there.

※

Later that day, he trod up the hot beach toward chair two. On particularly blazing days, families swarmed in the shade of the Pine Grove which lay to his right. A group of kids ran from the shade, on their way to the water, and he had to stop short to avoid walking into them. Most of the people whose blankets and baskets were in the grove swam in front of chairs one and two, so the lifeguards doubled-up there.

Out in the water more heads bobbed and jostled than he could ever hope to count. Pow picked his nose on the doubled-up chair. Troy—who Pow and he had convinced to come work at the camp this year—sat beside Pow.

"What's up, kids?" he said as he arrived at chair two.

"Not much, homes." Pow scratched at a braid above his left ear. "You hangin' in there today?"

"Yeah," he said, feeling a bit woozy.

Troy jumped down from the perch, his chair-sit over, and exchanged a horizontal hand-slap with Jim. Climbing up and plopping down on the hard, wooden surface, Jim started his half-hour sit. The lifeguards rotated regularly in this way to avoid heat exhaustion or sun-stroke.

Once Troy had strolled out of earshot, Pow asked again, "So, you sure you're okay today, Diffin?"

"Yeah, man. Why?"

"You were pretty fuckin' wasted last night," Pow said, briefly looking away from the water.

"Oh, I didn't know you were around, Pow."

"Yeah, I got in late last night, but you were trashed. I guess you must've blacked out the part of the night when I came in," Pow said with a hint of parental disappointment that Jim found odd.

"I guess."

They watched the tightly packed swimmers frothing up the waters before them. Eventually Pow said, "Yo, homes. I don't really know what to do with this Helen chick anymore."

"Why what happened?"

Pow sighed. "I went over to Helen's house to chill on my day off yesterday and when I got there, she's on the phone," he said. Pow swung his whistle in slow arcs. "She said something about some dude she saw making out with some girl. I couldn't help overhearing what she was saying, ya know? Turns out she's talking to this guy's girlfriend."

"Okay." He wondered what this had to do with anything.

"At first I thought she was trying to do the right thing," Pow said, catching his whistle in his fist, then turning to face him. "Diffin, she sounded all sweet and consoling." Pow sat back, slouching comfortably. "I sat there thinkin' 'aww, yeah. That's my girl.' But she gets off the phone, and I say how what had happened was too bad." Pow slapped his thigh. "Then the bitch cackles hysterically. Says how she made that shit up. She wanted that girl to break up with her boy 'cause the girl's parents were leaving town some upcoming weekend, and the girl didn't want a party, wanted to have a quiet weekend with her boyfriend, wanted to give him her v-card and shit," Pow said.

"Damn. What a cock-block," he said.

"Dude, she tried to break them up, so she could have a place to party. I told her that was fucked up, and she laughed and told me to lighten up." Pow sat, shaking his head as if remembering his initial disbelief.

He could tell that Helen's selfishness had upset Pow, so he decided to share his grief, too. "Yeah. Well, if it makes you feel any better, the reason I got so wasted last night was because Diana was supposed to come down and she didn't show."

"I heard. She at least called though, right?" Pow asked, concerned.

"No." He shrugged. "It's okay, though." He readjusted his shorts. "She hates the phone. She'd rather email or talk directly. It's one of her cute quirks," he said, even though it drove him crazy. Why the fuck couldn't she pick up the damn phone?

Pow shook his head as if to say, whatever. "Yo," Pow said, not looking away from the pond. "I read the craziest shit yesterday. Do you know how they used to catch monkeys in Asia?"

"Nope," Jim said, glad for the change of subject.

Pow poised his whistle at his lips, then continued, "They'd hollow out a coconut, tie it to the ground with a stake and put a piece of food or something inside. The monkey comes along, jams his hand in to get what's inside." Pow blew the whistle and signaled a swimmer to stop hanging onto the ropes. "Thing is, the hole isn't big enough for his fist to get out. But the monkey isn't smart enough to know all he's gotta do is let go and dump out the coconut. He doesn't let go, not even when the hunters come to round them up."

"Huh," Jim said, chuckling a little. "Stupid monkeys."

Jim watched a swimmer closely. He always found it hard to tell whether people were drowning or not. To him, most of the campers swam like they were drowning. He shrugged it off as the swimmer made some forward progress.

Pow elbowed him in the ribs. "Hey, I had the craziest fuckin' dream last night."

"Oh, yeah? Tell me about it," he said, expecting to hear some funny, half-remembered nonsense.

Pow raised his arms as if holding up a picture frame. "I stood on a beach, not this beach exactly, but sorta like it. Then a terrible fear overtook me, which was weird because it was a beautiful day. Then I noticed the sky changing from blue to purple and from purple to red. The red got deeper and deeper until it was black."

"Jesus," he said. Why hadn't Pow simply told him he'd had a nightmare?

Pow lowered his arms, crossing them over his chest. "The rest is hard to explain. It was like the sky got lower and lower. Then I realized the red sky was really a huge wall of flames and," Pow paused as if looking for the right words, "molten rock." Pow shook his head sadly. "People scurried around, pointlessly. The sand turned to glass under my feet," he said, getting excited. Then he spread his arms wide like an umpire signaling, safe and continued softly, "I remained still."

"Then what happened?" Jim asked, not even pretending to look at the water any longer.

"I woke up," Pow said, blowing his whistle at a swimmer who'd dunked his friend.

"Damn, Pow. How'd you remember that shit so vividly?" His dreams always seemed to be more like a foul taste left in his mouth, emotions without any memories attached to them. Usually he'd shake it off and get his day started.

"I've been trying to remember them. I've learned that the trick is respect; if you respect your dreams, they'll respect you," he said.

"What the fuck does that mean?" he asked, seriously wondering if Pow didn't have mental issues beyond mere A.D.D., or if maybe he really should be medicated.

"That if you try to remember your dreams, you can remember them and the more you try, the more you remember," he said, whirling his whistle again.

❧

Later that night, Jim sat on his bunk in the cabin. The sun had set, and the other guards were getting ready to go out. It was Saturday night. Gräbe passed him and stopped.

"Dude, you're not going out looking like that are you?"

He still wore his lifeguard shorts, sandals and a sandy, hooded sweatshirt. "Nah, I don't think I feel like going out," he said with a glance at the silent telephone.

Gräbe seemed to notice. "Damn. You know what you need to do? You need to go out and get laid."

He laughed, shaking his head.

"Seriously. Come out with me, man. I'll hook you up with some sweet x; you'll pop that shit, roll your ass off, meet a hottie, bring her back here and have the best sex of your life. When it's over, you'll forget about this Diana chick and how she's been messin' with ya head."

"I don't think so. I don't need to get laid. I just need to see Diana, but thanks all the same, man."

Gräbe turned around, thrust his arms in the air and stalked off.

Jim lay on his bed, thinking about what Gräbe had said, not about getting laid, but about going out and forgetting Diana. After some thought, he opted to stay in, nurse his hangover and hope to hear from her. Even if she blew him off again tonight, she might call, and then he'd at least hear her sweet voice and that would make him feel better.

Jim indulged in daydreams of Diana. He pictured her smile of crooked lower teeth, her Roman nose, her deep brown eyes, her bleached blonde hair and bangs. Funny, he'd always thought if he fell in love, it would have to be with some incredible beauty, some physical perfection. Now, he realized that perfect beauty doesn't spring from some objective ideal, but is born from traces of beauty: soft skin, bright eyes, blushing cheeks, mixed with flaws, grounding fantasy in reality. Besides, she made him laugh.

After the guys left, he drifted off to sleep, waking in the middle of the night to the guys stumbling back in. Troy ambled over and poked him. He had hoped to avoid late night drunk talk and wanted to pretend to sleep through it. But Troy poked harder and harder.

"What?" he asked, feigning the lethargy of a newly awakened person, still hoping he could be left alone.

"You'll never guess who was at the club, dude," Troy said in a loud, drunken whisper.

His heart rate picked up. He tried to relax, it couldn't have been her, but who else would Troy wake him up for? "Who? Not Diana, right?"

Troy's head bobbed dangerously backward as if he were about to topple back in surprise. "How did you guess?" Troy asked, about to start laughing.

"You what!"

"We saw Diana at the club tonight," Troy told him.

"What the fuck!"

Troy nodded.

"What the hell did she have to say for herself?"

"Akshally she wanted to know where you were," Troy said, jabbing him in the ribs with a forefinger.

He sat up. "What? She wanted to know where I was? Didn't she remember about coming down here?"

"She remembers telling you she'd see you this weekend. She said, she'd meant at the club," Troy explained, trying to keep his head from toppling over in one direction or another.

"Bullshit!"

Pow neared his bunk.

"Do you know about this bullshit, Pow?"

"What's that?"

"Diana. At the club tonight!"

Pow's smile faded and his head drooped. "Yeah, homes. She was there. I was trying to figure out how to tell you. She says she thought you would've been there. Guess it was a miscommunication?"

"Fuck no! She clearly said she was coming down here. She's getting creative now in how she blows me off!"

"Calm down, Diffin. I'm sure it's not such a big deal as all that. I told her what you thought the plan was and suggested she come down here today or in the next few days anyway," Pow said.

"Whatever. I can't believe this. She's blown me off, and I can't even be mad, 'cause she's gonna say I blew her off by not going to the club tonight. Sometimes I wonder why I try."

"Sorry, homes."

Troy put his hand gently on Jim's shoulder. "Sorry, man. Maybe you should call her in the morning?"

His whole body sagged. "I guess I have to," he said, falling back against his bunk. The whole cabin seemed to observe a mournful silence. He felt responsible for the sudden heavy air in the room. They should be laughing and joking about their night. Instead, he could sense that they felt bad for him and were going to sleep quietly. Their sympathy made him even more miserable.

8

As he tugged on his black, skater sneaker, a booming voice from outside the cabin caught his attention. He couldn't make out what it said, but he knew the voice.

DeGawain burst inside and bellowed, "Hey, fuckers! You guys ready to bust a move and shit?" DeGawain had on his bright orange, bowling-team jersey and some beige cargo shorts.

Yeats, another new lifeguard this season, closed his locker, finished buttoning a conservative blue shirt and dashed on some extra cologne. "Yeah, we're about ready." It only took one chair-sit to know that Yeats was quite a lonely, romantic guy. A very common type, he had all the drive, honesty and desire to be the best boyfriend any girl would ever have. Unfortunately, girls didn't want a guy like Yeats. He always came off as too needy or too desperate.

All the lifeguards were going out with DeGawain, except Gräbe who was going to stay in and pop pills alone. Not like their night looked to be any better. But they wanted to get out of the woods for a while. The idea was to drop by Panza's house to make some plans for later. He didn't really care if they simply sat around Panza's house and drank, and he didn't think anyone else felt any differently.

"Sweet." DeGawain's kinetic energy dissipated as he sauntered over to Jim's bunk. "You ready to skank it up, guy?" Obviously, DeGawain wanted to find a club.

"Fuck that. You know I don't skank," he said, clasping his shiny watch in place. Jim wore baggy cargo shorts and a black, polyester shirt.

"You know what I mean," DeGawain said, shrugging. "No need to get pissy."

"I'm sorry, kid. It's just—have you heard from Diana lately?"

"Nope. She still fuckin' with your head?"

"Yeah. Maybe she's had it with me?"

"I doubt that, guy," DeGawain said, grinning.

"Well, me too," he said, wondering what the fuck DeGawain was smiling so impishly for. He thought that he'd sound paranoid if he came out and asked, so he let it slide. "I wish I knew what the fuck was going on."

"I hear ya. Don't sweat it though. I'm sure everything's fine," DeGawain said, his grin growing broader. Then DeGawain grew serious, turned around and shouted, "All right, boys! Put on your drinkin' shoes and let's ramble on out of here!"

DeGawain headed outside. Nobody moved to follow. Troy pulled his gray hoodie over a surfing company t-shirt, and Pow, standing in his usual raggy, spacious jeans and dirty, white t-shirt, finished changing the colors of his elastics to red, white and blue; Independence Day was coming soon.

As the group climbed the hill leading away from the cabin, he thought for a moment about DeGawain's new reaction to his Diana problems. Did DeGawain want him to break up with Diana? Did he know something? DeGawain had known Diana first; maybe she'd said something to him. He laughed off the ideas. DeGawain would definitely tell him if he knew anything. He could count on that.

The whole crew snaked, single-file down a narrow path, low hanging branches drooping into the middle, lichen-covered granite pushing up in spots as if trying to trip the distracted walker. The path led to a dirt lot where most of the staff parked. Pow, DeGawain and he stayed in front, knowing the path well enough to navigate it in the dark without a flash-light; DeGawain and he regularly did it in pitch dark and drunk. As they emerged from the woods and Yeats's Saturn coup came into view, DeGawain bolted.

"Shotgun!" DeGawain shouted, sprinting for the car's front seat.

"Shotgun blitz!" Troy shouted and ran after him. There were two rules for calling shotgun. The first was that you had to wait until you were headed to the car and, in some circles, you could see the vehicle. The second was that anyone could call a shotgun blitz if you didn't stipulate, shotgun—no blitz. A blitz meant nothing more than a challenge for the seat, settled by a mad dash; first to touch the passenger door won the seat. The race was on until they ran into each other and fell on the dusty ground beside the car. Jim laughed as they wrestled in a cloud of dust, trying to pull free first and win the seat. All they accomplished was getting their clothes dirty.

The sound of a car engine distracted him from his entangled friends for a moment. A brown Chrysler LeBaron convertible rolled into the lot.

Troy won out on the...

He looked back at the convertible as it pulled into an empty spot a few car-lengths away. It was Diana.

She climbed out of the car, beaming an innocent smile.

He walked toward her and away from his friends. She opened her arms and he hugged her. Then he pulled away.

"Why didn't you come down last night?" he asked, still skeptical about what Troy and Pow had told him.

"Maybe I fucked up. I'm here now and it's still this weekend." She leaned close to him and whispered, "Your friends told me last night how upset you were. So, I came down right away." Then she hugged him and said, "And now I'm here, fucknuts!"

He couldn't stay mad; she smiled, and his anger evaporated. "It's okay. It's just that now it's too dark to really show you around. You'd love this place. It really is beautiful."

She'd miss the clouds sweeping and swirling in the big sky over the pond at their lazy pace, the deep green trees closely framing the pond with the occasional snow-white birch leaning out as if trying to touch the giant, opaque mirror, so calm, so flat in the early morning and yet so choppy in the late afternoon. Even the path they hiked now would be a wonder in the sunlight. But more than anything else, she had missed the sunset—filled with a whole new rainbow of reds, oranges and yellows so beautiful he hoped to imprint them on his mind forever.

But then, he got an idea.

The marshy far side of the pond, inhabited by mosquitoes and skunk cabbage, didn't have many campsites, and not many campers traveled there. But he knew about a few spots of dry land hidden away. He convinced Diana to spend the night with him across the pond in a little tent that he could strap to his hiking pack.

She called her mom to say she was spending the night with some friends at a camp in South County. Mrs. Huntington was a single mother who believed the best way to teach her children responsibility was to allow them their freedom. She trusted that any daughter of hers would make the right decisions. Except for the occasional lie, Diana proved her right. It was actually the very "smallness" of the lies that upset him. She thought nothing of them. He tried to remember that lying to parents was a necessity at times, but couldn't shake a bad feeling about it, especially considering her tight friendship with Helen.

But he tried not to get bogged down in doubt. He trusted Diana. He had to. A love without trust is a wounded, frail thing.

"So, what did you do all weekend?" he asked, trying not to sound bitter about having missed her for the past few days. The waning moon had been full two nights ago, but low clouds hid it and shut out the glow it would have cast across the pond's still surface.

"Nothing," she said, sighing. "I drove Nina around. After school Friday, I took care of the horses, rode them a bit, then I had to open up the pipe under the kitchen sink, because my mom lost a ring down there. But that didn't take long. It was kinda gross though."

Diana was different from other girls, she wasn't a "girly-girl" but there was more. She could fix anything, cook anything, find anything, or at least that was her spirit, a fearlessness, an adventurousness, an "I can do anything" attitude exuded from her. It was impossible to ignore and totally sexy.

Diana continued her running list. "I went to the club Saturday night, but you know that. Today I slept in a bit, then cleaned the house for my mom 'cause she had to work," she detailed her chore-filled weekend with the satisfied air of fulfilled obligations. Then she hugged his arm to her and said, "And now I'm here with you on a great hike through these dark woods."

"Are you scared?" he asked jokingly.

"What? With an experienced woodsman like you with me?" Diana giggled, and he wasn't sure if she was being completely sarcastic or not.

"I'm pretty experienced."

"I know, my little Eagle Scout." Diana said, and again he wasn't sure if he was being teased, or if she was serious.

Diana must have sensed his unease. She said, "I'm busting your balls. I know you know what you're doing, fucknuts. Relax, it's me."

The dry forested path had become a wetter, muddier ground by now. It had grown brighter, too. The clouds had drifted away from the moon, and a patch of wide-open, night sky surrounded the imperfect oval. In the brighter light, he noticed a few bats swooping over their heads, gorging themselves with a dinner of insects while cruising the night air. He bent down and picked up a handful of pebbles.

"What are you doing?" she asked. He told her to wait and stepped a few yards away from her. He told her to watch as he threw a pebble into the air barely below the bats' flight path. One bat dove toward them, hungrily chasing the pebble as it dropped, following it to a few feet above their heads before giving up. Diana screamed. She hadn't seen the bats, or maybe she'd thought they were small night-birds.

"I can't believe you made me scream like a bitch," she said, laughing at herself. They found more pebbles and took turns luring bats down toward them, each time getting a close look at the black, glove-like creatures with serrated wings.

When they grew tired of the game, Diana said, "Jim, can I ask you for a favor?"

"Sure," he said, tossing the remaining pebbles he held in his moist palm into the brush and heading up the path again.

"It's kinda weird, but it shouldn't be," Diana said, trying to walk side-by-side with him. "I mean... I don't want you to think it's weird, but I'm afraid you will."

"Try me," he said with an inviting smile.

"Well, there's this good friend of mine, Sam. He's a really good kid, but like I said, he's just a friend."

"Okay, so you have a guy friend." He didn't care if she had guy friends. It would only be weird if she tried to keep it a secret. Jealousy ruined more relationships than it saved, so he avoided it as best as he could. "I'm not some crazy, jealous freak," he said with a laugh.

"All right. Well, he was in this band or something... Anyway, the band broke up, and now the remaining guys are forming two new bands and... Look, the old guitarist wants to beat up my friend for pretty much nothing. He's got a group together, and they're going to jump him. And I told him I'd try to find him some help." Diana shot him a pained expression.

"Oh. Is that all?" he said, hitting his open palm with the flashlight playfully. "You want me to get some of my friends together to give this kid some back up?"

Somehow, Sam had learned that his former band mates planned the attack for a Sevendust concert, which Jim thought was great. He loved Sevendust and knew that Pow did, too. The guys would probably jump at the chance to go protect some skater, punk rock kid Diana went to school with, mostly to get away from the woods awhile, see a show and have an adventure.

"We'll rock out, pound some heads and then go chill elsewhere." he said enthusiastically.

"Thanks, Jim. You're the best," she said and pecked him on the cheek in stride.

He enjoyed sharing a comfortable silence with her as they strolled down the dark, moist path in the cool, summer air. After a few more bends in the path, a few inclines and granite-paved sections of earth, he veered off and stepped onto a large boulder jutting from the ground between two cedars. He reached back to help Diana up. She climbed right past his hand and took a few steps beyond him.

"Aren't you going to lead the way?" she asked playfully.

"Yeah, but this is it up here," he said. Up ahead, the path opened to a wide, dry campsite.

In a few minutes, he was building a fire while Diana sat inside the tent setting up the sleeping bags, trying to zip them together to make one. She insisted she could figure it out alone. He could hear her struggling with it behind him as he put the kindling together in a small teepee. By the time he was building a log cabin of larger pieces around the teepee, he heard triumphant zipping sounds.

The flashlight beam preceded Diana to the fire pit. He sat back, blinded and waited for his eyes to adjust.

"You put that together in the dark?" Diana asked, genuinely impressed.

"Yeah, well... it wasn't too dark over here. The moon was peeking out from the clouds a bit."

He finished building the fire, lit it, and soon they cuddled by its warmth, sitting on a bed of soft grass, leaning against a hefty log. She lay between his legs, the back of her head against his chest. Her hair smelled like raspberries,and his hands rested on her soft, flat tummy. Her arms rested on his legs, her hands idly rubbing his calves and knees.

"So," he began, stroking her belly. "How have you been?"

"I've been all right. I've really missed you," she said, twisting her head around for a long kiss.

"Mmm," he said. "I've missed you, too."

Diana snuggled into his chest and sighed contentedly.

"How's Jack?" he asked, wondering about the little rabbit he'd bought her for Easter.

Diana's whole body flinched and she pulled away, turning to look at him. "Oh my God! I never got to tell you!"

"What?"

"Helen killed him!" Diana said through wide eyes.

"How the hell did she do that?" he asked. Helen might be a sexy, little thing, but she certainly had issues.

"I don't know, but I know she did it somehow. I think she was jealous of him or something. I left her alone with him the other day while I was getting ready to go out. When I came back, she had Jack out of his cage and the minute she saw me, she like jumped and put him back. That night, he died."

"That's fuckin' weird," he said rubbing his chin. He'd definitely have to tell Pow about this. Even if it made no sense, or maybe because it made no sense.

"I know!" Diana exclaimed with a long, rising and falling "o."

"I'm sorry. Maybe I can buy you a new one?" he said, pulling her closer.

"No. It's okay," she said, rubbing the back of his knee. "I guess I have enough pets already with the horses and the dogs and all."

"I guess you do." he said. His hand wandered up

closer to her breasts. Her hand met his, not to halt it, but to guide it. He traced the circumference of her right breast through the lacy bra, then moving under it he fondled her nipple. He kissed her neck, and she leaned back into him, one hand on his forearm the other stroking his thigh.

They kissed and explored each other's bodies for hours while the campfire died down. By that time, he could tell he had made her face a bit raw from his stubble and he apologized.

"Don't be sorry. I'm not. It kinda hurts, but it was worth it," she said soothingly.

Staring into the dying fire, he said, "I love you so much, Diana."

"I know you do and that means a lot to me," Diana said, rubbing his right calf.

He dumped buckets of water on the fire pit and swirled the swampy ashes with a stick. Then, they moved to the tent and snuggled in the sleeping bag, until they fell sound asleep.

9

The night of the Sevendust concert the temperature dropped into the low sixties, the wind kicked up, and a line of kids snaked around the block from the Lupo's Heartbreak Hotel entrance. He and DeGawain crossed the street to join Pow and Troy who held a space in the line.

There they stood, he and his friends huddled together an hour and a half before the doors were scheduled to open. They shivered from the cool air, having left their sweatshirts and jackets in their rides, rather than risk losing them in the club.

"Where are those girls, man?" he asked.

"That crazy bitch Helen is probably holding 'em up," DeGawain said, his hands in his brown cargo pants. "Man, I hate that chick,"

"Yeah, aren't those bitches supposed to come keep us warm," Troy asked bitterly, rubbing his hands together against the chilly, night air.

"Fuck that Helen bitch. She prolly knows we'll stay and wait in this long-assed line for them until the doors open," Pow said, twisting a braid kept in place with a red elastic.

"Does she know you're gonna be in line with us?" he asked.

"Nah. Unless one of you told her," Pow said, releasing the greasy braid.

"How did you two break up anyways?" asked Troy.

Pow seemed to search the grimy, gum-spotted sidewalk for the words to explain his former relationship with Helen before giving up. "It's a long story, homes. I don't know if I wanna get into it."

"We do have a long time 'til doors open or this line goes anywhere," Jim remarked.

Pow shrugged his shoulders almost up to his ears. "Well, I'll just say she's a crazy, lying bitch."

"Whoa!" Jim laughed loud enough for the whole block to hear.

Pow continued, "Look, I could never be sure of when she was telling the truth or when she was off on some crazy, made-up story. Then, I find out she lied to me about her age."

"No way? How old did she say she was?" DeGawain prodded.

"Nineteen. Bitch is sixteen, in high school. You believe that?"

"Yeah, I knew that." he answered; DeGawain nodded.

"Why the fuck didn't you tell me, then?" Pow asked, disappointed.

"Didn't know you didn't know." DeGawain explained.

"Well, anyway. After that it made me doubt her crazy lies even more. I couldn't deal with that fake-assed bitch."

"Yeah, you gotta keep keepin' it real." Troy said mockingly.

"Whatever, homes. Bitch made me crazy, felt totally off center."

Troy stopped blowing on his hands to ask "So, why the hell are we here two hours early, again?"

"Simple. This stands to be a rather rough show, and the ladies would like to avoid getting elbows to their faces and whatnot. So, we're camped out here with these fanatics to capture some balcony space. That way we need not get rough with the hard-rock, heathen, plebeian types," DeGawain lectured.

"Unless we want to," Troy said with an impish grin.

"Which we shall. Which we shall," DeGawain assured.

"Speaking of getting rough, you're all down with the backstory we're faced with here, correct?" Jim asked.

Troy revealed his ignorance. "Backstory?"

"Well," he began, "this past weekend Diana came to visit. We took a hike to the far side of the pond and had a nice little night together out there."

"Did you bone her or not?" Troy asked. DeGawain looked away, hands in his back pockets, shuffling his feet.

"That's beside the point," he explained.

"So, you didn't fuck her then." Troy laughed.

Jim ignored him. "Anyway, she has a friend, Sam who was in this band," he went on to tell the story about how Sam was going to be getting jumped that night; he didn't quite get to the part where they were there to help Sam when Troy interrupted.

"How'd this Sam kid find out about the ambush?" Troy wondered.

Jim shrugged and related what he'd learned from Diana—that the guitarist from Sam's old band wanted to pound Sam, but first he had to rally support, and when he asked his old drummer for help, the drummer laughed, saying, "Yo, Sam is my friend, fool." Jim stopped to chuckle. "So, to make this long story a little shorter, tonight could be interesting and by that, I mean violent," he finished with an air of light-hearted excitement.

"Oh, so I've been unwittingly conscripted into battle, eh?" Troy asked, attempting to force his hundred-and-thirty-pound frame into insouciant serenity.

"Well, telling you was Pow's job. He must've forgot, big surprise," he explained, feeling genuinely sorry for roping Troy into a precarious position.

"Hey, come on man," Pow demanded with a lazy shrug.

"Hey, no big deal, Troy. Hang out and mosh. When trouble comes, you can hang back. We don't mind," he said

Trying not to make Troy feel guilty, he avoided looking at him, busying himself by rubbing his hands together and scanning the street for the girls' arrival or familiar faces or idly attempting to appreciate the historic downtown architecture. Pow stared at his feet, and DeGawain peered into a store front window.

After a couple minutes of standing with his head bowed, his hand nervously scratching the rear of his skull, a lot of weight shifting from left to right to left and back, Troy finally blurted out, "Look, I came here to knock some heads in the mosh pit, so what's the difference if I have to knock some heads in a brawl, right?"

No sooner had Troy committed himself to the cause, then a communal sigh of relief evaporated the tension, which Jim expressed with a quick laugh and a "nice."

Light-hearted banter and reminiscences ruled the conversation, until the arrival of the spirited sixteen-year-olds and Diana's fourteen-year-old sister. After the teasings of the where-ya-beens and the aren't-we-lates, an awkward moment persisted between Pow and Helen as they acted like they'd never known each other, or worse like they wished they never had.

Troy, somehow oblivious to the tension between Pow and Helen, noticed her shivering and offered to keep her warm, which she probably accepted from necessity, spite and lastly, perhaps, attraction. Jim followed the lead and wrapped his arms around Diana, leaving Pow, DeGawain and Nina solely in the chilly wind. Under the pretext of chivalry DeGawain took little Nina's nubile frame into his bearish embrace, holding her tightly, rubbing her soft, young arms, but his eyes seemed to linger on Diana. Pow stood stoic and reserved, shivering alone.

"Hey, where's that skinny kid you're friends with?" Diana asked. Jim shrugged, and the others looked perplexed, but when Diana clarified that she was asking about the "wacky, wild one," Troy figured that she meant Yeats. It turned out Yeats had scored a date, which made Diana smile and nod approvingly, especially since Jim had told her about his frequent lack of romantic success. He'd told her several times that he firmly believed that any girl who gave him half a chance would fall for his humor and kindness and never let go.

Fifteen minutes later, the group lounged on the balcony directly across from the stage while lots of kids and the occasional, oddball "old dude" streamed onto the dance floor below. The boys waited at the railing, bouncing legs and picking nails, eager to have the hard music stimulate their violent tendencies and ready themselves for the impending rumble.

Once Limp Bizkit struck the opening chords, the girls stood alone above the jostling, jumping, flailing bodies. Out on the floor, he lost track of his boys after he signaled for a nearby concert-goer to hoist him atop the crowd. He surfed the crowd well; he knew how to relax and give in to the will of the supporting arms.

He liked feeling out of control, in the power of something stronger, something that could lift him up and dash him down on a whim; it was a freeing feeling for him and it reminded him of being a kid again, having your dad pick you up and carry you, or having the older kids at the pool be able to throw you high into the air, splashing safely into the waiting water. When he finally dropped, he landed on his curving back, bracing the fall with his arms. He dusted himself off and found himself five heads away from the stage and one person away from the opening circle of moshers behind him. In the pit, Pow wildly performed his "move," which looked like he was jerking an impossibly long lawn mower cord, fist sweeping a wide arc from his knees to behind his head.

Jim worked up his courage and ventured into the continuous fray, swinging wildly and hopping straight across, purposefully ramming into Pow and exiting the other side, while others lingered, courting personal injury.

Finding a spot where the crowd packed tightly again, he went up to crowd surf again, but this time when the wave of hands beneath broke, he fell flat and hard on his unbraced back and couldn't breathe. He felt silly gasping for air in public, so he wove his way to the bathroom. After a couple of minutes, he managed to catch his breath, and when he was ready to leave, Pow breezed in.

"'Sup, kid?" Jim asked, before seeing what was, in fact, up. "Holy shit! Are you all right, dude?"

"Yeah, took a good shot is all," Pow said, holding his right eye. He waited for Pow as he splashed cold water on his face, hoping to slacken the swelling as best as he could without ice.

Once he'd found out that Pow didn't care and there was no beef, no asshole to bash, he thought he'd use this moment to ask Pow something. He rested against a stall. "Hey, let me ask you something."

"What, homes?" Pow asked, turning around.

He bit his nails a bit and asked, "What do you think of Diana?"

Pow shrugged slightly. "I don't know. She's cute. She seems like a cool enough chick."

He nodded, scrunching his face inquisitively "Yeah?"

Pow shrugged again. He turned back to the sink. "She is friends with Helen, so she might be crazy, but not necessarily."

He laughed lightly for a moment. "Pow, you believe everything is possible, though everything seems to also be 'not necessarily,' too. So, you really haven't told me anything."

Pow looked at him in the mirror. "I don't know anything."

"Right, you can't be sure of whatever it is you know. We've been through this befo…"

Pow cut him off. "No. I'm being serious, homes. I really don't know anything about her. I've never hung out with her and whatever Helen has said is suspect to me, homes."

His curiosity deepened with the mention of Helen "saying things" about Diana to Pow. "Well, what has she said?"

"I don't really remember. I stopped listening to her at some point. Mostly meaningless girl-bitching though, if you ask me," Pow explained and then continued, "which you did."

"Right," he agreed.

"Let's get back to the show, Diff."

Outside in the heavy heat of the dance floor's massed bodies, the music had ceased. Fred, the front man of Limp Bizkit, stood at center stage wiping his brow before his voice boomed across the crowd. "Okay, everybody, we, the members of Limp Bizkit, have received some upsetting news about a very good friend of the band. It seems Everlast, formerly of House of Pain, has suffered a major heart attack and is even now in a hospital emergency room. And since we can't do shit to help him, we are going to dedicate this next number to our boy Everlast. Get well, m'man!"

Jim's mouth fell open and his brows raised, both from the news that a member of one of his favorite rap groups had taken ill and at the mention of a song in his honor. He shared knowing eye contact with Pow, and they sprinted toward the mosh pit. All he knew about Limp Bizkit coming into this show was they had a song he liked called "Counterfeit" and a d.j. named Lethal—also formerly of the House of Pain. His mosh pit timidity vanished as he flailed and jumped with all the strength and energy he could muster for a hard-core version of House of Pain's hugest hit, "Jump Around."

When it was over, he panted contentedly all the way back to the balcony and Diana. She laughed at his excitement and his perspiration. "Did you see me in there? I was rippin' it up."

"I know. I saw you," she said with a smile that seemed to reveal intense affection and maybe even... Love?

He slid his arm around the small of her back and pulled her close. She put her arm around his shoulder, and they watched the show, while Helen, taking in the show, also silently watched them. He ignored her as best as he could and Limp Bizkit finished up, followed by a Led Zeppelin song pumping through the speakers at a reduced volume.

Sevendust began to rock the room to close out the show, and so far, there hadn't been an incident. During Sevendust's performance, Diana pointed out Sam, and Jim kept a close eye on him, a benign big brother from above. Sam stood at the mosh pit's edge, and some punks hung around the pit shooting angry glances at him.

The fight didn't start until halfway through the third song. A large kid with a handle-bar mustache and wavy, red hair grasped the arm of a smaller, lankier boy with a closely shaved head and an incredibly pale complexion and swung him round and round until the kid's feet left the ground and he swung in a wide arc, clearing out the pit. To his astonishment the larger kid, with perfect aim and premeditation, released the bald kid, letting him fly like a human missile, striking Sam squarely in the chest and sending them and many others sprawling to the ground.

Fists flew, 300-pound bouncers waded through the crowd like it was shallow water. He rushed away from Diana and gathered up his friends. Some punks started shit with the door-men and got pummeled and handed over to the cops. But most of the crowd rushed for the exit and met on the street. He and his crew were the last to leave, and as he cruised out, he turned. Inside, Diana stood alone on a nearly empty pit floor. She waved, and he thought her lips said, "thank you."

Cops on the street and on horses shouted for the crowd to move along and not to start any trouble. The mob mentality took over and, even though this group sought an internecine violence, it somehow silently, knowingly made its way around the corner and down a few blocks toward a large, dark, empty parking lot.

Suddenly Helen appeared between the two groups and cussed out the other group, "You're full of shit. I don't even know what we're doing here. You guys sit around and suck each other's dicks all day, so why do you even wanna try to fuck with these guys. We're gonna fuck you up for real! Why don't you go home and cry!"

He entered the lot, wondering if this would be a shouting match between the principal parties ending in a dispersion, or if "shit was going to go down." Usually, it would be the former, but it didn't take long for him to get his answer as a wisp of a kid came up to the drummer of Sam's defunct band and belted him across the side of the head with a Louisville Slugger. The two groups rushed into one, and all he could see were fists, elbows and knees. Helen had disappeared.

He stuck close to Sam and tackled the kid with the bat before he could land it on Sam's skull. He broke the kid's nose with a quick jab, hucked the bat across the street, into an alley and moved on. Behind him, Troy was knocked to his back. A red-headed kid about his size kicked his ribs. But before he could react to save Troy, Pow had stepped over their fallen pal, standing like a colossus and drilled Troy's attacker in the throat. DeGawain appeared to Jim's left side, his meaty arm brushing past his cheek and into a punk's face.

"You gotta watch what you're doing, Diffin," was all DeGawain said, striding on.

DeGawain took a bat to the forearm, and he tried to rush to his aid, but a blow dug into his kidney. He turned, and a fist struck his nose. Blood poured into his mouth, his eyes watered, he blinked a few times and rammed his forehead into someone's face. A huge weight took him down from behind. He wrestled on the hard, chilly ground, his neck tucked against his chest to avoid the headlock that thick arms tried to put him in. He noticed a kid slumped on the ground next to him, the kid he'd head-butted. Somehow, he squirmed out of the sweaty arms, rolled out beside the kid's girth, punched a left hook to his face, got up and kicked him in the ribs a few times.

He ducked, seeing something come toward his head, a hockey stick. He backed off, putting the downed big kid—now rising—between him and the long, curved stick. Someone else hit the hockey kid from behind with a skateboard. He scanned the crowd, finding his friends.

Soon more weapons appeared: broom handles, crowbars, more bats, but once the flash of a knife swept through his peripheral vision, he seized Sam by his shirt collar and split. Pow, DeGawain and Troy followed him, and, as they fled the scene, sirens whooped and hollered in the night. Sam cursed and spat, until his temper cooled and he realized that he'd been done a favor.

Cops, the news later told them, had arrested twenty "delinquents" in the rumble, and at least twelve kids were reported injured and hospitalized.

10

The keening kettle puffed billowing clouds of steam before his mother shut off the burner and poured their tea. He grabbed the milk. They fixed their drinks and sat at the cluttered kitchen table; bills and old mail piled up everywhere.

He generally preferred tea to coffee. Having been raised on tea, he still liked to sit down for a quiet cup and a book or sit and chat over tea. Some Americanized Irish assumed that tea was a drink for the English. He knew better.

His family had been in the States a handful of generations, having weathered the great potato famine in the countryside of Cork. It wasn't until after the turn of the twentieth century that the Sullivan's and the Ahern's of his mother's side had made the long voyage into diaspora.

On the other hand, his father's side, Orangemen from County Armagh, had in fact been Americans for perhaps a hundred years or more. They'd been Michigan woodsmen, and supposedly one of his paternal great-grandmothers had been Sioux. So, while his Protestant father sat home with the television every Sunday, his mother dragged him and his brother to pick up their grandmother and go to Mass. After church, they'd sit down and drink tea; he and his brother's cups being mostly sugar and milk. Eventually less and less sugar and less and less milk were necessary and before he knew it, he was a regular tea drinker. He drank coffee to get a caffeine jolt; coffee was for utilitarian uses; tea was for pleasure and relaxation.

"You worry me, honey," she said, putting a rough hand on the back of his wrist. He slurped his scalding tea and asked why.

"Because," she said, sighing heavily. "I'm afraid you're throwing your love away."

He wanted to slam his tea mug on the table, but had to place it down or it would spill and scald him. His mother rubbed his hairy forearm reassuringly. "You deserve someone who will love you back. Someone who will love you the same way you love them," she said removing her hand to pick up her cup.

"I want you to have somebody love you like I love your father," his mother continued.

"Hey, where is dad?" he asked more to change the subject rather than out of any real concern.

His mother's lower lip rose against the upper one, and her eyes searched the far wall. "He's at a scout meeting," she said, nodding slowly. His father had chosen to remain active in the Boy Scouts after he had finished. It gave his father a hobby, something to keep him occupied, and it gave his mother time to herself.

"Oh. This late? Is that usual?" he asked to make conversation.

"He's been having meetings later and later," she said distantly. "It's good, keeps him busy."

Usually, he didn't question his father's absences, he relished them. The home underwent a metamorphosis without him there, brighter, airier, more wholesome and less depressing. His mother would leave the television off, she'd put music on, and there would be more conversation, more human interaction.

After closing up the beach, he had gone home for a cup of tea with his mother. The clock in the kitchen read 10:35, and he figured he'd be leaving soon since his mother liked to go to bed early on her nights off. But he still had to complete the task at hand. The real reason he had gone home before his day off.

"Ma, can I ask you for a huge favor? A one-time deal, I swear," he began.

"What is it?" she asked with a hint of impatience.

"Since I can't go to the family reunion and all..."

"I can't either. Just because it's your father's family doesn't mean I wouldn't like to go, too."

"I know, but..." he didn't know how to broach the word "party." "I thought that maybe with dad away I could..." must get it out, "have a Fourth of July party," he finished in one long stream.

"No," she said, unflinchingly.

"Come on, ma." It couldn't end like that. The idea had sprung up in his heat-soaked isolation on a long chair-sit. It seemed brilliant. His brother William had been allowed to have a party a few years ago, when their parents were out of town. Of course, he'd missed it, working his first grueling summer as a dishwasher at camp Waetabee. It only seemed fair that he should be allowed one party.

"What am I supposed to do with myself?" Her face twisted as if she'd smelled something rancid. "You think I want to 'hang out' with your friends?" she asked.

"I thought you could spend one night at

grandma's." Ever since his grandfather died when he was a small boy, his mother and grandmother had grown very close. This idea also seemed perfect, since his grandmother had gotten very ill lately, and they'd be able to spend quiet time together. Even if his mother got home from work after midnight, there was still the morning. "And I'll clean everything better than it was before, I promise."

His mother remained silent. She seemed to be thinking about it.

"I'll think about it," she said.

He sighed. "That means no."

"Not really. I want to check with your father first."

"Oh, then that's definitely a no." He took a hearty sip from his hot mug.

They finished their tea; he hung around for a while. His mother put in a wash of laundry, scrubbed the dishes, folded the laundry and dried the dishes, and he tried to convince her—taking care to remind her about William's party. That was his best angle for sure. His parents had always valued fairness. She seemed receptive, but she would have to convince his father. That would be the end of that for a while.

Before he left, the phone rang. It was Yeats. Gräbe decided last minute to throw a party at his parents' summerhouse a half-hour away from camp. He got directions, changed clothes and drove straight down.

The Omni rumbled and groaned off the dirt-road, between the skinny birch and pine trees and up the windy driveway. He eased the old hatchback under a maple, leapt out and ran across the moist grass to a crowd standing by a low, empty stage. People bounced on a trampoline nearby. He recognized Pow's braids on one of them. Backslaps, "Hey, Diffin" and "Yo, The Diff's here!" and other variations greeted him.

DeGawain had invited Diana, so Jim grabbed a beer, and they hunted for her.

By the porch of the side door Diana awkwardly raised a purple bass guitar over Sam's head. When she finished placing it on him, her arms seemed to linger on his shoulders. He shook the impression from his head as he stepped closer. Sam slid away from Diana to slap Jim's outstretched hand, then thanked him again for helping him in the brawl and asked if he had any requests. He almost said: Stay away from my girlfriend. But of course, Sam meant musical requests, and he didn't really need Sam to stay away. He wasn't the jealous type. Sam mounted the stage with the rest of his new band. Diana wrapped her arms around Jim.

DeGawain, grinning savagely, stepped closer, smelling like onions and spilled beer. "You're getting pretty friendly with that musician, huh, Diana?"

Diana frowned without a trace of guilt. Jim pulled her tighter. DeGawain loomed even closer and snatched Jim's polyester shirt sleeve. "Remember where you got this shirt from, guy?" he asked. He wondered how drunk DeGawain was and what he might be getting at. Of course he remembered. The shirt was a special selection from a day of hungover shopping in a Brooklyn thrift shop.

The trip had been DeGawain's idea. Andy, an old friend of theirs from camp, had gone to Pratt Art Institute in Brooklyn; so, Panza, DeGawain and he piled into DeGawain's pick-up a week or two before Valentine's Day. The trip wracked his parents' nerves because a snowstorm had been predicted to dump a few feet of snow around the same time they headed out. They beat out the storm, no problem. Then in Brooklyn, they learned about Bodegas; go in, buy pretzels, bread, lunch-meat, a six—make that a twelve pack, easy. The ID process? "You twenty-one? Yes? Okay." Easy.

They'd sat in the dorm, drinking beers, playing cards and inviting girls from around campus to join them. It wound up being yet another weekend when he'd gotten lucky enough to meet a sexy, little girl who brought him away from his friends. A slender Asian girl whose name she didn't trust him to pronounce—call me "G," everyone else does—took him back to her room. For what? Lots of scantily clad necking. Everyone figured he'd screwed her, and it was once again easier to smile and let them assume he'd gotten lucky than to explain the truth.

But then DeGawain began relating the whole tale to Diana. He didn't even know what to say. If he told his friend to shut up, who knew what Diana would think had actually happened. The fat man opened the story with the snowstorm, told totally overblown. Then the excessive drinking and the day of shopping at the thrift shop. On the way to the store—because Andy brought a friend—he and Panza had toured Brooklyn laying in the flatbed, while brownstones and street signs like Myrtle and Willerby panned past.

Inside the musty building, he'd gotten sick in the shoe department and ran to find a trash barrel to puke into. Diana laughed at that detail, DeGawain histrionically imitating what his posture had been. Shaking his head, he rubbed Diana's back and tried not to laugh. He still hoped DeGawain might leave out the story about the girl.

Nope. That had simply been saved for last. DeGawain even described the girl, making sure to tell Diana that this girl had been very sexy in a way not at all like her: petite, Asian and clearly sexually charged. Something in Diana's posture, or the way her hands rested on his shoulders subtly shifted or sagged or—changed. All he could do was smile like a dope and tell her that he only thought that girl had been hot because he hadn't met Diana yet, which, of course, came off as fake.

He left to get beer. While waiting in the keg line, Helen appeared at his elbow. A strange glimmer flashed in her blue eyes as she gazed up at him. She seemed to be standing closer than necessary. Without breaking eye contact, her hand accidentally brushed down his arm hair. Accidentally? What the hell was she up to now? He charged ahead toward the keg, where—before he could fill a single beer—everyone insisted he do a keg stand. Not that he really needed convincing. He asked what the record time of the night was and easily shattered it by thirty seconds. When he got down, he filled two cups. Helen was gone. He went searching for Diana.

"Shut up, you stupid fuckin' bitch!" He found her by the trampoline, standing in front of the stage. Helen screamed as loud as she could at her. He walked over.

"No, you're a stupid bitch! And a fucking psycho!" Sam's band continued to rock out as if nothing was happening. "Nobody likes you here, either, so why don't you go!" Diana yelled back. It was the first time he had ever seen Diana mad. Seeing her upset saddened him.

Helen stormed up the wooded driveway to her daddy's Lexus and peeled off, driving way too fast on the dirt road. "Is she a little too wasted to be driving?" he asked.

"Who the fuck cares?" Diana said, turning to him. "Oh, well, I guess I do care a little." She took her beer from him. "I'm really mad at her, but I'd hate for her to get hurt." She smiled at him and wrapped an arm around him. "I'm glad you're here now. You can cheer me up."

"Hell, yeah." He turned around. "Let's start on the trampoline."

Beer flowed, and spirits shot down his throat all night. He ran around getting drunk with Diana, he even stage-dove off the trampoline onto the ground before the band. There wasn't a crowd to catch him, but he thought it would be fun. It didn't really hurt; he felt no pain.

That is he felt no pain until the next morning when he awoke in a big bed swimming in a dizzy sea of hangover and headache, body-ache and dehydration. He looked around to see where he was—a big bedroom with a humming air-conditioner and a private bathroom. He didn't remember going to bed. Next to him, thankfully, was Diana, sleeping peacefully. He realized he was naked, and then so was Diana.

A horrible moan of pain echoed into the room. He sat up slightly and saw a bulky body deposited in the tub. He sat up fully and saw DeGawain struggling from strange contortions out of the tub and splatting like a jelly-fish onto the tiled floor.

"My fuckin' head!" DeGawain said, holding his egg-shaped skull. He crawled on hands and knees across the tiles and onto the carpet of the bedroom.

"What the fuck are you doing?" Jim asked patiently.

"I have no clue, guy. Guess I thought the tub would be a cozy spot to crash last night." DeGawain crawled past the foot of the bed without looking up.

"Dude! What was wrong with the couches downstairs?" he said, glancing over at Diana, still asleep and not catching any of this.

"Shit, man you know me. I out drank everybody.

They all crashed first and left me with nowhere to sleep."

"What time did you come in here?" he asked, suddenly alarmed. Could DeGawain have seen anything? Had there been anything to see?

"I don't know. I don't fuckin' remember nothing," DeGawain said as he reached up from the carpet to open the door.

He shook his head. He suddenly remembered Gräbe offering him his parents' bedroom.

Then he noticed Diana's underwear on the floor beside the bed.

He suddenly remembered removing the underwear from Diana, slipping them off her smooth, tan legs. He also remembered sliding his freshly shaven face between those smooth thighs and licking and sucking and lapping away at Diana.

Looking closer at her panties, he almost puked. a pad with dried blood nestled inside the underwear.

He got up to check his face for blood in the bathroom mirror. He stared at his lips and cheeks, nothing. He was clean. Hopefully her period had recently ended. He couldn't remember. Would she remember that it'd happened? Would she let him do it again? He hoped so.

As he climbed back in bed, she woke up, and he held her tightly.

"Good morning," he said and kissed her.

"Good morning," she smiled back.

They snuggled together under the heavy blankets. "I love you," he said.

She kissed him.

11

Under the pressure of Jim's thumb, cold water jetted from the hose, cleaning a dark brown trash-barrel. A light breeze tickling his legs, he stood in his parents' driveway. His mother was at work, and it was the Fourth of July. She'd agreed to let him have an Independence Day party a few days before, and since his father hadn't been around when she'd told him, he wondered if his dad even knew. Not that it mattered. Everyone was already on their way. A keg of cold beer sweated in the Omni's back seat, waiting for strong arms to hoist it into a bin and pack it with ice.

The caked dirt on the plastic can turned to mud and sludged onto the blacktop. Across the street, DeGawain's foreign-made pick-up crept to a stop. The overweight ska-freak fumbled sheaths of red party cups on his way up the driveway. DeGawain wore his usual party ensemble: ugly, button-down shirt—a gross plaid mixture of greens and reds, cargo shorts and canvas shoes. Behind him skulked a pug-faced, chunky girl with short, reddish hair.

DeGawain shook his head sadly as he neared. "Oh. How the bronzed god has fallen!" he said. "Yesterday you surveyed your sandy domain. Now you're a common trash man."

Jim rolled the can over with his toe. "Funny," he said.

DeGawain dropped the cups on a chair and rested a meaty hand on Jim's shoulder. "But honestly, Diffin, it warms my heart to see you do some honest work for once."

He scowled. So, what if he didn't like hard work? His dad always harassed him about working hard, too. But wasn't that the other side of the American coin? Sure, everyone knows the shiny side. Work hard, get ahead; but there's the other side: slack off and stay where you are. What if he didn't care about getting ahead? Pow never worked very hard, never seemed to buy anything unnecessary and always seemed to have plenty of money and less stress than anyone.

DeGawain squeezed his shoulder. "Come on, Diff. You know I'm bustin' ya balls, guy."

Jim righted the barrel and sprayed inside. "I know," he said.

"We're friends, boys and shit. It's my job to fuck with you," DeGawain said, grabbing the cups. "Like brothers do."

He nodded, dropped the hose and emptied the murky water from the brown can. The dull, pungent odor of old rot splashed over the driveway. He leapt back to avoid getting his shoes wet. The girl DeGawain brought giggled.

DeGawain stopped halfway inside the house with the cups. "Oh, Diffin. I almost forgot. This is April."

He wiped his moist hands as best as he could on his shorts and shook the girl's soft, thick-fingered hands.

Her brown eyes twinkled through her reddish-brown bangs.

"Did you remember your bathing suit?" he asked, noticing her skirt and tank-top.

She hadn't. All week leading up to the party, Jim had stressed the importance of bringing girls to the party and of telling them about the pool in the backyard. DeGawain brought one girl and hadn't told her about the pool.

DeGawain's voice called from inside, "Can you believe that Irish bastard wasn't even going to invite me?"

He shook his head.

❧

A few days before, Jim raked the beach near chair three, while Yeats climbed up for the day's first chair-sit. Nobody had even gone into the pond yet. The bright sun glared, and a cool breeze swept across the pond. He could've used a sweatshirt.

"Hey, F... Diffin." DeGawain plodded toward him, kicking sand when he stopped. "What's all this I hear about a party?"

DeGawain looked misplaced on a beach, feet pointed away from one another, hands buried in pockets, squinting fiercely with a face completely neglected by the sun.

"Were you gonna invite me or what, guy?" he asked. "I hear you waterfront people had a big blast on the beach last week, too, bonfire and burgers and all that."

A screaming kid in a diaper ran past, and Jim shrugged. "I figured you'd hear about it and show. Come on, kid. You're my boy. Anywhere I'm welcome, you're welcome. That's a given." He frowned.

Apparently, he'd have to remember to explicitly invite him.

Another sand castle had been built in the same place as the one from a few weeks ago. A more elaborate design this time with turrets and a gatehouse—the kid who made it either had a really cool mold or a lot of talent. He felt worse about destroying this one, but he punched the flat part of the iron rake into the middle of it, crashing the structure into nothing more than level sand, ready for the next castle.

DeGawain dropped his head and poked at a rock with his foot. "Yeah, well you know how you waterfront staffers get kinda exclusive."

He looked up to the chair where Yeats watched the handful of people in the water, apparently not hearing DeGawain. Unfortunately, the rest of the camp staff shared DeGawain's impression. Maybe they were a little exclusive. It wasn't snobbery, not intentional. The lifeguards lived in close quarters together, so every year they seemed to either hate or love each other. The staff this year happened to get along well.

"So, what about this next party?" DeGawain whacked one wooden leg of the chair. "Am I invited to that?"

"Dude!" he laughed. "Of course you are. Didn't I say you were welcome wherever I was welcome."

DeGawain chuckled nervously, shading his eyes with a fat hand. "I heard your folks were going away for a week at least."

"My mom'll be around but she's workin'. I asked her to spend that night at my grandma's house, and she agreed."

The breeze blew in more cool air, the pond rippling from its touch. Jim shivered a bit. DeGawain stood silently beside him as the morning's first few swimmers splashed or swam convulsively. "Hey, you invite Diana yet?"

Jim dragged the rake down the beach, leveling the sand in front of the chair. "Well, I haven't talked to her yet. I left a message on her machine." The breeze died down.

"I see." DeGawain jammed his fist back into his pocket.

Jim stopped raking for a minute. "Why do you ask?"

DeGawain flashed a squinty smile and shifted to the shade beside the chair. "Wondering if you'd talked to her lately."

Jim's eyebrows knitted. "No. Not since we grilled on the beach the other day."

DeGawain said nothing, but nodded.

"What?"

DeGawain scratched his bald skull and said, "Uh, Helen told me that Diana's been spending a lot of time with that kid we protected the other night."

He shrugged and half-laughed. "Whatever," he said. "She told me he was a friend of hers."

DeGawain shielded his eyes with his paw and stared at him. "Hey, man. I hate to bear bad news. So, if you're cool with it, then I'm cool, too." DeGawain stared out at the swimmers. "I thought you should know what goes on."

"Yeah, forget about it," he said. "I'm not a jealous man, DeGawain." And besides he trusted Diana.

DeGawain turned like he had somewhere to go, then he stopped and said, "Hey, you know what? We're not hanging out this summer like we usually do. We need to start meeting up for lunch again."

❧

April dropped Jim's hand, and DeGawain tumbled out of the house. "We gonna get this keg going or what, guy?" DeGawain asked. They hoisted the cold, wet keg from the car and secured it in the barrel. They tucked it in with bags of ice and positioned it beside the island in the kitchen. April put a hand on Jim's right arm, raised an eyebrow and squeezed his muscles.

"You're stronger than you look," she whispered.

Was that even a compliment? He thanked her and politely pulled away. He wished Diana would show up soon. It'd be nice for her to show up early for once.

He grasped the tap—looking like a shiny bicycle pump with a spherical knob—from the kitchen counter and connected it to the keg, twisting it into place before dropping the lever. The tap clicked into position, and he wasted no time bleeding the line into the bin and pouring out three cold beers for DeGawain, April and himself. The cool carbonation tickled his throat as he tilted back his head, drinking down half the cup.

April poked his belly. "Marcus, you didn't tell me 'The Diff' was such a handsome drunk," she said, using DeGawain's first name.

"Hey, what can I say?" DeGawain shrugged. "Sorry, guy," he said. "But I don't find you physically attractive."

"Oh well." Jim chugged his beer and refilled it. Soon, a few girls from North Kingston who'd been at the beach barbecue rolled in with cheap wine coolers. Pow strolled in, obviously in a sedate mood, lugging several pounds of ground beef, which he took to the kitchen, making it his job to shape them into hamburger patties. Yeats and Troy showed up not long afterward with the buns and some condiments. More girls came, as well as some other camp staffers, and it was a party.

Without Diana there, though, Jim didn't really feel

like partying. The girlfriend of the guy throwing the party really should arrive before everyone else, whether to help get the house ready or keep him company while he hauled breakables into his parents' room.

Yeats discovered the stereo and blasted The Pogues louder than the system had ever played in its existence. With Shane MacGowan crooning about streams of whiskey, Gräbe strolled in carrying a metal juice dispenser with a spigot, which he deposited in the kitchen behind the keg.

"What ya got in there?" Jim asked.

"You'll see," Gräbe told him, grinning.

Pow headed to fire up the grill, and the guys went outside to watch him and get some fresh air. While in the kitchen, putting chips into a bowl, Jim decided to check out Gräbe's punch. He pulled on the smooth, black, plastic spigot, splashing red juice into his empty beer cup. It didn't taste like much, a slight hint of alcohol maybe. He soon discovered what had gone into the concoction. Hiding behind the metal container, empty and innocent, sat a bottle of corn liquor; grain alcohol, complete with flammable warnings and "must be consumed with a mixer" advisories.

He refilled his beer and decided to make the host's rounds and find Gräbe, too. If all the girls drank the juice mixture, Pow might not be able to sell enough cups for him to cover the keg. Although he wasn't sure confronting Gräbe about his powerful cocktail would make any difference.

Small groups of scantily clad people mingled in every room, everybody looking happy whether talking to someone or not, nobody had gone into his mother's room, and nothing appeared broken. So far, so good.

He'd already lost count at about six or seven brews.

Not that it mattered, he was drunk, and things were fine.

Needing to "break the seal," he headed down the hall. The bathroom door opened, and April popped out.

She stopped in the doorway and leaned on the jamb, running her fingers down her neck. "Hey, it's the sexy host boy." She traced the side of her breast through her tank-top. "Like 'em?" She smiled, stroking her breasts.

He blushed. "You know I have a girlfriend, right?"

"Yeah, silly," she said, still touching herself. "Does that mean you can't tell me what you think of my boobs?"

Beer setting into his brain, the question seemed fair. Her breasts weren't bad, bigger than he might like, nearly D cups. He figured he'd be polite though. "They're very nice," he said.

"Want a closer look?" she asked, lifting her shirt. Her breasts bounced free of the fabric; no bra confined the slightly sagging flesh; big brown areolas and pointing nipples breathed unfettered and in his face. He glanced right and left, wondering if anyone else was seeing this. DeGawain met his eyes at the top of the hall and ducked away, evidently embarrassed at having seen. April leaned in to kiss him. He told her, no, pushed by and locked himself in the bathroom. What did DeGawain think had been going on? He'd have to talk with him later to make sure he knew nothing had happened. DeGawain probably wouldn't tell Diana, but he had to make sure.

He drained his bladder and drank his beer. As he flushed the toilet, a high-pitched whine took off from outside the window and sailed away. He looked out the bathroom window into the driveway. Pow grilled burgers; DeGawain munched on chips; Gräbe and Troy attached pinwheel fireworks to the fence, lighting them and standing back. Whirling circles of sparks flew everywhere from the anchored center. Parched grass lined the fence, and if it caught fire and spread to the backyard, the blaze might burn down the neighborhood. He zipped his pants and rushed outside. As he jumped out the side-door and into the driveway, three salutes flew off, one after another, with their marked high-pitched squeals.

"What the fuck?" he yelled.

Troy spun around with a lit Roman Candle, popping off flaming ball after flaming ball of assorted colors into the sky. Troy told Jim not to worry.

"Son of a bitch," Jim yelled. "I'd at least like my fuckin' girlfriend to get here before we go laying out the red carpet for the pork chop patrol!"

At that moment, a flaming ball flew skyward and burst a brilliant red in the muggy night air.

Troy argued that the cops wouldn't come since it was Independence Day, but he knew better; East Providence cops were assholes; for years he'd seen them hassle people for less. Maybe in Warwick or Smithfield they wouldn't show, but here they'd probably come, find the underage drinkers, and the party would be over before it really got going, before Diana showed up. Troy explained that they should try to burn the evidence of fireworks in the meantime.

"Every-fuckin'-body's wasted around here," he muttered to himself, deciding to give up the fight. As the last pinwheel burnt out and the last Roman Candle popped off its balls, Pow shouted, "Yo! What the fuck! It's Yeats!"

Jim followed Pow's pointed finger. Illuminated by light from the final, fading Roman Candle blast, Yeats stood on the roof's apex.

"Yeats, what in the hell are you doing up there?" he shouted.

Yeats looked over the edge. "I can do it. No sweat!"

Jim backed away from the house to get a better view. "How did you get up there?" he asked.

"No, really," Yeats said, not paying attention. "It's gonna be great."

"He's gonna fuckin' jump!" Pow yelled.

"No!" he shouted. "No! No! No!" Yeats swayed both arms, bent at the elbow, back and forth as if he were about to go on a ski-run. Jim looked from Yeats to the four-foot deep above-ground pool in his backyard. Swimmers hopped out of the pool and ran onto the grass. A few huddled under Yeats on the deck, looking up.

Gräbe stepped up, shouting with his deep, gravelly voice of authority as if they were back at work. "Yeats, get the fuck down from there!"

Yeats paused for a moment to look at Gräbe before answering, "This isn't work," and turned back to concentrate on the pool.

"No, Yeats," Jim shouted. "It's not work, but it is my goddamned house!" Losing control of the party, he lost his temper, too. "Listen to me. That pool is not deep enough. You'll break your fuckin' legs. Or your back!"

"I'll be fine." Yeats flashed a silly grin. "Watch."

"No! Yeats don't be an idiot! Listen to me a sec. It's bad enough Troy's inviting the cops with fireworks, but if you get hurt, no one is sober enough to drive you to the emergency room. That's if you don't need a fuckin' backboard, then the cops will definitely be here!"

"What? Pow never drinks. He's sober at least," Yeats said, then turned to face them. "Or you could always call an ambulance, but watch I'll be fine!"

Suddenly, Yeats pushed his head and shoulders way

out over the side and pulled his legs up. Jim held his breath as Yeats's legs drifted out ahead of him, and he rode through the air on his back, splashing down rear end first. A huge wave soaked everyone in the backyard. The yard fell silent, and his heart pounded as hard as his feet pounded to reach Yeats. He dashed into the backyard with Gräbe and Troy trailing. The three of them surmounted the deck as Yeats's head broke the surface with a war-whoop.

"Wuuwhooo!"

Cheers went up. Relief rushed into Jim's system fast and free, until he got pissed again at Yeats's recklessness. He shouted incoherent threats and curses at Yeats and everyone in earshot, threats that he would never remember, being so drunk. He managed to communicate his message clearly enough, though. Nobody would encourage Yeats and nobody else would attempt the jump. He put Troy in charge of the pool as lifeguard and roof guard and went inside to chug some of Gräbe's juice and wait for Diana.

A half-hour later, even more drunk, he heard voices from outside shouting loud and drawn out, "heeeey!" Soon Diana appeared in the doorway wearing worn jeans, a pink T-shirt and a small, light blue vest. He stood up and rushed to greet her, planting a kiss on her blushing cheek before hugging her tightly and sealing their lips. "A sane, sober person arrives at long last," he said.

Diana pulled back. "Unlike you, you mean," she said, freeing herself from his arms.

He cocked his head sideways.

She put her hands on her hips. "You reek of booze. Don't even act shocked that I know you're wasted."

"Oh, come on, Diana," he said, wiping his mouth. "You're not mad, are you?"

"No," she said. "But you stink, fucknuts." She ran a hand through his hair.

"I'm sorry, Diana, but you should've been here," he said. "You should've seen what I've been dealing with. Fireworks blowing up everywhere! Yeats jumping off the fucking house!"

"What?" she asked, wide-eyed. "Is he crazy?"

"Yeah, you didn't know that?"

"That's nuts. Is he okay?"

"Yeah, I guess. He's walking. Lucky bastard."

Diana grabbed his hand and led him outside to meet her friends, consisting of Nina and her sister's very cute fourteen-year-old friends, Jenn and Mollie. Jail bait for him and most of his friends, but not for Troy. Standing behind the girls was Helen. He said, hi and shook her hand. Helen stepped away, heading into the house.

"You brought her?" he asked, once she was out of earshot.

"DeGawain told her about it," she said defensively. "I let her follow me here is all. It's not like I went and picked her up."

He rolled his eyes, then asked if she'd be spending the night or not. She said she'd love to, but she had to drive her sister Nina and her little friends home. And since Jim had wanted her to bring girls to make the party better, it was the only way she could do it.

They went inside to get Diana a beer, and he settled onto the couch in the living room with her. The party picked up and raged, complete with party fouls, drunk joke telling, flirtatious advances, mud tracked on the floors, dirt mysteriously smeared on the walls and mosquitoes invading the house. He swatted one such pest off his right forearm seconds before a shirtless Troy came in with Mollie wrapped in a towel. The pair traipsed down the hall and into the bathroom together.

He raised his plastic cup in silent salute and gave Diana a kiss. The night seemed to be going well for everybody.

About a quarter of an hour later, the close night air getting to her, Diana felt like going swimming. He gathered some towels and emerged from the bathroom in his lifeguard shorts, the only bathing suit he owned. The backyard had become a playground for underage drunks. A beach ball flew through the air, a couple of guys chased Nina around the back side of the pool, three bodies cannon-balled into the water while the rest of the swimmers raced around the circumference, creating a fierce whirlpool.

He nodded and smiled. He was a creator, the creator of the evening. Placing the towels down on the picnic table where a half-dozen or so party-goers lounged, he climbed the moist steps up the deck to enter and participate in his universe. The water covering the steps and deck chilled his feet a bit, and, as he mounted the ladder, Gräbe and Panza splashed him. Goose-bumps broke out over his back and shoulders. As he backed off the ladder, a sudden force struck him from behind, and he tumbled forward into and under the chilly, refreshing water. The current slowly swept him along the bottom, pairs of feet plodding around him.

When he stood up and threw his head above the current, Diana laughed, clutching her tanned belly. "Gotcha!" she shouted, before leaping into the waves to his left. As she surfaced, he took hold of her waist, spun her around and hugged her tightly.

She pushed him off with a laugh. "Whirlpool!" she shouted. "Come on, Jim. Come catch me!"

Apparently, nobody else believed that the creator should gain respect for his endeavors. He chased Diana around the pool for what seemed like hours. DeGawain brought him a beer, and he managed to keep people refilling it for him, which was more like it. By the time Diana left the pool and ran from him again, he was polluted. He chased her around the yard and into the house.

Inside, the ceiling fan whirled so fast it shuddered, as if trying to launch from its base. Jim tottered over to a chair and clutched the chain for the fan. After tugging it a few times, he refilled his now empty cup, mumbling about respecting his house. He looked up from the tap as the beer flowed out and saw DeGawain sitting on the living room couch with Helen and April. They whispered and laughed. DeGawain flashed him an expression, a look that seemed to express guilt and animosity at once. He could have been paranoid. He couldn't be sure.

Then Diana ran back outside. As he ran toward the door to follow her, he almost fell backwards. His mother loomed in the door, staring at him. He held his beer tentatively, realizing he stood in the kitchen shirtless. His mother didn't seem to notice the dirty floors or the bugs on the walls or even him standing bare-chested in the kitchen with a beer. Had she changed her mind about the party? Was she here to chaperone? She didn't say anything to him as she trudged down the hall. Damn. She'd decided to sleep in her own bed tonight; the party was over for sure.

"Henry!" she shouted at Yeats from the end of the hall. He raced down to discover what Yeats had done this time.

"What are you doing in here?" she asked.

Drowsily raising himself off the floor of his parents' bedroom was Yeats. "I'm sorry, Mrs. Diffin," he said. "I was looking for a quiet place to lay down for a minute."

"Ma, I didn't know," he said. The one damn rule she had been really intent on was that nobody would go into her room. He'd never counted on Yeats being such an uncontrollable drunk—jumping from the roof, now this. She got Yeats out of her room, shut off the light and gripped Jim by the ears, reminding him that nobody was to go into her room. Then she left. Off to sleep at grandma's house like planned. She'd fortunately only come by for a change of clothes, which she'd forgotten to take with her to work.

A little later, the party peaked out. Diana shunned his every embrace and advance.

Regardless he tried to wrap his arms around her by the grill. Diana pulled back, swatting his arms, almost spilling his beer. When he stepped toward her, she ran down the driveway and into the road, where she turned to sip from her cup. Was she still drinking or was that water? He wanted to ask her, but again once he got close, she ran.

Now he chased down the street after her, his bare feet slapping the pavement. She turned near the stop sign to watch him jog, one arm steady to keep from losing any beer. Was she having fun with him or was she mad? Before he got very close, she ran past him on the other side of the street, right by the house and down the street again. Helen rushed from the house to where Diana had come to a rest again. Tired from running barefoot with his beer, Jim quit running to walk toward the girls. Helen put an arm around Diana. Was she really that upset? Jim wanted to comfort Diana. What the hell was going on? As he got closer, the girls ran away from him again.

Standing in the street, he felt completely dejected and wondered if she wanted to dump him. Maybe DeGawain told her something about April flashing him? Maybe he told her something more? DeGawain really hadn't seen the whole thing.

Still puffing from running full of beer, he tried to ask Yeats for his opinion. But Yeats was busy spelling his name, first and last, in impeccable cursive at the foot of the driveway with his piss.

Giving up on talking to Diana, he went inside, filled another beer and plopped on the couch. DeGawain found him and asked him what was bugging him. He explained to DeGawain about April, about how nothing had happened.

"It's all good, guy," he said. "You know I'd never say anything to Diana. You're my boy. We were friends first, after all."

"Thanks, DeGawain." He swirled his beer. "You're one of my true friends," he said, instantly forgetting his paranoid suspicion.

"True, true," DeGawain said. "But you know what, guy? You're making a fool of yourself over Diana. She's not worth your time. You're 'The Diff' for shit's sake. You could be mackin' on like every girl here if you wanted. Instead you're sitting here feeling lousy."

"DeGawain, you're lucky you're my friend, 'cause otherwise I'd punch you in the face," he said, not looking up from his beer.

"Ah, that's the beer talkin'," DeGawain said. "Look. Diana's probably running away from you because you're trying too hard. That's not your style, guy."

He chugged his beer and went for more, leaving DeGawain alone. By the time Diana left, at about three in the morning, he'd just about given up on her. She gave him a quick squeeze and a curt peck on the cheek, then ran out before he could learn what she'd been upset about.

The numbers dwindled. The air grew chill. He put his clothes back on and joined Panza and Troy around the keg, drinking and pledging to stay up until they could kick it.

Outside in the driveway Helen, April and DeGawain stood in a tight circle. Every so often, one of them would turn away from the conversation to glance into the house through the windows. He continued to pound beers with Troy and Panza. Helen said goodnight before she left and April disappeared down the hallway. DeGawain joined them around the keg.

He performed a thirty second kegstand, and the others spent an hour on and off, trying to beat the record. Sated mosquitoes lounged up and down the walls and other bugs flitted around the lights. Troy and Panza crashed in the living room, wrapped in light blankets against the chilly summer night and the onslaught of mosquitoes whose appetite would soon return. He and DeGawain stood alone with the keg.

"Just us real drinkers, eh, tough guy?" DeGawain asked.

"Yeah, it is," he agreed with a nod and a gulp. "That girl is tough, man."

"Diana?" DeGawain asked. "Helen thinks she's crazy. Maybe she's right."

"Well." Jim sloshed his beer. "One of 'em is crazy, but which one?"

"Just when I think I know... I was sure it was Helen, but then with the way Diana treated you tonight. Jesus, guy, who's to say?"

"You think so, too?" he asked, suddenly concerned. "Why didn't you say that before?"

"I don't know, guy. Maybe she was embarrassed by you in front of her little, unsullied friends," he said, refilling his beer. "They must be unaccustomed to drunks like us."

"Fuck, man. I don't know what the fuck is going on."

"I tell you one thing though, guy." DeGawain leaned over the keg to get closer. "That girl April really wants you."

"Yeah?" he asked. "No shit."

"Yeah, guy. She was asking about you all night. Didn't she totally make a move on you earlier, too? Or was I seeing things?"

"Something like that," he said, forgetting that he'd already explained that to DeGawain. "She's not very hot, or even cute."

"She's got really nice, big titties, guy," he said with an impish grin.

"Damn, kid." Jim steadied himself on the wall. "I love Diana."

"Even if she's playin' you?" DeGawain asked, poking him in the chest.

"I don't know, kid," he said, still swaying. "I just don't know."

"All I know is that she told me she was sick of dealing with your drunkenness. She was really mad at you for something. Seems like she wants out, guy."

"No?" he asked, stricken. Her hug or the little kiss she'd given him before leaving escaped his memory. All he remembered was Diana running away from him all night.

"Don't sweat it, my man. Plenty of fish, right?" DeGawain said. "I mean, she never loved you anyway."

"Damn."

They drank more and more beer until they gave up on kicking the keg and settled for sleep. DeGawain headed for William's room. Jim stumbled into his room and a soft voice greeted him.

"Hello?"

"Who the fuck's that?" he asked, stunned. For a half-second he hoped Diana had somehow come back and sneaked into his bed to wait for him.

Sheets rustled in his bed. "It's me. April."

He couldn't see anything in the dark room. "This isn't going to work," he said, trying not to fall.

"Why not?" she asked, sounding hurt.

He got himself over by the bed. "That's my bed, and I'm sure as shit sleeping in my own damn bed tonight." Couldn't anyone respect their host anymore?

"Okay," she said, not moving.

Obviously, she didn't get it yet. "So, you can't, too," he said. "Why don't you go lie down with DeGawain." As he hovered by his bed, his eyes adjusted to the dim room.

"Why can't I stay here?" She stretched her arms over her head. "I've already got my pj's on." She lifted the sheets to show him. They weren't pajamas so much as a wifebeater and underwear. "I'm only saying I could sleep here. Couldn't we share the bed, like adults?"

He thought it over for a minute. Why couldn't he lie down in bed with a girl and not do anything? Besides, she didn't seem interested in doing anything anyway, despite what DeGawain had told him. He kicked off his shoes, ripped off his socks, dropped his pants, tugged off his shirt and wearing only his underwear, and crept into bed with April.

Not more than twenty minutes later, bordering on sleep, he slung his left arm over April's belly. April rolled over and pushed her tongue into his mouth. With his inebriated mind, he instinctively returned the kiss before he even realized what he was doing. When he did think of Diana, his booze-soaked, half-asleep assessment was that she had refused his every advance the whole evening and was likely to dump him soon. Even DeGawain had seen it.

The rest of the night overtook him as if it were a park ride, and he was simply a passenger. The whole house probably knew how long the ride lasted. April was loud. As it turned out, most rollercoasters took longer to finish than that night's degraded ride.

The next day April and DeGawain walked out the door as his mother came home. Her shriek coerced him out of bed despite the screaming headache and the 9:14 a.m. blazing on his clock. When he reached the top of the hallway and came to what had been his mother's immaculate kitchen, he understood her outburst.

The keg sat in its trash barrel; the ice melted and formed a series of lakes and rivers across the floor, which trampling feet had splattered with enough mud to conceal the floor's color and pattern. Mosquitoes still flitted about the walls along with other species of insects. Empty beer cups lay scattered and broken on the floor, table and countertops. The whole room smelled of spilled, stale beer and dirt, and, for some reason, the oven was wide open.

"James!" his mother wailed, thrusting her hands into her hair. "What have you done? My home! My home is a filthy, disgusting mess. You've ruined my home!"

He thought she was on the verge of a nervous breakdown. "What are you doin' home already, ma?" he asked, standing in his underwear. Troy and Panza had left, too, the blankets they used balled up on the couch and recliner.

"I live here, James. Remember?" she said, her hands now defiantly on her hips. "And what the hell happened in here? You were supposed to have a few friends over. It looks like you had a rock concert!"

"Mom, it's not as bad as it looks. Nothing's broken, and the mud is from the melting water," he tried to explain, his head surging. "I was going to have it clean before you got home, but you said you wouldn't come over 'til noonish." He looked at his bare wrist. "I thought I still had all day."

His shocked mother remained stock still.

"Ma, if you go back to gramma's for a few hours, I'll have the place even cleaner than it was before," he said, bare feet in the mud. "I promise, good as new and all that."

He ushered her out, assuring her that he would clean the house—better than before. As she drove off, he faced the dismal, disgusting kitchen. Suddenly, he remembered what he'd done and he felt dirty. He'd given up his v-card, his virginity to a random girl at a house party. He'd never gotten to confess to Diana that he'd been a virgin. She probably wouldn't believe him if he told her now. What was he going to tell her?

Alone, he chased down bugs, mashing them and cleaning their carcasses from the walls. His joints aching, his head throbbing, he lugged the keg out to the backyard, then swept up as much mud as he could, filled a bucket with scalding water and soap, scrubbed the floor one small, square patch at a time, threw away empty cups, washed counter-tops, vacuumed the carpets, sprayed air-freshener and finally, in the corner of the backyard, drained the keg—its golden contents, warm now, dribbling into a muddy, foamy puddle.

12

Lit by Diana's headlights, the wooded path of Diamond Hill State Park had appeared easier to navigate. Under a dimmer glow from the full moon, the path revealed its many rocks, roots, bends and hanging branches. He stumbled along behind Diana, trying to imitate her foot placements. While he searched for safe footing, he continued to search for the words he'd been unable to find all night. How to tell her.

She'd been so happy at dinner, talking about summer fun: days at the beach, nights out partying and how much better work was without DeGawain around. When was a good time to confess to a lover? He'd no sooner finished cleaning his mother's house, when he realized he had to tell her. That had been the easy decision.

He'd considered telling her under two conditions. While they were on a particularly fun or romantic date or while they were on an ordinarily pleasant one. Tonight's date ranked more and more on the fun and romantic side the closer they came to the granite rock face.

Diana, to his awe, had spontaneously suggested a rock climbing venture by moonlight. It struck him as daring and romantic, and he couldn't help but fall for her even more. She, on the other hand, simply couldn't believe he was crazy enough to take her up on it.

"You're the first guy I've met who'd do something like that with me," she'd said, her cheeks rounding into a huge smile.

He thought he'd take advantage of her surprise and elation to balance out the surprise and disgust she'd have once he confessed. But why ruin a good night and mar a wonderful memory? This was his simple and effective counter-argument for telling her on a less impressive evening.

As they entered a clearing, his eyes seemed to adjust to the dark, or maybe less trees obstructed the moonlight. She bounded and skipped toward the rock face.

"I think this is where we should start," she said, weaving up a steep path between rocks.

"You think?" he said, pausing in the clearing. "Don't you know for sure? You've climbed this dozens of times. Right?"

She put one hand on a large boulder and turned back to him. "Oh, sure, but never at night," she said, looking up at the rock wall. "Everything looks kinda different in the dark, ya know?"

"Yeah," he said, as something scurried in the underbrush. "But I assumed you'd done this at least once before at night."

Diana slid three steps to her left, still searching for the exact place to start. "Nah, I told you, fucknuts," she said, trying a few different handholds. "Nobody else but you was ever crazy enough to agree with me. Other people always talk me out of it." She swung around on him. "You're not backing down, are you?"

He scanned the dark gray stone with its craggy juttings and deep shadows. "Me? Nah, don't be silly. I was just curious," he said, realizing that it was too late to back down.

"Okay," she said. "Follow me. I'll eventually find the handholds I always use, and you can sorta follow in my footsteps."

He didn't like the sound of her "eventually."

"Or maybe you should call it handsteps," she added with a laugh.

Her relaxed manner put him at ease, and he could see pretty well by the time he began scaling. At first it was scampering over large rocks, and when they'd reached the actual wall of rock, they found themselves already ten or eleven feet off the forest floor. Once they'd started really climbing, he discovered deep clefts and crevasses marked her chosen starting point, and before long, he was twenty feet from the ground. With her shoes several feet above his head, she stopped.

"Everything all right up there?" he asked, closing in on her soles.

"Uh, yeah," she said. "I can't remember where to go from here though."

Great. Stuck on a rock face all night or having to jump. The way he'd come didn't look like it could be backtracked. He gripped the rock, spread-eagle in the quiet night, waiting for her to figure it out. His muscles burned, and his calves trembled by the time she exclaimed, "Here we go!"

She altered her course to the left a yard or so and continued straight up. "I forgot about shifting over like that," she said, moving deftly up the stone-face.

He kept his eye on the shadowy place where she'd slid over and found himself about thirty feet off the ground by the time he reached it. It took him at least a minute to find a secure hand hold, and a moment of doubt struck him as pebbles drizzled onto his head and left arm. He half expected her to come tumbling next, but she was a good ten feet up and passing a pine sapling growing from a crack. Sweat coated his back and stuck his shirt to his flesh by the time he gained the pine.

"This tree safe?" he asked as he reached a hand up to it.

"Sure," she said, still steadily climbing.

"You used it?" he asked, grabbing hold of it.

"Nah, I never use it."

Having already put his weight on the tree, he frantically searched for a fresh hand hold. Over forty feet above the rocky ground, he dug his hand at an awkward angle into a dark, six-inch crack. Pulling, scraping, angling, burning and willing his way for the last twenty feet of the rock face put him at the brink, his body stretched out like an "X."

"Reach up," she said, sitting atop the cliff face in the clear moonlight.

Easy for her to say. Which hand should let go in preference of the summit? The idea of moving either hand terrified him. On the verge of his goal, he couldn't quite release a tangible hold.

"Oh, come on, you scaredy-cat," she said.

Her silly challenge calmed him, and he reached up with his right hand and gripped the cliff-top.

"All right!" she shouted, her surprise and excitement striking him as a back-handed compliment.

He pulled himself up and refused Diana's help in a moment of masculine pride. He straightened and took a deep breath of fresh air and looked around.

"Beautiful view, huh?" he exclaimed.

"That's what I'm saying!" she said, standing. "That's why I thought we should come here."

She chose a cozy spot for them to sit overlooking barely lit Cumberland and nestled in his arms, their feet dangling over sixty feet from the ground. He could tell her now. He knew he had to do it, and why not now?

"What a beautiful night," she said, leaning her head on his shoulder. An owl hooted in the distance.

He could ruin her evening with a few words. Wasn't it his responsibility? *Diana, I cheated on you.* The words wouldn't form. She rubbed his leg.

What if he told her, and she flipped out? She was a strong girl. She could kill him from where they sat with a good hard push if she got mad enough. He peered over the edge. Craggy boulders and a root-strewn path lay in the half-lit darkness below; there'd be no way he could survive the fall.

"Careful, fucknuts," she said, pulling him back from the edge, then kissing him. They snuggled in the night, overlooking Diana's small town as more and more lights winked out.

After nothing but street lights remained, and a night chill fell, the two descended on the less steep side of Diamond Hill and soon arrived back at Diana's car. They got in, and, instead of starting the car, she kissed him. He leaned over to her side, to get closer, hovering over her, and eventually they slid around, somehow winding up with her on top. He sat in the driver's seat, holding her firm, round ass, kissing her soft lips, feeling like he was stealing time from her by not telling her what had happened.

After a while, she leaned back on the steering wheel and said, "Why don't you drive me home?"

He felt as though he'd gained her special trust now

that she'd asked him to drive the LeBaron. Every moment from the woods to her house tortured his conscience. He knew he didn't deserve this trust and yet he enjoyed it. But how could he bring up Independence Day after they'd had such a great time? He drove to Diana's house, kissed her goodnight, got into the Omni and drove home.

愛

That Sunday he went to church with his mother. His father stayed at home on the couch, and his grandma had been too sick for months to make it to mass with her oxygen tank and fragile balance. His mother strode across the ugly blue carpeting and between the rows of dark-stained, wooden pews. She sunk to one knee and blessed herself before sliding in; Jim did the same, but faster. Once on the cool wood, he knelt, folded his hands before him and closed his eyes.

God... His mother, grandmother and—he'd been told—his grandfather preferred to pray to the Virgin. Others called out to Jesus, but he always addressed his thoughts and prayers to God by which he meant the Trinity. *God, please help me. I know I'm a pretty bad Catholic, missing church, never making full confessions and everything, but I know regardless you still love me. Help me to do the right thing with Diana, grant me the right words and help everything to work out for the best.* Before blessing himself, he asked God to look after his grandmother's soul, to take care of his brother and to continue supplying his mother with patience in her marriage.

He sat back in the pew and shuffled his feet on the filthy tile floor, eyeing the chipped, cracking wood of the pew before him. The choir sang. His mother chatted with an elderly woman behind them. People he grew up with in Riverside filled the seats in St. Brendan's. McNulty, one of the kids who'd jumped him in junior high, sat a few rows over, close to the front. All the other kids thought McNulty was the most religious one in the grade from as far back as elementary school. Probably because he never missed church and always wore his crucifix outside his shirt.

The priest and the rest of the entrance processional glided down the center aisle carrying the tall metallic cross with Christ writhing forever in the same position. One of the altar boys looked like an O'Rourke. A family of "good Catholic" Micks who lived in the neighborhood known as the gully, which lay down by the salt-marshes. There were about six boys as far as he knew, and every one he ever met smelled like dirt and liked to cause trouble; it seemed each one had his own specialty: stealing, fighting, instigating fights and any other manner of delinquency. But they all looked the same, this altar boy was definitely of the same brood; the O'Rourke features were all there: wide floppy ears, dirty, wavy hair, pale, freckled skin, lanky limbs and the same bone structure surrounding the eyes, a protruding brow and nearly non-existent cheekbones.

Mass dragged on. The Gospel reading of the week was from Matthew chapter six, some of the later verses. Before the reading started, he drew a tiny cross over his forehead, his mouth and his heart along with everyone else. The entire church fell silent, listening for their lives, dressed in their Sunday best as the words hung in the air. Words about storing treasures in heaven rather than on earth, about being as carefree as the lilies, not taking pride in food and clothing.

Later, he wished peace on the people around him, shaking hands and wondering if they meant the words they said anymore, or if it'd become mindless ritual. His mother took his hand, kissed him and said she loved him, instead of "peace be with you." After taking the Eucharist, he once again prayed for God to help him live a better life. After church, he asked if they could stop by and have tea with his grandma, but his mother said she was too tired.

≈

A week later he took Diana to see the movie Twilight with the aged Paul Newman, James Garner and Gene Hackman running around in orthopedic shoes and pretending to be a lot younger than they really were—acting, on screen, as if their life was really in its prime. He'd admitted to himself that he and Diana might as well be over, the trust broken, and she needed to know. They made out in the Omni after the movie, but he eventually pulled back to begin his repentance.

"Diana," he said, still hoping she might understand. "I have to tell you something,"

"What is it?" She seemed to sense something bad from his tone.

"I've been meaning to tell you for weeks now..." He couldn't finish, but knew that by bringing it up, he had to. Like jumping off the dock on a chilly morning, once airborne you couldn't change your mind, you were going in. His face flushed, his ears tingled and warmed.

"What is it, fucknuts?" she asked, frowning but forcing a laugh.

His palms sweat. He stared at them, at his steering wheel, at the emptying movie theater.

She cocked her head, waiting for him to continue.

"Well, you remember my Fourth of July party? We had a little fight," he said, preparing to blurt it all out.

"I thought you were dumping me that night and I was very, very, very—oh God—I was so very drunk that night. I didn't know what I was doing." He gazed into Diana's expectant eyes and wished he could tell her nothing happened.

"Well, Diana... After you left... I hooked up with some fat, dumb bitch, because I thought you were breaking up with me." He looked away, breathing out slowly.

"What?" she asked, her back to the door. "What do you mean hooked up? Did you fuck her?" She stared into his eyes, interrogating him with her glare.

"Yes," he answered.

"I see," she said, sinking into her seat and staring forward.

"Are you mad at me?" he asked, not knowing what else to say.

"Am I supposed to be happy?" she asked, her head swinging toward him.

"No, I'm trying in my own lame way to apologize. I don't think I deserve your forgiveness, but I'd like you to understand that I was drunk and I thought you didn't want anything to do with me anymore." A group of laughing people bounded past the car. "I'll do anything to make it up to you."

"The first thing you can do is take me home," she said coldly.

They drove to Diana's silently. At her front door, he turned to her with eyes near brimming with tears and asked, "Can I please see you again..."

"I suppose," Diana said, climbing out of the car. As reluctant as her answer sounded, it gave him hope.

13

Jim climbed the basement steps with his clean laundry and set the basket in the dining room beside his bag. The music no longer played. His mother poured soda in the kitchen.

"What happened to the tunes, ma?"

She scowled, holding up one hand to quiet him.

"That crap gives me a headache. Is that okay with you?" his father's voice grumbled from the darkened living room. He'd been closing the thick curtains. As his father ambled around to the front of the couch, he came into sight. His mother swept past with the glass of soda for his father, who installed himself on his regular couch cushion.

Jim stood in the middle of the dining room. "Yeah, of course. I didn't realize you were home, dad. What've you been up to?" he asked, creeping toward the edge of the living room.

"Errands," his father grunted, wielding the remote control. Jim sat in the arm chair against the far wall. By the time his mother sat on the couch with her glass of water, John Wayne occupied the television screen.

"What time do you want to eat dinner, honey," she asked.

He considered the question and his father turned the volume up on the television. She said something else he couldn't make out, and then his father grumbled something about a commercial. Until then, Jim hadn't realized that she'd asked his father about dinner and not him.

"How many times have you seen this movie?" she asked playfully.

"It's a brand new one," his father responded, joking rather than answering the question. He also left the volume up. His mother let out a long sigh; the same sigh Jim often let out when dealing with his parents, which aggravated them beyond reason.

At the first commercial, his father turned the volume back down, and his mother said, "So, what about dinner?"

Jim kept his vision locked on the screen while he listened. The Pillsbury Doughboy swooped into some random woman's kitchen to bring her dinner rolls.

"I don't know, in a little bit."

A little girl with a steaming mouthful of roll poked the iconic character in the tummy making him giggle.

"Well, do you want a salad?" she said. "Cheese and crackers? I'm starving,"

For fast-acting heart-burn relief and your daily calcium supply reach for...

"Well if you're hungry why the hell are you asking me?"

Another sigh. "Well... I did think it would be nice if we ate to-geth-er," she said facetiously.

Another Wayne movie was coming on next, no need to change the channel.

"Okay," he grumbled.

"Salad or crackers?" she asked, getting up.

Hot girls dancing at a bar, everyone drinking cheap beer but somehow the whole world was partying. Besides network programming, a common trend ran through the commercials which struck him at that moment: food, drink and the medicine for having over indulged in both. How American.

"Surprise me," he said, turning the volume back up as cowboys sitting around a campfire filled the screen. All the westerns might get boring, but they were better than the news lately. All the national news wanted to talk about was a young intern named Monica Lewinsky, and the main topic on the minds of the local newscasters was the huge corruption scandal in city hall uncovered by the FBI's Operation Plunderdome.

He ate salad with his parents in silence and gunfights, then before dinner he went into the den to try and write to Diana. He sat online with an email window open without writing a word, hoping her screen name would pop up in his buddy list window. His mother called him to dinner before she'd logged on or he'd gotten anything down. He banged out a few words before washing his hands for dinner: how he was sorry, how he'd wanted to tell her sooner, how they'd had too much fun rock climbing for him to tell her that night, how he couldn't wait to see her again, couldn't wait to start making it up to her.

After a dinner of meatball grinders, he settled into the armchair again to watch more television with his family.

After clearing her throat, his mother asked if he'd

been eating and sleeping enough at camp. He told her he had.

"Have you been getting out of bed on time?"

"Mom, if I didn't, I'd be back home," he said.

"What does that mean?"

"It means he'd be fired, dear," his dad grumbled.

His mother laughed. "You're not drinking too much are you?"

Jim rolled his eyes. "No, ma."

"Because alcoholism runs in the family," she said.

"I know, ma," he said. And he did know. His brother had come to visit him when he lived on campus, and they hiked to a party together. Jim got smashed as usual, and William told on him. He'd been concerned, he said. Jim hated when William played the concerned big brother card. His mother lectured him about how she'd often helped her father up the driveway as a girl because he was so drunk, he could barely walk. He'd been a functioning alcoholic, a dentist with a successful office of his own, but every holiday, weekend, or special occasion he had a bottle in his hand. Now, despite the fact that William was the president of his fraternity and drank as much, as often and to a usually rowdier effect, Jim had been labeled the family's problem drinker.

"You know, but you really don't care do you, James?" his father, surprisingly interrupted.

"I care," he said, twisting in his chair to face them.

"You care about getting drunk. Your mother and I were nice enough to let you have some friends over and you turned the place into a madhouse. She gave you one rule. Nobody in our bedroom, and when she comes home after work, what does she find but one of your no good, drunk friends sleeping on our floor," he said.

Jim looked at his mother. She'd said later that it didn't bother her so much, that after all it was Yeats, but at first, it'd startled and upset her. She didn't say anything now, but stared Jim down as if damning him.

"But it was just Henry," he said.

"It's always 'just' something though isn't it, James? When are you going to take responsibility for your actions?"

"I already told mom that I was sorry."

"Sorry isn't always good enough, James. One of these days your recklessness is going to get you into more trouble than sorry can solve."

Had this already happened? With Diana?

He sighed.

His father mockingly sighed over and over again. "What kind of answer is that, James?'

He got up to leave.

"Don't you walk away from me," his father said, on the verge of yelling.

Jim stopped in the middle of the dining room and spun around.

"I don't want to talk about this anymore, dad. All you and mom do is criticize me. I never do anything right or well enough. I think I should leave."

"Doesn't that tell you anything, James? Maybe you should grow up? Straighten out and fly right?" he said, repeating one of his favorite phrases. This one rated up there with shape up or ship out and other Navy-isms.

He looked up and away, slowly shaking his head. He said, "No. I think you should get off my back."

His father rose. "You want us off your fucking back?" he shouted.

"Martin, don't," his mother whispered.

He felt his ears heat up, turning red.

"Off your fucking back?" his father said louder, spit flying from his tight, thin lips. "How about you get out of my fucking house if that's the way you feel, you ungrateful twerp."

Twerp? He figured he could take his old man out in a few swings or at least get him down and make him wish he'd never talked to him like that. His father stepped closer. Instead, he simply said, "Dad."

"What?" his father said in his face. "We feed you, clothe you, help you pay for college even when you failed out—"

"I didn't fail," he said.

"No? They kicked you out of the honors program, James! What the hell else do you want?"

"It's not like they kicked me out," he insisted. "I got two D's, but that's passing."

"Not in my house it isn't. You failed, James, and we still support you. Now you want us off your fucking back?" He came close enough that Jim could smell his terrible breath, see his cracked, rotten, lower incisors. "I'm serious. We can get off your back, all right. Get the hell out and don't come back." Some of his father's stubble was gray. His mother stood off to the right.

"He doesn't mean it, James," she said soothingly. "Martin, please calm down."

His father turned away from him for a moment and said, "Don't. Don't you tell me to calm down when my lazy, ungrateful, drunk son tells me off."

"I didn't tell you off," Jim interrupted. "I only meant that I want some room." He knew he shouldn't keep talking, that by defending himself he would egg his father on, but he had gotten tired of his father talking about him that way, always twisting the facts to make him seem like a big loser.

His father swung around on him. His face scrunched up; eyes transformed into magnified slits of cold blue; he raised his fist and shook it slowly as a warning.

Jim stared back and tried to project his frustration and anger through his eyes like beams into his father's stubborn face.

"Boy..." his father said.

He stood still, glaring at the twisted nose hairs, the beer fat plump around his eyes, the big round ears sticking straight out, then back into his eyes, again trying to communicate with his stare. When his father's fist finally made contact with Jim's left jaw, it moved his head to one side. With his head turned to the right for a split second, he considered his reaction.

His brother William had always said, "If that bastard lays a hand on me, it'll be the last thing he ever does." He knew his brother would throw his entire mass directly into his father's chest. If this incident occurred on television, the son would either punch back or go running away like a wounded deer. But what would Jim Diffin do?

He slowly straightened his head, slightly raising his chin as if presenting it for another, cleaner shot and glared back at his father with more contempt than before. But now he tried to ask his father, Do you feel better now, old man? He thought the question so intensely he imagined his father heard, as that ruddy face slackened and the rage left it. His father turned away and retreated silently down the hall, leaving Jim standing alone in the dining room. His mother still stood in the living room. Her face seemed to be apologizing. He tried silently to tell her it wasn't her fault. She hurried down the hall after her husband. Jim gathered his balled-up, clean laundry and walked out the door.

A strong breeze swept off the pond like an inexhaustible whirling emptiness. Boys chased after one another on the water line. A small boy allowed his younger sister to bury him on one side of the chair.

Pow climbed up beside him, plopped down, draped a dark green towel over his pale legs and twirled his whistle across his knuckles.

"Did I ever tell you I had that dream again the other night?" Pow said.

Jim shook his head.

"Well, I did. And this time it was different."

"Really?"

"Yeah, I got to see the end."

"The end?" Jim asked. "It started the same though?"

"Yeah, the same stuff as before, but it kept going this time. It wasn't bad. It was good. Everything burned up, even my body had been like totally consumed. Ash fell on my burnt bones. The clouds looked like coal.

Half-dead people crawled past me, beggin' me to somehow end their misery. But I felt some kind of stillness within me, so I didn't move."

"This doesn't sound good, dude." A young mother—so young Jim preferred to think she was a baby-sitter—ran by, chasing her toddler.

"I know," Pow said. "But listen, homes. People blossomed."

"What?"

"Flowers, beautiful flowers busted right from their chests, hips, shoulders, skulls. Then I started sproutin'. My feet shattered the glass under me and sunk into the ground. My back straightened. I grew into a huge, oak tree, homes," Pow said, pausing as if remembering the moment.

He tugged a braid, seeming to search for the words to continue. "Then it was like, hurricane force winds blowin', takin' away most of the smoke and sweepin' up all the charred shit. It rained, too, soakin' my bones and freshenin' the air. The sky opened up. All blue. It was beautiful, homes. The fear was gone. Everything was warmth and sunshine." Pow grinned and nodded.

"How many times have you had this dream?" Jim asked. Often Pow's dubious sanity had caused him concern, but if this dream from apocalyptic beginning to metamorphic ending was still plaguing him, then he might need some psychiatric help.

"I don't have it any more. Like I somehow saw the end, and now it doesn't happen anymore. I dream about other shit now."

"I'm glad to hear it," he said. "So, you sleep more peacefully now?"

"Totally, homes."

"I still can't believe you've never done drugs."

Pow clutched his stomach and laughed. "I know," he said, still chuckling.

Down the beach, Troy blew his whistle at some boys wrestling in front of his chair. They didn't stop; he stood up and blew harder.

An old man tramped past their chair. The man hadn't dressed for the beach, wearing a polo shirt, khaki pants and orthopedic shoes.

"Did I mention I finally told Diana?" he asked, knowing he hadn't told anyone yet.

"Wow, no way?" Pow said, tilting his frame so much Jim worried he might tumble out of the chair. "Well, you said you were going to. How'd she take it?"

"Seemed to take it well," he said, spinning his whistle.

Pow adjusted the towel over his legs. "So, she forgave you?"

"I think so. She didn't say, 'Jim, I forgive you' or

anything like that, but I asked her if I could see her again and she said, 'yes.'"

"Really?" Pow asked.

"Well. She said, 'I guess so,' which I think is as good as yes. Anyway, I'm working on this great plan to make it up to her, to make sure she can't help but forgive me."

Jim spotted a bobbing head as it moved clumsily toward shore. His body tensed on the seat's edge until the head steadied, clearly having reached shallow enough water to stand. He swatted at a fly buzzing past his ear.

"How is that going to happen?" Pow asked, pushing his sunglasses higher on his white-smeared nose.

"It's a plan I have. I don't want to talk about it, might jinx it." He stood up and blew his whistle at a pair of kids hanging on the outer rope.

"Listen, Diffin. I won't preach, but you really shouldn't worry about her forgiving you."

He scowled as he sat back down.

"Here's the thing, homes," Pow said, angling to face him. "You did something you're not proud of, betrayed the girl you love. But her forgiveness isn't going to fix things."

"How do you figure?" He looked down, dangling his whistle on the foot board, making it dance between his feet.

"Personally, I think even if she says she forgives you, your relationship is still fucked. The trust is gone, and you can't have love without trust."

"Fuck that, kid."

"Seriously, homes," Pow said, checking the water briefly. "What I mean is you have to forgive yourself, fix yourself, and you can only do that through some self-examination. Maybe you should figure that crap out before you get into another relationship. Of course, you might not know for sure if you've figured it out until you're tempted again."

"Dude! Why're you hatin' on my relationship?" he asked. The sun beat down hard; sweat ran down his back. "You'll see, kid. I'm gonna straighten this shit out, sweep her off her feet all over again. She'll forgive me, maybe even fall in love with me, too."

"Hey, I could be way off, Diffin." Pow faced the water again. "But you really should look into getting to know 'The Diff' a little better. If you can look inside," he said, putting five fingers onto the center of his chest. "Then you can get centered and shit; you won't have to do anything special to get a girl to love you. You'll simply attract her, and she'll love you without realizing it."

"Whatever, dude. That's enough of your new age funk." Jim scanned the water for a swimmer to yell at, needing to vent some frustration.

"Yeah," Pow said. "What the fuck do I know. I don't even have a girl." He almost laughed.

"That's because you don't try," Jim said seriously.

"But that's exactly my point," Pow said, lazily swinging his whistle.

14

He sauntered down the hill from the dining hall with a bounce in his step, despite the table he carried on his back. He was coming from the kitchen, where DeGawain had been finishing up the dinner service. The waterfront cabin lay dark and quiet at the hill's bottom and beyond it, on the beach, sat two dining hall benches, barely long enough for two people. He lugged the table out into the sand and checked the sky. The sun was about an hour from fully setting. He balanced the table, top side up, across the rowboat's bow, dropped the benches behind the stern seat, shoved it off and rowed out to the floating dock.

❧

Last week—the evening of his birthday—he hung out around the dining hall in the dirty general staff lounge. Chipped and faded wooden signs, indicating activities the camp no longer offered or warning the campers about bears that hadn't been a problem in years, decorated the walls. An old television with an outdated video game system and a handful of games had been donated along with a Ping-Pong table, a jukebox and a pin-ball machine for the staff, so they wouldn't have to leave camp at night to entertain themselves. That night he didn't play any games. He just sat on an old—also donated—couch. Waiting.

Diana had promised to come down and bring him a cake. But that was before he'd told her about the Fourth of July. She said she intended to keep the promise, even if he was a cheating sleaze-bag. But the hands on the clock crept around past nine-thirty p.m. when she'd planned to come at 8ish. Had second thoughts struck her? Maybe she'd decided he wasn't worth it, birthday or no birthday, promise or no promise.

His doubts fled once he saw her beaming smile grace the room's fluorescent lighting. She carried a cake, severely dented on top, wrapped in cellophane and covered with bits of dirt and twigs. It seemed like she hadn't gotten over what he'd done and, to prove it, brought a fucked-up cake.

She greeted him with a peck on the cheek, then shook her head over the beat-up cake. "I fell in the woods on a root, or something."

Her scent, a fruity hand lotion, overpowered the dingy, must of the staff lounge. "You didn't take a main road?" he asked, checking to see if she hurt herself. She didn't have any dirt on her knees and her elbows didn't look scuffed.

"No," she said, finding a table to put the mangled cake down on. "I took that small path you always use." She carefully removed the wrapping, trying to keep the debris off the frosting.

Shaking his head, he asked if she didn't have a flashlight. Diana pulled something from her pocket and shook her head. She popped candles into the craggy cake surface. When he asked her why she'd done that, she told him he made it seem easy. She finished jabbing candles in, borrowed a lighter and presented the cake to him, seven candles burning in a circle. She laughed and explained she'd been holding the candles when she fell and didn't find them all.

Diana and the staff in the lounge sang happy birthday to him. He cut his mangled cake, which they shared with whoever was there or passed by. After cake, they strolled down the hill to kiss and cuddle in the cabin's tower. Diana seemed somehow distant, said she was tired before any clothes came off, and so he guided her down the back path to her car. Before she left, she gave him a long, good-bye, birthday kiss.

❧

Out at the floating dock he positioned the table, estimating where the sun would set, so Diana would have the best view of it and then rowed back to shore. He called the kitchen from the deserted cabin. DeGawain said he was finishing his clean-up, but he'd whip up the meal as soon as he finished.

Diana would be showing up at any moment. Then, after calling DeGawain to bring down the food, he'd row her out to the table and row back to pick up the meal. He'd spent over a week getting the pieces together: DeGawain cooking some fancy pasta alfredo dish, Gräbe allowing it and the other guards vacating. He'd told Diana to show up around seven-thirty, because he had a surprise for her. The elaborate plan would hopefully help win her full forgiveness.

The katydids buzzed loud and strong in the hot, humid early evening. It got so humid sometimes that the best description was simply to say that it was sweaty out. Even though it was after seven, his shirt stuck to his back, and he mopped sweat from his forehead. If he thought he had enough time, he'd take a quick dip in the pond. Instead, he sat still and calm in the doorway overlooking the water.

As the sun dipped and the clock neared eight, he worried she'd miss the sunset. The sunset was key. Dusk was so beautiful over the pond. She couldn't miss the spectacle, the centerpiece, the entertainment for the meal. The air changed, the sweat under his shirt giving him a slight chill. He called DeGawain at the dining hall, but Diana hadn't walked by yet. Bats swooped along the edge of the beach, reminding him of their hike around the pond. A breeze rolled off the water chilling him, so he pulled a sweatshirt from his locker and sat back down to wait. He could barely even see the chairs and table on the dock anymore. The sunset's colors shifted from lurid reds to subtle purples.

At about ten to ten, the sun down, the moon rising, he heard a scuffle outside the cabin door. He leapt up to open it. She might've missed sunset on the dock, but at least she'd see the setup, the trouble he'd gone to. When Yeats entered the door, he slumped back into the chair.

"Sorry, to intrude," Yeats said. "I didn't want to miss you two eating out there in the sunset. I thought it'd be nice to come down and sneak a peek at you, like a movie scene." He switched the light on. "I'm sorry she never came."

"She might yet," he said, squinting.

"That's true," Yeats said, opening his locker and rummaging through it. "Do you want me to leave you alone?"

He shook his head.

Yeats sat down on his bed. What seemed like a full minute passed in silence until the phone rang. He sprang on it, hoping to hear DeGawain's voice tell him she was on her way, and he'd bring the food.

"Diffin?"

"Yes, DeGawain?" he asked, his voice rising in expectation.

"She there?" he asked.

"No," he said, sitting down on Gräbe's bed. "Guess that means she's not there either. I hope she's all right, not in an accident or anything."

Yeats crossed his legs and picked at his shoelaces.

"Me too," DeGawain said. "But, uh, Diffin... Not sure how to ask you, but what should I do with all this food?"

He shrugged, looked over to Yeats who still sat quietly on his bed. "Bring it down," he said. "Yeats's here. We can all split it."

Yeats's head shot up when he heard his name. At least they could sit down and have a good meal together, so that something could be salvaged of the night.

"If she shows up late," he said, thinking into the phone. "I can at least show her what she missed out on between the dirty plates, the dinner set up and all." She might simply be running late again.

"Okay," DeGawain said and hung up.

Jim reached over and slammed the phone down, allowing his body to stretch out on Gräbe's bed.

"Sorry, dude," Yeats sighed.

"It's all right," he said, propping his head, so he could face Yeats. "I deserve it, after what I've done."

"Maybe," Yeats said.

"I mean I did cheat on her," he said, sitting up.

"Yeah, but she did say she forgave you," Yeats said,

pointing his finger for emphasis. "I mean, if she's trying to punish you, then she should dump you."

"That's the last thing I want," he said, shaking his head.

"I know," Yeats said. "I'm just saying. She shouldn't punish you. It's not her place. Knowing you, you'll find a way to punish yourself."

He shook his head. Yeats was probably right. Funny how someone can sit on a lifeguard chair for a few hours a week with another person and really get to know them. "Maybe if I'm to be forgiven," he said. "Then, this is like my penance."

"Maybe," Yeats said, with a dismissive gesture. "But you should talk to her. Make her decide if she's really going to forgive you and forget about what happened when you were mindlessly wasted, or if she's gonna stick around and walk all over you."

"I guess," he said. "I'll talk to her, but how mad and indignant can I really be with her after what I've done?"

"Don't be so hard on yourself," Yeats said. "You're still a person who deserves to be happy, no matter how unhappy you made someone else."

Before he could respond, DeGawain walked in with the grub.

"Dinnertime!" DeGawain lifted the platter up and down for emphasis.

He settled around the platter with them, and they dug into the creamy penne, with moist, garlicky chicken and juicy broccoli. He stuffed his face while DeGawain heaped food on his plate, and Yeats picked at a plateful. As the food ran out, his friends started talking, probably trying to cheer him up, dodging the subject of Diana.

He laughed with his friends for hours and when he did go to bed, he felt grateful for their efforts to cheer him. Unfortunately, he didn't sleep until the sun had risen, up all night thinking about his girlfriend—or did he even have one?

୬

On Saturday, he left camp with Troy and Yeats, headed to meet DeGawain and Panza at the club, hoping to either get Diana off his mind or see her there. It'd been three days with him calling about twice a day without reply. He felt sure she was screening her calls or telling her mom to say she wasn't home. Depressed over Diana and angry at his helplessness, he drove through East Providence on his way to pick up a shirt he'd left at his parents' house, so he could wear it to the club.

As he sped down Pawtucket Avenue, two cars pulled out from the supermarket lot—one in each lane, cutting him off. He clenched the steering wheel and pushed down on the accelerator. Swerving to the left lane, where one car had pulled ahead of the other, he cut the wheel and jumped out between the cars, passing them. The next thing he saw was a cop car coming from the opposite direction. Sure, that the cop had seen his aggressive driving, he switched to the right lane and, watching the cop pull into a parking lot—no doubt to turn around—he banged a hard right down a side street.

"Where are you going?" Yeats asked, reaching forward to hold onto the dashboard.

"Pork-chop patrol saw me make that move," he said. "Then he pulled into the grocery store lot." No way did he feel like yes, sir-ing and no, sir-ing a cop right now. "I'm gonna lose him before he even starts pursuit."

"Ah, fuck," Troy said from the back seat.

He pulled the first right then another, creeping to a stop and killing headlights and engine. Having heard about this maneuver before, he wondered if it could possibly work. How could the cop find them? Should they ditch the car and hide in the bushes?

"Duck down," he said. As soon as they'd ducked, a cop car, flashing lights blaring siren, blazed by with enough speed to make the Omni lurch forward. He waited. The pig actually hadn't seen his little car. After it seemed enough time had passed, he started the engine, leaving the lights off and drove through the residential streets toward the Veterans Memorial Parkway and a quick exit from East Providence. He threw his lights on after making the first turn and, as he neared the parkway, he cursed himself.

"Dude," Troy said. "That's a dead-end."

"I know," he said, punching the wheel. "Now." He pointed to the guardrail. "Fuck." On the bottom of a ridge, beyond the guardrail cars sped past. Fucking side-streets. As he put the Omni in reverse, headlights approached. He killed the lights and engine again, but the same trick didn't work twice. A siren whooped, the lights flashed, and the cop parked behind them.

"Damn," he said, rubbing his face, wondering what kind of trouble this meant.

The cop paced warily, with his hand on his holster and his flashlight pointing at the driver's side. He flashed his light into Jim's eyes and ordered, "Slowly, slowly, step out of the vehicle."

"Yes, sir," he said and followed instructions. Exactly what he wanted to avoid.

Seconds later, another cruiser parked behind the first, and an officer climbed out and moved into position, flashlight blaring, hand on holster, watching Troy and Yeats. The first officer pushed Jim against his dusty hatchback. His arms were spread on the car's roof, and his face smeared the gritty dirt from the hatchback window. The cop swept Jim's feet farther apart, and his right hand pushed on the back of Jim's skull. He'd never had to "assume the position" before.

"What the fuck were you doing?"

"I don't know, sir," he heard himself say. "I'm just an idiot. I was just being an idiot." It seemed like the only thing left to do. Really, what more could he say.

"What have you got hidden in here?" the cop demanded, leaning closer to his ear, smelling of after-shave alcohol. "What are you carrying in this vehicle? Why did you run from me, you punk?" With each question the force on his head increased. It felt like his head was being crushed.

"I don't know, sir. I'm just an idiot. I was just being an idiot."

"Who were those guys that cut you off?" This time the cop moved Jim's head from side to side as if to shake answers from him.

"I don't know, sir. I'm sorry. I ran because I thought you were going to pull me over for driving like an idiot."

"If you hadn't run," the cop said. "I was going to pull over the other cars. I thought they were fucking with you, had something against you, cutting you off like that. So, what've you got hidden? You're sure there's nothing hidden?" The cop leaned in close to his ear again and whispered, "I can bring dogs out here in fifteen, ten minutes to check. Any drugs, alcohol, or weapons stored in this vehicle, you better tell me about them right now or it'll get a whole lot uglier for you."

He thought quickly to make sure he had no alcohol, or anything that could be misconstrued as a weapon in his car and said, "No, sir, nothing like that."

"So, you expect me to believe you ran away from me like that simply because you swerved in traffic?" The cop pulled away to apply more pressure to Jim's head. "What's the matter with you?"

Resisting an urge to tell the pig: you fucks always pull me over for stupid shit, he said, "I don't know, sir. I'm just an idiot. I was just being an idiot."

The cop, obviously tired of interrogating him, took him to the back of his cruiser and put him in. He watched through the metal grating as the cops took out Troy, questioned him and locked him in the other car. Troy's lower lip trembled. Would they arrest all of them? Was being an accomplice to evasion an actual offense? Jesus, what kind of an asshole gets his friends arrested?

The cops made Yeats open the trunk and all the doors for them—all the while maintaining their defensive postures, one cop holding Yeats under the flashlight, while the other searched the car. It was the first time he'd gotten to get a look at either cop. The middle-aged one with the mustache he figured had been the one questioning him. The other one, balding with a potbelly, must have been the second responder.

When they finally called off the search, they freed Troy and put him and Yeats in the Omni. Would they be released, but not him? After the pigs talked at his friends for what seemed forever, they eventually released him, too. On his way to the Omni the mustached cop gripped his right biceps and slammed him into the car's side.

"You go home right now," he said, getting close. "Don't drive around town for the rest of the night. If I see you on the road again tonight, or catch you trying to run from a cop again, I swear, I'll bash your punk fucking head right through the pavement!"

He agreed, but as soon as the cops had left, he drove to his parents' house to get his shirt and wash his face;

he had Omni dust all over it. Troy and Yeats waited in the living room with his parents, probably telling them about the whole adventure. If they were in the house, at least his old man would act civilized. Before he left, his dad made some kind of remark about respecting authority. Jim hardly listened. The cops had hassled him, but that was nothing new. They'd probably enjoyed themselves. His mind was already out dancing.

When he drove out of East Providence, he took the Wampanoag Trail where fewer cops patrolled and headed into Providence to meet the guys.

15

Although the club the other night had been a fun distraction, it would've been better if he hadn't constantly searched the crowd for Diana. That had been Saturday, but by Monday without a word from her, he was freaking out. Once his shift ended, he walked over to a pay phone near the dining-hall. The guys had gotten tired of listening to his phone calls—never mind the bitching that always seemed to follow. With the black plastic receiver to his ear, he counted each ring. A woman's voice answered on the fourth ring.

Jim swung the metal cord. "Mrs. Huntington?"

"Yes. Is this Jim again?"

"Yes. It is, Mrs. Huntington." He hoped he wasn't getting on her nerves. "Diana there?"

"No, Jim."

Damn. He tried to judge her voice as to whether she was telling the truth or not.

"She's over at the barn with her horse. After that I think she has to drive Nina somewhere. But, as usual, I'll be sure to tell her you called."

He couldn't tell. It sounded plausible and likely to him.

"Thank you, Mrs. Huntington," he said and dropped the phone back into place.

Later that night when he badgered the guys over whether or not Mrs. Huntington could be lying to cover for Diana, all they said was, "Maybe," or "Who knows," and eventually, "Let's go get a bite to eat at the R'n-R."

The R'n-R was a trucker stop on the Rhode Island/ Connecticut border. A narrow shortcut from the camp wound through the woods to within a block of it, but most of the campers and staff who ate there took the highway.

The back road, as it was always called, was dangerous, even for trucks. The camp always warned patrons never to take the uneven, winding, narrow road. Only one truck could pass at any time. Places of it wound between old stone walls or natural ridges, half the time creating the effect of driving down a ditch. The staff tried to regulate the comings and goings up and down it. If they drove down the path, they'd delay at the diner until very late at night to drive back, assuring—hopefully—that at that hour everybody was heading in and not out.

When he said he wanted to drive the back road with his Omni, everybody laughed. At first, he'd only been fucking around, but when nobody believed he'd do it, he couldn't resist.

He took Yeats and Troy with him. Yeats wanted to drive the highway—but having wrecked his car en route to the lifeguard test that past Sunday and with every other car filled up—he didn't have any choice. Gräbe drove his truck before him and DeGawain drove his truck behind. The ride to the trucker stop went well.

His car slid in the mud a few times and it jolted like a W.W.II jeep over rough ground, but it'd been fun.

At the diner, he indulged in the all you can eat "Midnight Special" of two eggs, two pancakes, two pieces of bacon and a side of toast with bottomless coffee or tea for $3. More staff from the camp showed up, rangers, kids who ran the mountain bike center or gave nature hikes. Everybody ate there frequently enough to know the waitresses' names and refill their own bottomless coffees. He might have had one or two too many cups of coffee, or maybe he was feeling especially daring that night, probably a combination of both.

He stayed late with everyone, and as they left the restaurant, lightning streaked across the sky; the wind ran through the trees, making them shush-shush at the thunder. There was an energy swirling, and he fed off it and the coffee and his despair. He pulled up the rear, cranking his radio. Rain dumped on the Omni; lightning brightened the street leading to the back road. Rammstein's "Du Hast" blared through the speakers as heavy rain drops drummed a steady beat on the roof. He sensed Yeats and Troy shooting each other looks as he accelerated toward the wooded path.

The curves and ruts kept them at speeds of five or so m.p.h. But as the storm picked up, so did the pace of the trucks ahead of him. It didn't make any difference that the trucks had better tires, better shocks, better handling in general and were designed to drive off road. He pushed down on the pedal and paced Gräbe's truck now ahead of him.

"Dude, slow down a bit, okay?" Yeats asked, putting one hand on the dashboard to steady himself.

"I'm all right," he said, calmly.

In the rearview, he could see Troy holding his buckled

belt and heard him muttering prayers. Jim didn't slow. He straddled the road, hurtling down it. The radio switched tracks to Rage Against the Machine with "No Shelter." The song's fast tempo and angry lyrics cracked and sparked across the factory speakers as the storm continued to rock at the same pace. At a sharp turn, he barely slowed, tapping lightly on the brakes.

The tires lost grip. Jim spun the thin steering wheel in his hands, but the car sped off the path. Trees loomed ahead. Nothing left to do but deal with it. Out of the mud—the tires bouncing over moss, dead fall branches and leaves—he could steer again. Dodging trees, saplings, bushes and boulders in the dark, images of tow trucks leapt through his mind. So, he treated the Omni like a go-cart, never letting off the gas, weaving between the trees. Rocks kicked up and thumped under his feet; stumps and logs pounded the underside, and brush scratched from all sides as they lurched and careened through the woods. No matter what, he would not get stuck. The red lights on the rear of Gräbe's truck served as his beacon, like dead-reckoning It was his one hope to regain the road.

Suddenly, the Omni burst free from its off-road excursion and back onto more familiar terrain. Once on the road, the car violently fish-tailed, but he gently turned into the skids, and soon they followed the caravan again. Realizing nobody had suffered so much as a scratch, the psychotic thrill of a near death adventure seized him. He renewed his crazed pace all the way back to the main campgrounds. His heart beat fiercely, and he could hardly contain his excitement as his passengers sat speechless, apparently still trying to understand what had happened.

Pulling into the camp parking lot, he leapt from the car, screaming, "Did you see that shit?" He ran around, jumping and pumping his fist in the rain. "Did you all see that shit?"

"Yeah, you're fuckin' nuts!" DeGawain said, rolling down his window.

He jumped on the Omni's rear bumper and bounced it. "Can you believe this fucking thing? It's fucking invincible! This piece of crap can do anything!" He whooped into the night. "Holy shit, I can't believe that."

The rain poured down, chilling him and cooling his adrenaline and caffeine rush as he hiked to the beach in the dark with the others. Back at the cabin he peeled off his soaked, mud-caked shoes and hung his wet clothes from the rafters. So much moisture clung in the air that his sheets held in the damp. A puddle had formed by the beach-side door. In the morning he'd have to rake the beach because of all this water.

16

Early the next afternoon, he headed out to relieve Pow from chair four. The sun had blazed all morning and burned some of the moisture from the freshly raked sand. Across the pond, a family of swans ventured out for a swim.

"So, I heard about your escapade last night," Pow said. "How drunk were you, homes?"

"Not at all," he said, a bit startled. "Who the fuck told you I was drunk."

"Nobody," Pow said, whipping his whistle in circles. "I assumed. Diffin. Doing some crazy shit in his Omni. Must be drunk."

"Damn." He climbed onto the chair. "You know I never drink and drive."

"I'm pretty sure you never have, that doesn't mean you never will," he said, then added one of his favorite aphorisms. "Past performance is no guarantee of future behavior, homes."

"Whatever, Pow."

"Look, homes," Pow said. "All I'm sayin' is you're

gonna kill yourself one of these days, and you know what? She's not really worth it."

"What?" He adjusted his sunglasses and pulled down his floppy hat. "I love her."

"Yeah, but does she love you?" Pow asked, climbing down from the chair.

"Don't fuckin' bring that shit up." He dug in his pocket for his whistle. "You know she doesn't love me. But she will at some point, I have faith in that."

"What if your faith is misplaced?" Pow squinted up at him. "You hurt her, confessed to her, did your best to attempt some kind of reconciliation." Pow put his whistle around his neck and squished his hat in his hands. "You're begging for forgiveness, but the most important thing is that you forgive yourself."

"It doesn't matter if I forgive myself," he said, finding his whistle in a pocket he'd never used before. "She has to forgive me that's what—"

"No." Pow smacked him with his hat. "Quit that nonsense, homes. Listen to what we're talkin' about: confessing, reconciling, forgiveness. Next you'll be talking about being in a state of grace because of some sick penance you performed."

He clenched his jaw. A few Hispanic boys did back flips and walked on their hands, proving their machismo to one another.

"It's kind of sick." Pow shrugged. "And I'm getting sick of your sickness. I'm hoping you get sick of it, too."

"What the fuck, Pow," he said. "I love her, I fucked up, why shouldn't I suffer?"

"First of all, she doesn't love you, homes. Maybe she never would've, maybe she would've—who knows—but it's time to call it quits."

"Quits?" he asked. "If she's tired of me, she'll dump my ass, kid. I love her too much to quit."

Pow slouched and kicked the sand. "Hey, maybe you're right. I'm sorry to get on your case, homes. You know I don't know what the fuck I'm talking about." He looked up and swatted him again with his hat. "I won't bring it up again, a'ight?"

"Sounds good to me," he said, trying to pay attention to the water as Pow trudged away. Not far from his chair two toe-headed boys wrestled in knee-deep water. In case they carried it too far, he put his whistle to his lips and got sand in his mouth. He sputtered and spat over the side of the chair.

When he straightened up, the boys hadn't stopped. He blew his whistle; it didn't make a sound; instead, a line of sand blew from the hole. Someone had fucking filled it with sand and pebbles. He looked around, shaking it.

On the next chair over, Yeats stood up and signaled for him to whistle at the boys. Jim felt completely impotent without his whistle. He held it up and shook it, trying to get the sand out and show Yeats that something was wrong with it. Yeats nodded, then whistled at the boys, and they quit roughhousing.

Jim scanned the beach. Pow lounged by the cabin, holding his belly, laughing. Jim leaned back, shaking his head. "Pow," he muttered. He smacked the whistle in his palm to get the sand and pebbles out. Why the fuck Pow would fill his whistle with sand?

When his chair-sit ended, Jim jogged over to chair number two where Pow lounged, pulling on his braids. "Pow," he said, expecting some response, some explanation or at least a laugh. Instead Pow sat still, his whistle poised fractions of an inch from his lips. His face appeared empty, as if he gazed at something miles away. Jim whipped him with his lanyard. Pow flinched and shook his head.

"What's up, homes?" Pow asked, lowering his eyes.

Jim asked him if he'd been asleep, but Pow said he'd been concentrating on his heartbeat. It allowed him to stop thinking and simply "be," to live in the moment or some crap.

"Yeah? Fuck all that," Jim said. "What's the deal? Fucking with my whistle?" He ripped his hat off his head, gripping it tight.

Pow didn't say anything. He placed the whistle between his lips and rested it there, not moving. Sweat ran down Jim's face. He should've been relaxing in the shade, in the cabin, drinking water instead of standing in the hot sand wondering why his friend had gone nuts. He asked him again why he'd filled the whistle with sand.

Pow pulled the whistle away from his lips an inch and said, "It's like wind blowing through the grass, homes."

Jim wiped sweat from his face and rubbed it off on his crumpled hat. "Have you had any water today, Pow?" Dehydration and constant heat really took a toll throughout the day. A few times Jim had forgotten to drink enough water and thought he saw colors trail through the sky. But Pow put the whistle down and held up his water bottle, half-full and beaded with condensation.

"Dude, you're nuts, aren't you?" Jim asked.

"Maybe," Pow said.

"What the hell does wind in the grass have to do with my whistle filled with sand?"

Pow's face took on that distant look again. "What does wind in the grass have to do with your whistle filled with sand?"

"Pow," Jim said, wondering now whether his crazy friend was fucking with him. "Come on. What does it mean?"

Pow wound a braid on his index finger. "A family of swans swimming across the pond."

Jim scanned the water. No swans anywhere in sight.

"Diffin!" Gräbe called out from the cabin. "Get over here! I got stuff for you to do."

"Okay!" he called back. "So, what about it, Pow?"

"Diffin!" Gräbe shouted.

Jim shook his head and trudged toward the cabin. Somehow, he felt like Pow's shenanigans might relate to his Diana troubles, specifically the conversation they'd had earlier. But then again, Pow had probably recently read some book on absurd humor and wanted to try it out.

17

Since Gräbe initiated Friday night barbecues on the beach back in July, they'd managed to keep it quiet, and the administrators of Camp Waetabee hadn't found out. Now that it was the last week of operation before they locked things up for the off-season, Gräbe wanted to throw an obnoxiously large version of the regular Friday night parties.

Apparently, Gräbe didn't want to return next summer, but he couldn't be sure that the camp wouldn't lure him back with its easy duties and decent pay; he wanted to move on with his life and thought if he could throw a big enough party and get caught, the camp wouldn't ask him back. This'd been one of his ulterior motives for the barbecues in the first place and why he'd allowed Jim to attempt his sunset dinner on the dock.

After dinner, DeGawain rushed down to the beach and burst into the cabin. "Diffin! I just heard from Helen that Diana's coming to the end-of-the-summer barbecue tonight."

DeGawain couldn't tell him when she was coming,

why she was coming, if she was coming to see Jim or simply because she wanted to hang out with everyone. None of that was really as important as the simple fact that she was coming, and he'd have a chance to talk to her at least one more time. So long as she continued showing up, no matter how late, hope stayed alive.

But later that night, waiting for Diana's expected arrival excited his stomach and bowels, frequently dragging him off to the toilet while everyone else straightened the cabin, built a bonfire, gave money to Gräbe for a liquor run, or made last minute phone calls to give directions or extend more invites.

When people started showing up and empty beer cans began littering the beach, Troy smacked him on the back. "Hey, Diffin," he said. "Lighten up will ya? This is a party. Have a drink already."

Yeats pretended to stumble toward him. "Yeah—uh—weigh-ya's yaw beeyah?" he asked, impersonating Ted Kennedy. The question was all Yeats ever said in his Teddy voice. It originated from a story Yeats's dad told about being at a Democratic fundraiser in the eighties with the old, crusty-nosed patriarch. Teddy stumbled around the room, trying to be a gracious host, breathing noxious fumes and asking any empty-handed guests where their beers were.

"Come on, guys," Jim said seriously. "That's the shit that got me in trouble to begin with. Diana will be here soon, and then I'll have a few with her and that's all for me tonight." He thrust his hands in his pockets and leaned against the cabin wall beneath the window.

Inside the cabin Gräbe whispered to Pow, "Unless she don't show, then The Diff'll be gettin' ripped."

Ignoring them, he pulled up a chair, fired up the grill and occupied himself with cooking the burgers. Every new arrival captured his immediate attention until he saw that it wasn't Diana. He threw sizzling patties on the grill to keep busy. Sitting hunched over the grill, he tried not to pay attention to his surroundings—instead, focusing on the grill.

The coals burnt flamelessly, cinders flaring bright orange across the mostly gray pile. Whenever grease dripped, a hissing fire leapt up, but the violent flares did little compared to the steady, passive heat of the calmly intense cinders, burning themselves out behind bars and doing all the work. Only the ashes, their energy already exhausted, remained unaffected.

He stood with a half-smile, contemplating the coals until something jabbed him in the ribs. Turning, Diana's face glowed in the flickering light of another grill outburst. He pulled her to him and held her as tightly as he could without crushing her. Diana hugged him back as tightly; he tried to find her lips with his, but she pulled back to glance behind him.

"Are you gonna burn those things or what?" she asked.

While he'd been day dreaming, the burgers had charred and shrunk into meaty hockey pucks. One of the patties had ignited, and the others sat dried and useless. Using the spatula, he hurled them onto the beach with the rest of the rocks and garbage.

"Want a burger?" he asked, happy to see her. Now what he needed to do was get her alone for awhile and talk to her about their relationship.

"Not if you're gonna cook it like those, fucknuts," Diana said, leaning into him.

She called him fucknuts like nothing had changed. Maybe everything would be okay. "Ha ha," he said. "Nah. I tell ya what. I'll cook us some burgers if you grab us some beers." If she agreed to that, did it mean anything?

"Sounds like a plan," she said. Maybe it meant she'd get him a beer if he cooked her a burger.

She seemed happy enough, laughing and joking with his friends on her way to and from the coolers. His pulse literally quickened at the sight of her, giving him a minor adrenaline rush. Diana returned with his already cracked beer can.

They sat together on the beach, quietly devouring their burgers and drinking their brews. The sand underneath him chilled his rear. He wanted to slide closer to her, to feel her warmth, to hold her tight, to know for sure where they stood, but he didn't want to push it, especially in front of everyone.

Gräbe and Troy lit the fire they'd built earlier in the day. It didn't take long for the lifeguard crew and their guests to get totally trashed. Once Yeats started jumping through the fire for kicks, Jim turned to Diana.

"What d'ya say we get outta here?" Tentatively, he put an arm around her. "Go for a walk?" Her facial expression didn't seem to change at his suggestion. He'd hoped she'd react in some way that would reassure him.

"Where do you wanna go?" she asked, her demeanor unchanged. Either everything was absolutely fine, or she expected him to know that they were only friends now. Why couldn't she give him a sign he could read?

He shrugged. "Nowhere in particular," he said, although he'd spent a lot of time between bathroom trips earlier, planning a route. "Let's go somewhere a little less..." he watched Troy imitate Yeats's fire-dive, "insane."

"Okay." She rose, taking their greasy paper plates to the trash.

They slipped away from the glowing beach and wove through the Pine Grove. Beyond the grove a path led through the woods behind a series of campsites, ending near the sailing center. He took her hand and guided her down the path under moon and starlight. Tension gripped his throat. He didn't know how to bring any of it up. He wondered if he even should or if he should keep putting one foot down after another and see what happened. But the stillness of the path, contrasted with the slowly fading yelps from the beach, closed in on him, and he felt compelled to speak.

What words could break the silence? "You stood me up the other night," he blurted, realizing how stupid he sounded. He tried to qualify his blunt statement. "I mean, I know I deserved it and all..."

"Yeah," she said, holding his hand.

Afraid to ask the question because of what the answer might be, he held off and led her around a bend, away from the water, back toward the center of camp.

After helping her avoid a muddy section of the path, he asked, "You still mad at me? Is that why you didn't come?" He held his breath.

"A little bit," she said. "I'm mostly disappointed."

"You said, you forgave me," he said, pushing some low hanging briers out of his face and holding them, so she could pass. "Did you lie about that or have you changed your mind." Lie? Too strong a word, but he'd already said it.

"I didn't lie, Jim," she said, sounding irritated and dropping his hand.

"I—I meant—what I meant to say..." He took a deep breath. "Why didn't you come?"

"I'm not really sure, Jim," she said, growing sterner. "There's no excuse for what you did, you know. If you thought I was breaking up with you," she paused and stood still in the path, "then you should've found out for sure before fucking some stupid, ugly slut!"

She'd yelled loud enough to possibly awaken some of the campers, but at least she was venting. These were the words he'd wished she'd said weeks ago. "You're absolutely right," he said, with that stupid smile on his face that often got him into trouble. "I was drunk. I know it's not an excuse. I'm not trying to... It's a reason. Not an excuse, but a reason." He hoped she'd see the difference.

"I don't see the difference," she said, crossing her arms over her breasts and widening her stance.

He cleared his throat and rubbed his arms in the cool night air. "With an excuse," he said. "A person expects to be excused because of what he says. A reason is why something happened without any expectations of forgiveness or anything."

Her eyebrows raised and her head tilted. "You don't want me to forgive you?"

"That's not what I meant," he said, shaking his head. "I don't want you to forgive me because I was drunk. I'd like you to forgive me because I love you and wouldn't ever intentionally do anything to hurt you." He knew he sounded lame, like an abusive husband. There was no excusing him, but even if she never saw him again, she should know the reason he did what he did wasn't to hurt her or because he was some sex-crazed maniac. He'd been stupid. That was all.

Diana stepped closer to him. She looked angry.

"Don't expect me to forget, fucknuts," she said, punching him in the chest.

He shook his head. "I'm not asking... Wait!" he said, opening his arms. "Does that mean you forgive me, for real this time?"

"Yeah," she said, accepting his hug. He held her tight, kissed her on top of her head. He told her about the night he'd arranged for her, but she'd already heard about it. They turned, walking up the path again.

She put her arm around his hip, and he held her shoulders. "I kept saying to myself, 'why should you drive all the way down there to see your no-good, cheating boyfriend?' I couldn't answer the question," she said. "So, I stayed home. That sunset thing sounds nice though. I'm sorry I missed it."

"Me too," he said. "Maybe I can plan something else like it sometime."

She kissed his cheek. A few minutes later he took her off the path, despite her worries. He led her to a huge slab of granite poking out of the ground. She examined it. Growing all over the rock was a bioluminescent lichen. She'd never known such a thing existed and seemed very excited, which made him happy. As they neared the end of the path, he plucked a few leaves of bull-brier for them to munch on. She'd never eaten the sour apple-flavored, wild-growing leaf before either. With the summer nearly over, he was glad that she could appreciate some of Camp Waetabee with him, even if it wasn't the sunset. They still had the bats, the trails, the lichen and the bull-briar.

When the walk ended at the assistant cook's cabin, Diana threw him a doubtful look. DeGawain's assistant had left for the next few days and he'd given Jim permission to use his cabin—really a shanty on four concrete slabs—if he needed it for Diana.

He took her hand and kissed her forehead. "Why don't you crash with me in here tonight," he asked. "We could be alone."

Diana stepped back and examined the brown shack in the dim light. "I don't know, Jim," she said. "Whose is this, anyway?"

"It's the assistant cook's," he said, kissing her cheek.

"He's outta town, visiting a friend. He said I could use the cabin anytime he was away."

"Well," she said, drawing the word out. "I guess."

He smiled and opened the creaking door for her. Following her in, he flipped the light on, and they kissed. The inside of the cabin smelled like cologne and spilled mouthwash. A few dirty socks lay about. They kissed and stumbled over the spiral patterned rug on the floor and toward the neatly made bed. Blue cloth covered the two windows. She pulled off his shirt and unbuttoned his pants. He tugged off her top and popped off her bra, hitting the lights before they fell on the bed.

They fumbled together, getting her tight jeans off; but once the last leg was free, he kissed her recently shaven legs from ankle to inner thigh and kept kissing up her hip, her stomach, her shoulders, the nape of her neck and finally her breasts. Drinking in each inch of her unbelievably soft skin.

Despite his tenderness, her body felt tense and rigid. He thought he knew why. She thought he expected to snatch her virginity. Going with this intuition, he said, "I don't even have a condom on me or anything cuz I wasn't planning on sex." He kissed her lips. "Just so you know."

"Good," she said and her muscles softened. They fooled around for hours, stopping short of intercourse.

The next morning Jim woke up spooning Diana, her back curved into him. Birds sang a wild chorus all around them. He smoothed Diana's hair, lacing loose strands behind her ear. The sun barely sneaked in around the edges of the make-shift curtains. He would have to get out of bed soon. Today was the last day for campers. Once they left in the afternoon, the staff would start cleaning the camp, breaking down and packing up for the long off-season. But before that could happen, Jim would have to get back down to the beach to help the other guards clean up their barbecue mess.

Diana rolled over and planted a kiss on his lips. She smiled and wrapped her arms around his neck. They held each other under the blanket's embrace. When they did talk, it was about not wanting to get out of bed, not wanting to leave the cozy warmth of being beside one another.

Eventually, Jim climbed out of bed. He really had to get to work. They dressed in the chilly morning air of the dim cabin. Before Diana left, she kissed Jim and held him tight. "I love how much fun I have with you, Jim," she said.

"I know," he said, proud of himself for not saying it, not telling her he loved her.

All morning he cleaned the beach with the other guards. After lunch, the campers cleared out, and the staff swept through policing for garbage in waves. They climbed ladders to take down signs; hauled kayaks, canoes and rowboats into the dining hall; loaded sailboats onto trailers to be carted off to storage in town; rolled up tents at activity centers and picked up even more garbage. After a week of packing everything away and cleaning, Jim threw his clothes and personal items into his car. Yeats—still car-less since his accident—tossed his bags beside Jim's in the Omni. They climbed in and drove off.

Yeats sighed as they rolled through the camp. "We can't move home to our parents' houses after a summer like this."

The archery range looked strange, nothing but an empty field now. The nature center's windows were boarded up, the trading post's, too.

Jim shrugged. "What else can we do? Unless we can find decent jobs."

"Or," Yeats said as the Omni passed the Camp Waetabee gates and onto a country highway. "We could find halfway decent jobs and split rent."

"You think we could work that?" he asked, turning the radio down.

"We just lived and worked together all summer. I'm sure we could do it outside camp. And we won't even have to work together."

"Yeah," he said. "We need to jump on that idea. We could have the guys over all the time. It'd be like the summer never ended; only the weather changed." The Omni belatedly accelerated out of a turn, roaring and sputtering.

"Hell yeah," Yeats agreed.

Jim nodded, cranked up the music—AC/DC's "For Those About to Rock"—turned off the country road, out of the woods and toward the highway.

PART III

FALL

"The highest good is like water, which benefits all things and contends with none. It flows in low places that others disdain and thus is close to the Tao. In living, choose your ground well. In thought, stay deep in the heart. In relationships, be generous. In speaking, hold to truth. In leadership, be organized. In work, do your best. In action, be timely. If you compete with no one, no one can compete with you."

— Lao Tzu

18

Jim wheeled the lawnmower into his grandmother's garage. Sweat soaked his body, beading on his forehead, and grass clippings clung to his forearms. He entered the house through the garage. As he passed the washer and drier and crossed the connecting room, his mother said, "I don't know what to do anymore, ma."

"I hate to say it, dear, but this is something only you can do. You have to figure out how you feel about it all and about him," his grandmother responded. An oxygen tank sat beside her with a tube running to her nose.

Jim entered the kitchen where his mother and grandmother sat at the table. "What's going on?"

"Oh, nothing, James," his mother said.

"No, really," he said as the kettle whistled. His grandmother got up and plucked a potholder from a drawer.

"Adult talk," his mother said.

"I'm an adult," he said, getting the milk.

"Girl talk, then," his mother said. He shrugged and rolled his eyes, handing his grandmother the milk.

The three of them sat around a small, round, brown table with full cups of tea. His grandmother stirred hers, then dipped the spoon in, slurping a sip to test the temperature and the mixture of milk and sugar.

Years before, he and William would walk the half-mile to this house after school whenever their mom worked. His grandmother's eyes would smile a welcome through thick, black-framed glasses as she offered Ritz crackers, Hostess donuts, Chips Ahoy cookies or a cup of tea. The house perpetually reeked of Ben-Gay, a detail he and William frequently joked about.

She'd sedate them with a card game that allowed her to go through her usual line of questioning such as, "How's school going?" She expertly dealt the cards, a lollipop hanging out of her mouth in place of a cigarette. After smoking since high school, she'd quit one day by trading them in for lollipops.

Now he sat sipping tea, realizing how she had always worried and cared about everybody and still did, even with death looming. That very day he and his mother had found her lying on the couch, clutching her rosary and praying for someone. If anyone in the family needed extra help, she prayed; even when people didn't need help, she worried and prayed. And when someone died, she prayed for their soul.

Her husband—his grandfather—had died when Jim was five, but his grandmother never remarried. His mom used to say that her idea of remarriage was dying and reuniting with her Patrick again. She was blessed with that kind of incredible faith. The largest crucifix he had ever seen on a wall hung vigilantly over her bed throughout her marriage and remained there now.

"Jesus was there to bless every time they did it," his mom joked.

Her house was the hub of family gatherings and activity. She'd sat in her rocking chair quietly taking in the talk, rarely adding anything. Maybe her hearing was worse than everyone thought, or maybe she simply enjoyed watching everyone interact.

Her shock at coming down with emphysema had been understandable, yet sad. She didn't know how much tar had built up over the years in her lungs, and it mattered little that she'd quit. The damage had been done. She hated to admit it but her daughter, the nurse, had been right. She was stubborn, but more than lovable.

Her life was the lives of her family. She concerned herself with their concerns, not in the manner of a meddler or a news bag. She was a humble, deeply spiritual and selfless woman.

Jim sipped tea, unable to get over the change that had come over his grandmother as her lung capacity dwindled and she began the long, painful death that would eventually drown her in her own lung fluid. Her eyes seemed sunken, duller. More liver spots covered her sagging skin; her hair thinned, her posture worsened.

On the ride home, his mom turned to him and said, "I have to put my mom in a nursing home."

"What?" he asked. That had always been something of a family joke. Whenever he got really mad, his mother told him that it'd be okay because one day he'd put her in a home. He knew she didn't want to go to a place like that and never dreamed she'd put her own mother in one.

"I've talked it over with her," she said. "And we decided while you were still mowing the lawn."

"What about the visiting nurses?" he asked. Anything but a home.

"They're getting too expensive for your grandmother, and I can't help her, either."

He wanted to argue, to figure out some other option. He hated the idea of his grandmother being shipped off to live "in a home" somewhere. But looking into his mother's eyes, he knew she hated it worse than he did.

Later that night, his parents discussed how to pay for the taxes and utilities on his grandma's house after she went to the nursing home.

"You'll have to get your sister and brother to help you," his dad said.

"Excuse me," Jim said.

"What is it," his mom said, sighing. "We're busy trying to figure this money out."

"I think I can help," he said.

≈

He led Diana into his grandmother's living room. He was giving her the tour. His grandmother had moved to the nursing home a few days before.

"How exciting," Diana said. "Your own house to live in."

"Well, Yeats and I will both live here."

"How did you convince your mom this was a good idea?"

"Somebody has to pay the taxes and utilities on the house. They can't shut off the heat and water, or the pipes will freeze. I told them I'd pay for it with Yeats's help, and eventually they agreed."

Diana touched a doily that lay under a glass lamp. "You'll redecorate though, right?"

"Of course. A lot of this stuff will be stored away

in my grandma's room since it's kinda like all the inheritance my mom and my aunt and uncle have."
He showed her the room where they'd store stuff, then showed her the room that would be his. His mother and aunt had grown up sharing the room, and now he would live there; Yeats would have his uncle's old room.

On their way out, in the kitchen, he pulled Diana close to him. He kissed her, one hand gently holding the back of her head. Her hands ran all over his back. He undid Diana's jeans and knelt before her. She lifted her left leg up on his shoulder and rested her hands on his scalp. He kissed her belly and slid down. He looked up to her face. He loved to lick her and look into her eyes, or catch her head thrown back, pleasure expressed on her face. This time she gazed out the window, moving her head as if she was trying to get a better view between the nearly closed curtains. He looked down.

19

Before Jim saw Diana again, he and Yeats had moved into the house at the end of Ginglow Street. Together with Jim's mother they hauled the valuable furniture and other breakables into his grandmother's bedroom. Antique wooden tables, a mahogany desk, the old glass lamp, the doilies, the giant picture of Jesus, anything remotely important and all the family photos cluttered on and around the king-size, four-poster bed.

They left the beat-up, old armchairs and the couch in the living room and the rickety dining room table in the kitchen. Pow made a gift of one of his sofas, so more people could crash. Jim and Yeats made it even more their place by lining the mantel with empty booze bottles, hanging posters, and Yeats brought in his life-sized cardboard cut-out of Elvis to chill out by the front door. In a few more weeks, friends brought a traffic light and, later, a parking meter. Nobody asked where they came from. When the cable guy showed up, he asked if it was a fraternity.

Jim hated calling it his grandma's house and calling

it his house seemed silly; so, he'd made up a nickname for the house: Ginglow's End. So far, it'd caught on. Diana had been busy during this time with the first few weeks of her senior year at Cumberland High School. Jim missed her, but he'd been busy with moving in and his junior year at R.I.C. He was going full time again this semester and had to keep his grades up.

Finally, in late September, he and Diana made plans. She would drive down to Ginglow's End where he'd show her around again, before taking her out. When her LeBaron pulled into the driveway, he rushed out to meet her in the driveway. She climbed out of the car, and it struck him how in person she was always more beautiful than in his memories.

Diana pointed to Jim's mother's car beside the LeBaron in the driveway. "New car?"

Jim shook his head. "No." Jim told her how the Omni had finally died. Apparently, the drive through the woods had mortally wounded it. To fix it, he'd have to spend more money than he bought it for. The "new" car was his mother's. He was borrowing it while he shopped for a new ride.

After they hugged and kissed, he told her he had something to show her. Reshouldering her purse, she followed him to the far side of the garage where a low wall of flagstone held in a wilted Rose of Sharon.

"Look at this," he said, lifting a loose stone. She came over and snuggled next to him and peered under the brick where two identical keys lay next to each other. She looked at him as if to say, so what? "I want to keep a key under this brick, so I can tell my friends about it," he said. "That way they're welcome to come by here even if I'm not here. Ya know?" He shrugged. "In case they need to get out of their parents' houses."

Diana put an arm around his waist. "That's very nice of you, Jim."

"Thanks," he said. "But there's two keys and I only want one under here. So, I think you should take the other one." Diana didn't move. She looked at him and then at the keys. Suddenly she stooped, snatched a key and hugged him around the neck.

"Thank you, baby," she said, still squeezing him.

Inside, Diana didn't seem too impressed with the decorating job. She did, however, say that it was an improvement over the grandma decor. Unfortunately, she hadn't brought a change of clothes, because she wasn't able to spend the night. She needed to wake up early the next morning to take Nina to a doctor's appointment.

Jim drove them out of Riverside and into Seekonk, Massachusetts, a small cow-town on route forty-four. Across the state line, east of East Providence, it had a long strip of restaurants and a pair of cinemas on the old country highway. They ate dinner and caught a movie, but afterwards it was still early enough that Diana didn't have to go home. She thought that rather than go back to Ginglow's End, where Yeats was probably watching cable television and scratching himself, they might find a quiet place to spend time together. She directed Jim down backroads through Seekonk into Attleboro, and eventually they popped back into Rhode Island somewhere in Cumberland.

Jim parked his mother's white Saturn behind a backstop in a small park. Getting out of the car, Diana led him away from the baseball diamond and down a winding path. The distant street lights burned halos into the sticky fog. Diana pulled her hair back in a ponytail and took Jim's hand. The tiny path curved gently around a small, dark pond and into a wooded glen on the far side. A smooth, large rock reclined under the wide arms of a tall maple. Diana motioned for Jim to sit, and when he did, she slid onto his lap. He realized he could sit on the rock and lean on the tree's smooth bark as Diana sealed her lips to his.

The street lights now reflected in the dark pond's surface as well as lighting up the night fog. The moist air tickled his ears. Diana's soft flesh pushed close to him. They'd been talking lately about their sex life, or lack of it. Diana said she'd be willing to go down on him. He hoped that was why she'd brought him here.

He couldn't resist, the night had gotten to him. "I love you, Diana," he whispered.

She pulled back, smiling. The lights behind her cast a shadow over her eyes. "Jim, I'm sorry. You must think I'm horrible." She smoothed one hand over his cheek. "I'm falling for you, Jim. Believe me. I'm just not sure I quite—"

"It's okay, Diana." He rubbed her thigh. "Don't force yourself to feel something."

She kissed him. They spent another hour kissing and groping. Before they had to leave, Diana told Jim how much she liked his t-shirt. It was an old Camp Waetabee staff shirt, a ring-tee. They didn't make them like that anymore, and it was one of Jim's favorite shirts. She asked if she could have it. In the humid night air, Jim didn't think twice. He pulled the shirt off his back and gave it to her. She laughed, saying that she didn't mean right that moment. Still, on the drive back to Ginglow's End, his bare back rested comfortably in the bucket seat of his mother's car, his shirt clutched in Diana's hands beside him.

❧

A few weeks later, Jim paid the phone company for a phone jack in his bedroom. Now, he could get online at his place. One afternoon, surfing the internet for lyrics to a Big Bad Bollocks song entitled "Whiskey in Me Tea," and writing an email to his brother William, Helen sent him an instant message.

> Helen939: y do u think u love Diana so much?

Jim minimized the other windows he'd been working on. He stared at the question. How weird. Helen always seemed to be trying to stir something up. But what could she be getting at now?

> Diff07: I just know it.
> Helen939: But she doesn't even love u. You're nothing but a fun toy to her. So, how can u say u love her?

Jim's leg bounced. He knew she was fucking with him, but he couldn't help getting upset.

> Diff07: Why don't you stay out of it? It's really none of your business.
> Helen939: Why don't u admit that you only say u love her to get in her pants?

Christ. Before he needed to punch out his computer screen, he went to the kitchen for a soda. When he came back, Helen had written more.

> Helen939: Nothing to say to that, huh? You're such a loser horn-ball.
> Helen939: Hello? Yeah, that's right. Why don't you leave her alone?

Not even sure why he was still writing to this crazy bitch, he typed away.

> **Diff07**: Hey, hey, hey. I was in the other room. y don't you cool the fuck out? I've never told a girl I loved her before. I don't have to say that crap to get laid.
> **Helen939**: Whatever. u fuck ugly fat bitches without saying that. Diana's right here with me and she thinks you're full of shit, too.

He fell back in his chair. "What?" he said. No fucking way. She had to be lying.

> **Diff07**: Fuck you.
> **Helen939**: She's wearing your camp waetabee shirt. did you really pull it off as soon as she asked for it? u'll do anything to get your dick wet, huh?

Jesus. Why was he still talking to this bitch? He should really get off-line and call Diana. If his cell phone worked better, he'd go out to his car to call her. Unfortunately, that piece of crap had been giving him such a hard time lately, it probably wasn't worth it. Whatever. Diana probably told Helen about their date, and now Helen was using that information to fuck with him.

> **Diff07**: you're full of shit. Diana knows that I love her and that I'm not trying to get laid.
> **Helen939**: y do you keep asking for blowjobs then?

Oh, man. Diana had brought up the fallatio thing... Hadn't she? Now that he thought about it, he couldn't remember.

> Diff07: That's between Diana and me.
> Helen939: then y did she tell me about it?

Jim shook his head, swept the cursor over to privacy options and blocked Helen's name. He finished writing his email to his brother, gave up on the lyrics and logged off.

20

A few weeks later, a friend of DeGawain's had a birthday party in Pawtucket. On the night of the party, Jim worked at his new job—lifeguarding at a fitness center. The fitness center didn't usually hire a lifeguard, but Jim called them several times a day, so they hired him. By the time Jim got out of work and arrived at the party, everybody, even Diana, was drunk. Since he'd borrowed his mom's car again, he stayed sober. When the cops showed up at midnight to break up the party, Jim rounded up Diana and Nina and invited people back to Ginglow's End.

Halfway home, snow started tumbling down, quickly clogging the streets. By the time Jim pulled up to Ginglow's End, he had to gun the accelerator to get up the driveway. With the snow, nobody would probably come to hang out, but that was fine, too.

Getting the Huntington sisters inside, proved more difficult than skidding up the driveway in the snow—one trashed and one on some sort of wild trip. First, he would get Diana, all rubbery-legged, to walk by holding her hand, or placing her arm over his shoulder, but then he wouldn't be able to get Nina's attention. Nina ran around the street and rolled in snow. Jim propped Diana alone in the doorway to convince Nina to come back.

Eventually, he threw Diana over his right shoulder, accidentally hiking up her skirt and revealing her white cotton underwear. Even though the neighbors were probably sleeping, he shimmied the skirt down, then took Nina's hand and took them inside.

He led Diana to his room where he changed her into warm, dry clothes. Afterwards, she followed him into the living room and lounged on a couch. But by then he couldn't find Nina. He checked outside, and, sure enough, she lay in the deepening snow, making a snow angel without her coat on.

"Nina!" he called, shivering.

"What?" she yelled.

Not wanting to have to go back out in the snow, or have to put his hands all over his girlfriend's underage sister to get her inside, Jim leaned in the doorway, begging Nina to come in. After Jim waited in the doorway for at least ten full minutes, calling out to her, she came skipping and hopping into the house. That done, Jim went immediately to the refrigerator. He had some catching up to do. Cracking a brew, he emptied it in five or six continuous, solid gulps.

Nina saw the sink full of its typically disgusting, sullied dishes and said, "I can't sit in here and do nothing. Do you think I can wash your dishes?"

She seemed hyper enough that Jim was rather sure she'd soon go off on some other trip, so he agreed and cracked another beer. Jim found Diana wandering around as though she'd never been to the house before.

After failing to convince her to go to bed, he went to

the refrigerator for yet another beer. If the girls were going to be insane, he might as well join them.

Jim led Diana back to the living room and glanced out the picture window. Snow continued to pile up on the street. The plows hadn't come yet, and Yeats still hadn't made it back. Jim wasn't sure Yeats should've been driving, but Yeats insisted.

Diana snored behind him. She'd also slid off the couch and onto the floor. Jim picked her up and lay her back on the couch. He tried asking her about Helen's strange instant messages at the party, but she'd been way too drunk. Besides, looking at her snoring on his couch, he couldn't believe she'd been sitting beside Helen that day. If she thought he was pressuring her for sex, she would definitely tell him. Diana was a lot of things and shy wasn't one of them.

Getting nervous about Yeats, Jim grabbed another beer. In the kitchen, Nina danced around, probably to music in her head.

When he came back to the living room, he leaned down to kiss Diana on the forehead. "Do you need to go to bed now, Diana?"

"No," she whined. "No bed."

"Oh, Diana, you're whining," he teased. "What's that all about? I thought you hated girls who did that crap."

Diana's response came with more whining and the promise of tears. She rested a hand on his arm and burst out, "I knoooow. I'm such a bitch tonight."

"What do you mean?"

"I'm acting like a weak, light-weight bitch!" she said, letting go of him and beginning to sob.

"But you're not," he said, sternly. He told her a major reason he loved her was because she was strong. Then, with a laugh, he told her not to be a whiny bitch and to get over it.

She laughed, too and smiled up at him. "Thanks, fucknuts," she said, her eyes still closed.

Deciding to check on Nina again, he glanced into the kitchen where the young teenager happily scrubbed away over the sink—completely out of touch.

Carrying Diana to his bed, he stripped her, leaving her in her underwear and a t-shirt. He pulled up the sheets, pausing at her knees to admire the blush of her cheeks, the tenderness of her belly button and the delicate curve of her smooth thighs, then he covered her and tucked her in.

Jim cracked still another beer and chugged half of it. Then headlights lit up the curtains to the kitchen. Seconds later, Yeats flew inside, followed by fat snowflakes.

Yeats burst into laughter as he slammed the door against the cold wind. "Man, it took me foreeeeever to get home!"

Jim handed him a beer. "What happened?"

"I got lost," Yeats answered with mock satisfaction, then refusing the beer. When Jim frowned in confusion, Yeats reminded him that he was on G.H.B.

The substance known as G.H.B.—officially Gammahydroxybuterate and unofficially, Georgia Homeboy and other quirky nicknames—had a bad reputation as a date-rape drug and a good reputation with ravers as an excellent drug to come down from ecstasy with. It was a powerful depressant formerly used legally for two purposes: treatment of alcoholism and for improved recovery from anaerobic work-outs. It gave all the feelings of alcohol with the benefits of a deep, rejuvenating sleep and no memory loss. But, if coupled with other depressants like alcohol, it'd been known to cause comatose states and death. Since the federal government banned it, Gräbe'd found it and sold large quantities from his Providence apartment. Jim, not being big on drugs, had never tried it.

Nina poked Yeats in the back.

Yeats turned.

"All done with the dishes," she said. "Anything else I can do?"

He and Yeats exchanged knowing glances for a moment, then simultaneously shook their heads. Nina was a well-developed and beautiful fourteen-year-old girl, but fourteen was still fourteen.

"I've got laundry," Jim answered, assuming she'd refuse that option.

"Sure!" she beamed. "Where is it?"

Moments later, Yeats put his feet up on the coffee table, and Jim came back up the hallway from his room. Nina trailed him, carrying his laundry basket. After putting in the first load, Nina joined them, sitting on the floor next to Jim. She seemed to hang on their every word.

Stories went back and forth for hours, until Yeats eventually said, "Yo. I got work tomorrow. I need sleep."

Nina moaned, asking for Yeats's laundry. So, Yeats handed over his dirty clothes and said goodnight, leaving Nina and Jim alone in the warm living room.

"I think your laundry must be done by now," she said. "And I've got to start on his now."

"Get me a beer while you're up?" he asked.

When Nina came back, she had his warm, clean laundry and an ice-cold beer. She pulled a footstool next to his armchair and folded the laundry.

"You don't have to do that, Nina," he said, feeling a bit guilty.

Nina gleamed a smile. "I know," she said. "I want to."

"What are you on, by the way?" He had to ask.

"Acid," Nina answered without hesitation.

His shock left him silent for a few moments. "Are you serious?"

"Yeah. What's the big deal?"

"You're fourteen. Do you know what that shit does to you?"

"Do you know what that shit does to you?" Nina retorted, pointing to his beer.

"That's not the same; you're still developing, and I'm pretty much done. Besides, booze is way less harmful than acid."

"Whatever," she said, turning back to the laundry. "I'm old enough to decide what I want to do with my body."

"You really think so?"

"Age is really all relative you know. At my age a couple hundred years ago, I'd be engaged to get married, maybe even married, maybe with kids!" she said, spinning around again.

"I think it's sad," he said, as if to conclude the argument.

Nina didn't say anything. She finished folding the last pair of socks and jeans, then carried the basket down the hall into his room.

When she returned, she changed the subject, "My sister's wicked passed out, huh? She can be so lame."

"She was really drunk."

"Whatever," she said, resting a hand on his leg. "I think it's time to put Yeats's wash into the dryer. Do you want another beer?"

He jiggled his can a bit, chugged it and nodded. Nina came back and sprang into his lap with the beer. She put her arms around his neck and locked eyes with him.

He opened the can and swigged down a third of the beer. He looked back up to Nina and shook his head.

"What?" she asked, rubbing his ear. He didn't think she was trying to be sexy by playing with his ear. Being tripped out, his ear probably felt nice between her fingers.

"Acid," he said. Still—her warm rump rested on his crotch. He hoped he wouldn't accidentally get aroused. If he did, what would she do? What would he say?

Fortunately, his statement broached a whole new discussion or argument, boiling down to the age relativity issue. Nina argued the same points, until she got flustered, while he calmly rested his hand on her back and tried to refute her claims. He and Nina, being drunk and drugged, argued to pointless repetition. Eventually, he said, "Let's talk about something else."

"Okay," Nina said. "Or let's do something else." She smiled seductively, giving him the wrong idea. "Let's go for a walk!"

"No way," he said, explaining that he was wasted and that it was snowing.

Nina looked out the window. "It's not snowing."

Sure enough, it had stopped. Jim tried to come up with another excuse, but alcohol had numbed his brain.

"And," Nina said. "I can't sit here anymore."

Jim took stock of his situation. He sat with his girlfriend's kid sister in his lap, both of them fucked up in their own ways. If Diana got up for the bathroom or for anything, this would be hard to explain, especially with his past. The fresh, chill air might banish his rising libido.

"Okay," he said. "Let's go, but not far or for long."

Nina leaped from his lap, then pranced around the room. He spread his arms to stretch, and Nina rushed to hug him.

"Thanks for doing my dishes and laundry, babe." Had he said babe? She didn't seem offended. After he let go, the memory of holding her slender, yet busty frame lingered in his mind.

Outside, the temperature had dropped even more, but the wind had died down. Chunks of snow dropped from the front yard's old, oak tree. He plodded down the driveway while Nina hopped from side to side swaying her arms. They trekked up the street like that. Nina's skipping made her chest dance about, and the rhythm they set mesmerized him. The cold early morning air bit his nostrils. He closed his eyes and took a few deep, relaxing breaths. The air served as a potentially sobering force, and he felt confident this walk would remain innocuous. They strolled to the top of Ginglow Street onto the main road and down some side streets. Nina continued to frolic about and found everything fascinating.

"Smell this fence," she said.

He leaned his nose close to the chain-linked fence and shrugged.

"Oh, you're too drunk to smell it!" She laughed, taking his hands in hers and trying to force him to dance with her. He'd been sobering up and felt drained, cold and ready for bed. He couldn't move his feet enough to dance, even if he wanted to. She pulled at his arms and skipped around until she tripped on his feet. He tried to keep her from tumbling into the snow, but she went headlong toward the ground and brought him down with her, their two bodies rolling over each other with him winding up on top.

Nina's green eyes, cheeks and especially her full, little lips smiled enticingly up at him as his face slowly dropped closer to hers. She held the small of his back and seemed to welcome his descending lips. His nose touched hers, and his forehead fell onto her forehead. He swept a stray strand of hair from her face, gently leaving it behind her ear. She felt warm beneath him, her body so firm he didn't think he couldn't restrain himself. He rubbed his lips together.

A plow truck whizzed down the street yards away from where they'd fallen. He rolled off of Nina. After a brief, awkward silence, Nina was up and skipping again. Guilt plagued him the rest of the walk, and it became easier to ignore Nina's silly, drug-induced ramblings.

Twenty minutes later, he put Nina to bed on a couch though it didn't seem likely she'd sleep. In his room, he stripped and stretched out beside Diana, who mumbled something and rolled over onto him. He welcomed her embrace and felt better for it.

The next morning was warmer, and a fog rolled in. On the way to their house, he took Diana and Nina out to breakfast. Diana thanked Jim for taking care of them.

Nina slurped orange juice.

At least he hadn't done anything to regret.

21

When Jim came back from bringing Diana and Nina home, the snow from the night before had begun to melt. Yeats's Saturn Coupe remained on the left side of the steep driveway, awkwardly angled into the bushes betraying the intoxicated parking job from the night before. The house had been left unlocked.

Inside, Yeats stooped over, one hand on the open refrigerator door, peering in. Yeats turned for a moment as Jim stepped inside, squinted without altering his posture and grunted a greeting.

The house smelled of stale beer; dried mud covered the kitchen floor; bottle caps hid in every corner. Bills, junk mail and old homework crowded the kitchen table and counter space. CDs lay on the floor by the stereo separated from their cases, some of them probably containing the wrong CDs. He and Yeats were such slobs.

In his room, laundry sat in a basket, folded, fresh and clean. A half-finished beer can sat on the nightstand, spare change from his dresser had fallen all over the floor around it, his sheets hung down to the ground, papers cluttered every piece of hardwood flooring near his computer desk.

Back in the living room a pile of empty cans stood and lay in various postures and several crushed shapes and sizes on his grandmother's coffee table. A pile of coasters tottered on one corner, several having already plunged to the oriental rug. Yeats sat behind them facing the television.

"What'cha watchin'?" he asked.

Yeats didn't answer.

"Yeats," he repeated a little louder.

"Oh, huh? Sorry, man. I'm so fuckin' tired after last night," he said.

Still standing at the edge of the room, Jim nodded to the television.

"Oh, sorry. I'm not really watchin' anything," Yeats answered. "I was kinda zoned out."

Jim laughed. "How 'bout Nina doin' our dishes and laundry last night?"

"That was the coolest." Yeats seemed to wake up at the memory.

Jim scratched his arm. "But do you think it was right? I mean, we kinda took advantage."

Yeats touched his lips, rubbed his chin and slowly shook his head. "No. I see what you're sayin', and it makes some sense especially since she's underage and all."

"Yeah, fourteen," he interrupted.

"Fourteen? Really? I guess I did know that. All the same, I think she was way too tripped out on acid for us to tell her she couldn't do that stuff. And on top of that, we gave her a project, which I'm sure kept her from totally geekin' out on us."

"Good point," Jim said and left the room.

In the kitchen, he stood with the refrigerator door open, one hand on the door: dill relish, butter, mayonnaise, slimy-wilted lettuce, a few pizza boxes he couldn't remember either he or Yeats having ordered, mustard, ketchup and a smattering of unidentifiable stains. He had made dinner out of relish once, tasted exactly like pickles. But that had been on a leadership camping expedition, and the kid in his group in charge of dinner had burned it again. He would have had to hike miles for anything else. This was a bit different.

All the same, he got a fork. After a few bites, he lost interest and figured he'd swallow his pride and drive the mile or two to his parents' house and scrounge. Besides, he really should return his mom's car.

"Anything in there?" Yeats asked, standing in the middle of the room behind him.

"Nah, not really," he said, replacing the lid on the relish and hiding the fork in his palm. "Actually, I was thinking about visiting the folks tonight, drying out, getting some free food."

Yeats looked down, wagged his finger for a second and said, "I was thinking the same exact thing."

❧

When Jim got to his parents' house, the fog had thickened, leaving only a few houses in each direction visible. He pulled up in front of the house, leaving his dad's parking spot empty. Inside, the windows were cracked open, curtains pulled aside; everything looked breezy and bright. The stereo blasted the Cranberries—a gift from him; he knew his mom would like the Irish rock band and hopefully listen to less Barbara Streisand or worse, George Strait. He kicked off his shoes, took two steps toward the kitchen when his mother raced around the corner and shouted.

He jumped. His mother leaned against the wall, holding her chest, eyes wide and panting. "You scared the shit outta me, James!"

"Hahaha." He shrugged. "You scared me, too."

She pushed off the wall and wrapped her arms around him. "Good to see you, hon," she said. Then she stepped back, looking him in the face. "Are you okay?"

"Yeah, ma." He went to turn the music down. "Where's dad?"

She glanced off above him and said, "He's at another scout meeting."

He nodded. Good, it'd be nice, having some sane time alone with his mother. "Wow," he said. "They're really keeping him busy with this volunteer commissioner stuff."

"So. Have you had dinner yet?" she asked, opening a cabinet in the kitchen.

He sat down at the table. "It's only five in the afternoon, ma."

"So?" she asked, her face jovially demanding an answer.

He shook his head, "No, ma. I haven't eaten."

"Did you bring laundry?" she asked, digging through the cupboards.

He looked off thinking of the whirlwind girl on acid cleaning house for him and Yeats and then... the mistake he almost made. "Uh, no," he said. "No laundry, ma."

"How about tuna casserole?" She turned away from the cupboards.

"Sounds awesome."

"Tea?" she asked, one hand on the burner knob.

"Yes," he said, sinking into the chair.

He drank tea with his mother while she, kinetic as always, did the dishes, peeled potatoes, opened the tuna and simmered the cream sauce. They had a quiet dinner together—Jim wolfing down his and getting seconds before his mother finished her meager first helping. Later, they sat next to each other on the dark leather couch and watched television.

Looking at the clock on the VCR, he asked, "So, how late does dad stay out when he goes to these meetings anyway?" It was already past nine.

"Well, he's actually coming out of his shell and getting very buddy-buddy with those guys. The meetings end, and he gets talking to them all. He's turning into another Pat McGuire," she said, letting out a tight laugh.

He smiled. "Huh. I doubt anyone, especially dad could out-talk Mr. McGuire."

"Well, he's always had the gift of gab around me. But now he's using it with other people." She pushed to her feet. "Want some wine, honey?"

He turned from the television screen. She always drank horrible sickly-sweet wine, heartburn wine. "Sure, ma," he said, thinking it would be nice to share a drink with his mom without needing a holiday.

Before the commercial break was half over, she zoomed back into the room with two glasses of wine. She handed him the one without ice in it and still standing said, "It's good to see you, honey. You don't have to stay away because you have your own place now." She eased herself beside him, then turned to him. "Cheers, James," she said, and they clinked glasses. "I don't know what we'd do without you and Henry helping out the way you are, taking care of the house, paying those taxes and everything."

Mud-caked kitchen floor, caps everywhere, crushed

cans all over, druggies and drunks over all the time...
"Sure, ma," he said. He did, after all, pay the property
taxes as rent, take care of the water bill and the oil bill,
so the pipes wouldn't freeze.

"So, any special occasion for the wine, ma?" He felt
he had to ask.

"No." She took a big sip. "I've been drinking a few
before bed lately and since your father isn't home yet, I
thought you'd drink with me."

"Really, ma?" he said, already getting phlegmy from
the cheap wine. "You usually only drink when your
sister's in town."

"Well, I haven't been sleeping well. So, I figure a little
night cap can't hurt."

"Sure," he said, waving his hand. "They're saying
now that a glass of wine or two a day is supposed to be
good for your heart."

She finished her glass in one big pull. "Well,
sometimes it helps me sleep."

"Why're you sleeping so poorly, ma?" he asked and
tried to finish his wine, so she wouldn't have to wait for
him to get more.

"Oh, honey," she said, frowning at her empty glass.
She swirled the ice and sipped the water from the
bottom. "My arthritis has been killing me."

"You have arthritis already?" He glanced up. She was
forty-nine.

"Mhmm," she said, rubbing her right knee. "It's
terrible in my knees."

They had a few more glasses of wine, enough to make
him sleepy.

"Do you mind spending the night on the fold-out in
your old room?" she asked.

He emptied his glass. "Well, I'd rather sleep in my
own bed I think, ma."

She reached her glass up high over the couch's arm and set it down slowly on the end table. "Oh, James. I'm terribly exhausted and really don't feel like driving on those slushy roads," she said.

He turned his head to roll his eyes. "Okay, ma. I'll spend the night," he said. "But in that case, I'm really sleepy. I had a long night last night. Do you mind if I don't stay up with you until dad gets home?"

She pulled her chin in toward her neck, puckered her lips and shook her head.

He brushed his teeth with a spare toothbrush his mother kept for him. Then he took out his contacts, kissed his mother goodnight and went to his old bedroom. He removed the rock-hard cushions from the couch and pulled out the bed, which clinked and clacked with metallic and springy sounds. The mattress still had sheets from the last time he'd crashed.

His old room—his mother had always talked about making it into a sunroom or whatever. Now it was somewhere between his room and something else. The walls were still the same blue, his Patriots poster still hung on the closet door, a few other relics of his younger days lay here and there, a soccer ball, his old bureau along with pens and scattered papers on top and his old television in the corner. But the room had also started changing. A few house plants hung from two of the corners. Pictures of him and his brother from at least ten years before sat on top of his television. A sewing kit had been put away next to the couch, which was also a new addition and a few of his mother's clothes hung in the closet next to his old scout uniform.

He threw off the light and pulled the covers to his chin. The foghorn's familiar droning lulled him to sleep.

Hours later he awoke from a dream. He had been

running and getting nowhere, sobbing and shedding no tears. He half sat up in bed, took a few breaths and rolled over to try and get back to sleep.

A strange, distant sound seeped into the room. The foghorn still moaned deep and soothing, but there was something else. He propped himself up on an elbow, trying to hear. It sounded like someone crying. Who could be crying? Could it be his mother? He'd never heard her cry before. But this wasn't merely crying, it was a half-stifled sobbing.

The room was cold and dark. He got up, turned on the light and listened at the door. Then, he pulled on a t-shirt and shorts. Wouldn't his dad be home? What if he stepped out to find his mother crying with his father trying to comfort her? That would be a strange intimacy to violate. He snuck out of the room, slipped into the bathroom and softly closed the door behind him. He peered through the blue aluminum blinds. His mother's car still sat alone in the driveway—no sign of his dad.

He opened the door slowly and padded up the hall. The light in the living room made him squint. His mother sat beneath the lamp on the couch where he'd left her three hours ago.

"What's the matter, mom?" he asked, stepping into the center of the room. "Is dad all right?" He never knew his father to be out this late.

She looked up through slitted eyes and wiped her nose with a balled-up tissue. "Your father's fine," she said, her voice breaking.

He sat beside her. "What's the matter then, mom?"

"Nothing to worry about, James." She sniffed, then blew her nose with a fresh tissue and cleared her throat. "You should get back to sleep. It's late."

He stretched his arm around her. "Are you sure, mom? You don't want to talk about it?"

She met his eyes, tilted her head to the side and remained still.

"Mom?"

She curled and uncurled a piece of tissue paper. "Oh, James," she said, fresh tears rolling down her glistening, raw cheeks.

"What is it, mom?" he said, pulling her tight.

She wiped her red nose. "James, it is about your father."

"What?" he asked.

"He's having an affair," she spat, the last word coming like a curse. Then she fell back to sobbing, leaning toward him. He held her as she rested her dark brown curls on his shoulder. Her tears dampened his skin through his cotton shirt.

"Oh, my God," he said under his breath. He might be having a bad dream, but his mother's shuddering shoulders were too real.

He held her close. "Are you sure, ma?" He didn't know why he asked her. Maybe it was because everything had become so real, that it seemed unreal.

"Yes. He told me himself," she muttered. She heaved and cried on his shoulder, weeping in his arms like a girl.

"How? Why? Who?"

"At work... Some plain-Jane hussy half his age... some mid-life crisis bullshit," she answered.

"Holy crap. What are you going to do?" He sat pathetically still, not knowing what to do, feeling like he was saying all the wrong things.

"I don't know, James. I really don't know."

But she always knew what to do. Before he'd even been old enough to go to school, they were at the mall together when an old woman collapsed. All the other adults watched, helpless. Big, strong men stood still, but his mother handed him her shopping bag and helped the woman, giving chest compressions and mouth to mouth until the ambulance arrived. His whole life, if he didn't know how to handle something, he always knew she could help him—whether matters of life and death, or mundane personal problems.

"Are you going to get divorced?" he asked. Unbelievable, divorce—as a boy, once his aunts and uncles split up, he always thought it was simply a matter of time until his parents did it. More and more of his friends' parents got divorced as time went on; it seemed like a rite of passage. But his parents never did. His mother was so hard-working, so ebullient, so charismatic, so crass, so trusting, so real; his dad had always been more likely to rest on the couch, barely getting up when company came, always uncomfortable with certain types of talk, so reserved and paranoid. Time went by and divorce drifted out of his mind. But now.

"I don't know, James," she said, sniffling. "You know I don't believe in divorce."

"Does he want one?" he asked. He felt strange talking this candidly about such personal matters with his mother, but the more she talked, the less she seemed to cry.

"He said he doesn't care," she said, sitting up a little.

"What the hell does that mean?" he asked impatiently. "Do you want me to kick his ass?"

She smiled and maybe almost laughed. "No. He's still your father, James. No matter what that asshole does. He'll always be your father, and you have to respect him."

"Doesn't sound like there's anything to respect," he said angrily.

She shrugged her shoulders and wiped at tears streaking her face and neck.

"How does your head feel?" he asked, sliding his arm off her shoulders and turning to face her. "Do you have a headache?"

She shrugged again. "A little."

He stood up. "Let me get you some water and aspirin."

"Okay," she sighed.

When he returned to the living room, he asked, "So, how did this come up? Did you ask him where he'd been one day, and he told you?"

"No. I suspected him. I went to his work. I followed him after he left." She paused, swallowing the pills. "I approached the two of them together. Asked if that was his mistress. He looked right through me and said, yes." She glanced away, her eyes welling again.

"Mom, you don't have to tell me if it's going to upset you more." He sat back down, rubbing her shoulder.

"No. It's okay. It actually feels good to talk about it." She smiled, sipping more water.

"Does anyone else know?"

"My mom, but I hate talking to her about it. She's wasting away on me, and I don't want to visit her to complain about my failed marriage." She trailed off. "Failed marriage," she mumbled.

Once more, he put his arm firmly around her. "I'm sure she doesn't mind. She probably likes seeing you and she must know that telling her makes you feel better."

She gave him a weak smile. "Anyway, that day your father admitted the affair, then told me to go home."

"Told you to go home? Are you serious?" He shook his head. "He's got some fuckin' nerve, huh?"

She drank more water. "I really don't even know him lately. He wasn't really living here all summer."

"But, he was here this summer. I saw him."

"He would come home on your day off, so you wouldn't know," she said, putting her hand on his knee. "He'll be home sometime in the morning probably. I talked to him earlier tonight. He knows you're here."

"Wow. That'll be strange." Maybe for once his family would talk about something as a family.

"James, you have to promise me one thing," she said, gripping his hand.

"Anything, mom. Anything."

"You can't let your dad know that you know," she said. "If he ever found out that I told you, it would ruin any chance he might come to his senses and come home to us."

That would be exactly like his stubborn, son of a bitch father, too. He was always right, even when he was wrong. He'd been disgraced he'd say and never come back and blame it on her for the rest of his life. Besides, even if he did come back wouldn't he only go back to bullying everyone in the family? Go back to being waited on hand and foot by his hard-working wife?

"But, mom. Is that what you want? I mean... You still want him back?"

"I don't know, James. I do still love him. I can't help that. He's my husband, and we've been through a lot together, more than you could know. And even if I'm not sure I want him back, I don't want to lose any chance I have."

"All right, mom."

"No. James, promise. I'm telling you he'd never forgive me if he knew I told you."

"Okay, mom. I promise I'll pretend that everything is still normal, but only if you promise me one thing."

"What?"

"Anytime you need to talk about anything, call me. Okay? I don't want to think that you're over here crying alone in the middle of the night while dad's out carousing, and I'm right down the street."

She smiled, and another tear ran down her face. "I promise, James."

22

"Nah, Yeats, I can't. I told you before," Jim said into his new cell phone, a recent gift from his mother. "Today's Diana's birthday, and I'm taking her out to celebrate." He stepped toward the entrance to the health club where he worked. "All right, I'll talk to you later, kid." He pushed the "END" button and wedged the phone into his baggy, front jeans pocket. Smiling at the receptionist, he strode to the manager's office.

He shifted his weight, as he watched his manager, Bruce, rifle through the checks. Bruce paused and pulled one envelope halfway out. He searched his desk, then the floor around Jim as if he were looking for something.

"Jim, I've got some bad news," Bruce said, finally looking up.

Jim gawked at him. Damn, an hour's reduction.

"The regional supervisor was here last night and he says that the company has to make some changes."

His lungs seemed to rise into his throat. His gaping

mouth quivered as he attempted to respond. He couldn't make a sound, so Bruce continued.

"We need to lay off some people. We're cutting back in maintenance, and since you're the newest staff member, and we're not required by law to have a lifeguard…" he trailed off, and Jim swayed.

Jim's eyes drifted out the window to the shiny black '98 Eclipse parked in the lot. He'd arranged a five-year payment plan last week for the car and had based the payments on the job he'd just lost.

"Wow, that sucks," Jim managed to say.

"There's nothing I could do. I know it's rough," Bruce said, extending the envelope.

Do you know, though? Do you know I'm not just a kid? Do you know I'm on my own and can't leave Yeats hangin' for the rent? I bet you think I live in a cushy house with my mom. You bitch!

Bruce rattled on. "I'll leave you on the payroll, and if any hours open up in the pro-shop or anywhere, you'll be the first to get a call, okay?"

Bullshit! "Okay." He smiled. "Thanks a lot, Bruce."

Jim took the check and clutched it tightly. He trudged out of the building on shaky legs. "Now what am I gonna do?" Jim asked as he opened his car door. He squeezed his check tighter and answered, "First, I cash this."

After cashing the check, he sped home. Once he stepped inside, he glanced in the fridge. "Still empty," he mumbled, shaking his head. In the kitchen, dishes sat in the sink, covered in glop made from mayonnaise, soda, lentils, beer, pizza crusts and cigarette butts. Jim averted his eyes and shuffled to his bedroom. He opened the top drawer of his bureau, removed and counted his money and figured he had enough for another month's rent, a car payment and eighty bucks to hold him until he found a new job. Hopefully, Gräbe's offer still stood.

A voice in his head, that unfortunately sounded a lot like his dad, told him to save the cash, and if Diana really cared for him, then she'd understand. Jim dropped enough money for his payments in his drawer and pocketed the rest. "Diana has to have a happy birthday," he whispered to the mirror.

Half an hour later, freshly shaved and showered, Jim parked his car before Diana's house. He bought a bundle of ten assorted yellow and white daisies, Diana's favorite, which he had picked up on the way and strode to the front steps. He rang the bell and seconds later she eased open the door.

"Wow," Jim exhaled, extending the flowers. She wore a knee length, white skirt with a yellow button-down top that matched her hair.

"Thanks for the flowers, Jim. You really didn't have to." She turned back into the house, and Jim stepped inside.

She put the flowers in a vase, shouldered her purse, and they climbed into Jim's Eclipse. After three songs had played on the radio, Jim pulled into the restaurant parking lot.

"I wish I could take you somewhere fancier," he said as he opened the car door for Diana.

"It's okay, Jim," she said, smiling. "We're not even dressed for fancy."

Inside the restaurant, nobody else waited, and the hostess seated them right away. They perused the menu, until the waitress came by for the third time.

"I'll have a bacon-swiss-burger, medium, please," he said.

"Grilled chicken Caesar salad for me," she said.

"Are you sure, Diana? It's your birthday. You can have anything you want."

"I know. That's all I want, though."

The waitress nodded and dashed off with the order. Diana leaned back into her chair, and Jim leaned forward.

"So, how's school going?" he asked.

"It's school. Ya know? Same old shit."

"Yup, I hear that," he said, trying not to think of his parents. "Anything new at work?"

Diana sat up straight and placed her elbows on the table. "Marcus is driving me crazy! He thinks he can boss me around because he goes to Johnson and freakin' Wales. I mean, he may know more about food, but it's a pizza joint. How much more is there to know!"

Jim couldn't help laughing, despite Diana's anger.

"It's really not funny, ya know? Now the other freaks who work there are listening to him and not me. He's not even a manager, and I've worked there longer! It's cuz I'm a girl. That's the real reason."

Jim wanted to say, at least you have a job and it still pays you well. Shut up! Instead, he smiled and nodded as she ranted about how unfairly the pizza industry treated her. But really, if life were fair, he'd have a job, and his mom wouldn't be home alone every night, crying her face raw.

"Well, he does study culinary at J and W. . ." Jim said to make conversation.

"So what!" Diana shouted.

"I was gonna say that I can understand where your dumb co-workers are coming from," Jim explained.

"Yeah? Well, I think they see me as a girl and him as a guy and so they respect him more."

"Damn the man," Jim said casually.

Their food arrived, and the heated discussion ceased.

Between mouthfuls of food, Jim quizzed Diana about what she wanted to do later. Halfway through the meal, Diana finally answered, "maybe a movie."

"Any movie in particular?" Jim asked, while chomping on some fries.

Diana shrugged. "What's playing?"

"You don't know either, huh?" Jim asked.

"Please, as if I have time to watch TV. I have school and a sister to drive around, not to mention pain in the ass work!"

Jim glowered for a moment, but she missed it, and he immediately felt guilty. "How about we go and see what's playing once we get there?"

Diana shrugged, again. "It's what we always do anyways."

Jim stuffed the last bite of beef and bacon into his mouth and waved the waitress down. Before swallowing, he mumbled, "Check, please."

The waitress sailed past, dropping their tab. When Diana reached into her purse, he snatched up the check.

"How much is it?" she asked.

"Don't worry about it," Jim smiled. "It's your birthday."

"You don't make all that much money. Let me help out here."

Jim thought about it for a minute; he had lost his job. But there was no way he could be so selfish as that. He wasn't selfish, never would be.

"No. Happy birthday. It's on me." Jim calculated fifteen percent in his head and added a dollar. He pulled thirty-five dollars and twenty-seven cents from his pocket and placed it on the table under the check.

At the theater, Diana decided of all the movies playing within the next ten minutes, she wanted to see Life is Beautiful. Tickets, popcorn and soda left Jim another twenty-five bucks down. He watched the movie with his arm around Diana until it fell asleep. He wanted to pull his arm away, but opted to let it suffer for the birthday.

Once the movie ended, Jim stood, his arm tingling. Then, with leaden legs he and Diana scaled the inclined movie exit.

"How'd you like the movie?" Jim asked, squinting as they entered the bright lobby.

"It was incredible," Diana said, wiping a tear. "I can't believe that even when everything was shitty for that guy, he still made sure his son had a good time."

"Yeah, imagine that," he said, wondering how many fathers and sons really had such relationships. "So, what do you want to do now?" he asked as they entered the dark parking lot. "Go for a drink maybe?" Because of Gräbe he knew of a few bars that didn't card. He only had money for a few rounds but birthdays come but once a year.

"No, thanks," she said, leaning her head on his shoulder. "I'm getting tired now actually and I have stupid work tomorrow."

There she goes with the work again. He hated keeping things from her, but she deserved a happy birthday. Telling her about his job and his parents would be a total downer.

"Back to my place then?" Jim asked hopefully.

"Sure, but I don't want to stay up too late."

Back at Ginglow's End, Yeats watched late night television alone.

Yeats turned down the volume. "Hello, lovebirds."

"Ugh, we're going to bed, Yeats. Keep it down, all right?"

"Ha ha, yeah, you keep it down, you crazy kids," Yeats said with a silly grin.

"I'm gonna brush my teeth, Diana. Meet me in bed?" he asked.

"Sure."

After brushing his teeth and washing his face, he slid into his bedroom and where Diana slept soundly. He tucked her in, went to his top drawer and pulled out the wad of bills and coins from his pocket. "Nineteen and change left," he whispered to himself. A few tanks of gas? A meal or two? He dropped the cash onto his bureau. He undressed, climbed into bed, pulled Diana close and smiled.

23

Days later, Diana lay beside him in bed again, nestled under his arm, her head on his chest. She breathed so softly he could hardly hear the gentle rhythms as he ran his fingertips, barely touching her skin, along her bare back. She idly wove her fingers through his belly hair. His face was raw from kissing her for around an hour, sliding his naked body against hers, masturbating each other.

She'd jerked him off, her legs straddling him in an arousing simulation of sex. He could feel her vaginal warmth on his penis as she pulled and pushed in time with her hips. He wondered where she'd ever gotten the idea. It turned him on immensely and while it didn't finish him off, he enjoyed the erotic effort.

Now they lay and had lain for hours together, not talking, gently touching one another and breathing easily. Their fooling around had made him forget what had really been bugging him, what he really wanted to talk to her about: his parents. He needed to talk to someone about it, but didn't know who. With their naked bodies snugly together, it occurred to him that there was nobody so close to him as Diana. He brushed his fingers up her back, stopping at her scalp where his fingers played in her straw-colored hair.

"Diana," he began awkwardly.

"What is it, Jim?" she asked—almost demanded.

Jim paused. What could she be upset about? He pulled some stray strands of hair over her ear. "Are you upset?"

"No, Jim. Everything's fine," she said. Somehow though, when a woman, even a young woman, says that everything's fine, it never was in the end. Jim wondered if he should bother sharing his family secret with Diana right this minute. He could tell something else preoccupied her mind.

Despite her tone, he started again, "Well, Diana."

"I know what you're thinking, Jim," she said.

This startled him. She must have felt him twinge, because she continued, "It's really obvious, Jim. It's practically been written on your face all night."

Did she really know him that well? Or maybe, somehow, having already lived through her own parents' divorce, she could actually see a particular look in a person's face. Was there a look? The look of a person whose parents were splitting? Maybe there was and maybe he had that look, and she'd seen it, but hadn't wanted to say anything. But now, since he brought it up, she could admit she'd known all along.

"Is it really something you can see on my face?" Jim asked, amazed.

"Jim, I'm not an idiot."

Was it that clear, really? "I'm not saying you're stupid, Diana. But I didn't think it was the sort of thing you could... tell from a person's face."

"Jim, it's always on your face," she said, rolling over

to face him, her chin propped on his chest. That didn't make any sense. How could it always be on his face? He hadn't learned about his parents until recently.

"I don't think we're on the same page here," he said.

"That's exactly what I was going to say," she said, rolling the opposite direction and right out of bed. She gathered her clothes. First, she put her underwear on, then found her bra and shimmied it up her arms.

As she fastened it in back, Jim asked, "Diana, what exactly are you doing?"

"I thought we'd agreed," she said, then bent over to pick up her jeans. She gave them one whip-like shake before putting a leg in. "You want sex, Jim. It's all you have on your mind."

"What? That's not what I was going to say at all," Jim shouted. His heart-rate quickened. He leapt from his bed and held Diana's arms. He felt silly and powerless standing there before her, flaccid and chilled while she was practically fully dressed. "I think we need to talk about this some more. You're not leaving me, are you?"

She pulled on her shirt, tugged her hair from inside it, and her lips tightened into a grimace. "I'm sorry, Jim. There's really nothing to talk about. Actually, I've already talked it over with Helen and Marcus."

"What?" Jim scanned the floor for his underwear—something to cover himself.

"It's not fair for either of us, Jim," she said with one hand on the door handle. "You have a girlfriend who won't fuck you, and I have a boyfriend I'm not ready to fuck. Honestly, I thought I'd try tonight. That was Helen's idea. But I couldn't. I'm not ready, Jim, and it's not fair to you."

"Since when do DeGawain and crazy-assed Helen get to decide anything about us?" Jim asked, finding some boxers at the foot of the bed.

"Don't be so mad, Jim. When you think about it, you'll realize I'm right," she said.

"But, Diana," he said. "I don't care about the sex. I haven't even been thinking about it. Everything about tonight was great. I don't need any more than that,"

"Yes, you do, Jim. Don't fool yourself." Her eyes watered a bit as her cold, tough routine failed. "This isn't really working."

Jim felt dizzy. "You can't be serious, baby."

Diana stepped back to where Jim stood in his underwear. She hugged him and he tentatively hugged her back. She pulled away, kissed him on the cheek and looked him in the face. "Don't worry, fucknuts. Everything will be fine." She wiped a tear from her cheek and asked shyly, "Still friends?"

Jim smiled when she called him fucknuts. He pulled her in for another hug. He rubbed her back and said, "I don't want you to go."

She stormed out of the room, and he slumped on the floor beside his bed. She marched down the hall, said something like "good-night" to Yeats and Troy who watched television in the living room and then the screen door clanged shut. Slowly, Jim got off the floor. He lumbered down the hall and into the dimly lit living room.

"Diana's gone," he said.

"Yeah, we saw her leave," Troy said.

Jim tried to smile, but frowned. "No. I mean really gone," he said. "She talked to DeGawain and Helen about us and they convinced her that since I want sex and she's not ready, we shouldn't be together."

Yeats turned off the television. "What the fuck is that all about?"

"Whoa, that's fucked up," Troy muttered.

"I mean, if she's going to talk to anybody about the relationship it should be you, right?" Yeats said.

"That's what I'm sayin'," Jim grunted.

"Dude," Troy said. "Shots." Troy hopped over the coffee table and ran toward the kitchen. Jim plopped into an armchair. Troy came back with the chilled bottle of 80 proof peppermint schnapps from the freezer and three shot glasses. He poured three out on the coffee table, handed the first one to Jim, the second one to Yeats and raised the third above his head. "Fuck the bitches," he said.

"No," Jim interrupted. Yeats and Troy pulled their glasses away from their mouths.

"What to then, Diffin?" asked Yeats.

"I don't fuckin' know, but I'm not ready to be angry at Diana. How 'bout a good old-fashioned toast?"

"Sure," Yeats nodded. "Got one in mind?"

Jim bowed his head and held his glass before his face. He raised his head suddenly and said, "Yeah, I got one." He raised his glass high and said, "When we drink, we get drunk."

"Yeah, we do," Yeats said, drawling out the "yeah."

"When we get drunk, we fall asleep," Jim continued.

"Sometimes. That's true," Yeats interrupted again, raising his glass a bit for emphasis.

"When we sleep, we commit no sin," Jim said.

"That's a good point." Yeats motioned with his glass again.

"When we commit no sin, we go to Heaven," Jim said a bit louder. "So, let's get drunk and go to Heaven!"

They clinked glasses, dribbling sticky schnapps before downing the first round. They poured out another round and drank to J.F.K. The next round went to Bobby, the next to Michael Collins, then "Slick" Willie Clinton, "Buddy" Cianci, Bobby Sands, Gerry Adams,

Martin McGuinness and by that time they forgot they were toasting anyone and slammed back shots. Jim wandered away with the last few ounces of the bottle and opened the refrigerator.

He found the water bottle Yeats had hidden in the crisper. He poured a half a shot glass of G.H.B. from the water bottle.

"What are you doing, Diffin?" Troy asked. Jim put the water bottle back into the crisper. He hadn't heard Troy come in and hoped to get the concoction together without anyone knowing.

"Nothin'," he said, dumping some schnapps in on top of the drug.

"Yeats!" Troy yelled. "Diffin's trying to fuckin' kill himself with Georgia Homeboy!"

Yeats came rushing, stumbling around the corner. "What are you doin' Diffin?" he slurred.

"Nothin'," Jim said, considering the shot glass in his hand. "I've got a great tolerance. I'm sure I'll be fine. Maybe this shit'll get me to that extra level of fucked up that I need."

But now that he held the alcohol-G.H.B. mixture and saw the incredulous look on Troy's face, the concern in Yeats's, he wondered if maybe he wasn't making a very good decision. Would he actually die?

"Jim," Troy said.

Yeats strode toward him, his face gone blank. Jim stopped thinking and threw back the shot. The strong taste of sweet peppermint schnapps overpowered the reputedly awful taste of the G— Gräbe had said it tasted like sweat from an ox's balls. Jim exhaled.

"What the fuck, Diffin!" Yeats yelled. "Go fuckin' throw that shit up. I don't want to be calling a fuckin' ambulance tonight."

Troy wandered closer. "He's right, Diffin. You should go puke."

Feeling more confident now that he'd gone through with it, Jim blew past them. "Fuck that. I'll be fine." He selected a CD, popped open the top-loading player and dropped the disk in carelessly. "And if not..." He shrugged. "I won't be feeling any worse." He secured the disk in place, closed the top and hit play.

He cranked the volume as House of Pain's first album, *Fine Malt Lyrics*, pumped. The bass chords dropping one at a time, the old-man voice looping over and over "The House of Pain" until the voice fell a few decibels, and Everlast explained, *"The time has come... for everyone to clean up their own backyards... before they go knocking on their neighbors' doors."* This slowly blended into random phrases all mixing and overlapping one another, *"The House of Pain is cleanin' up and sweepin' up," "alcoholic liquidity," "crack a brew,"* with Everlast finally screaming himself hoarse *"It's the House of Pain!"*

Following this opening, the first song on the album, "Jump Around" began. Jim knew that this song, if anything, would help his already drunk friends to cut loose and forget what they considered his mortal danger. It didn't take long before all three were jumping around the room like idiots, eventually making the CD skip. This only provoked laughter, and they fixed the music and moved the jumping insanity to the living room.

Yeats told him that G made him feel drunk, but he never blacked out and, instead of hungover, he woke up feeling especially rested. But for a long time, Jim didn't think he felt anything. All the same, he drank water while Troy and Yeats chugged beer. Eventually, Troy passed out on the couch and Yeats wandered off to bed.

Jim turned off the music and sat down at the kitchen table to rest a moment.

Once they were asleep, and he was alone in the quiet house, he got a bit nervous. He'd been fine these past few hours, jumping and laughing, throwing couch cushions and a football around the living room. How long did it take to die from mixing downers with G.H.B.?

"Georgia Home Boy," he said aloud and laughed. Grievous Bodily Harm. Which was the cooler nickname for the stuff? He wasn't sure, but he hoped the latter wasn't the more apt.

When he woke up the house was quiet. He felt restless. It didn't seem that late. For some reason, some compulsion, he rushed outside and ran past his car, sprinted down the driveway and up the road, turned right up Willet Avenue down Pawtucket Avenue and in what seemed to be a few moments he was in downcity Providence. He danced amid the taller buildings like it was a nightclub. He found an open club and ran inside, danced for what seemed like hours in the midst of heavy music and wispy people. He felt empty. He ran to Cumberland. The sun threatened to rise. Diana's door was locked. He sat down outside on the cold steps and fell asleep.

"Jim."

He opened his eyes and lifted his head from the kitchen table. Troy stood over him.

"You're alive, fucker," Troy said with a laugh.

Jim shook his head and, even though his neck was stiff from sleeping in a hard-wooden kitchen chair, he felt more rested than he ever had in his entire life. It was six in the morning, but he didn't go back to bed. He cracked a beer and sat on the couch, planning on calling Diana in the afternoon.

24

Jim sat planted in the couch, unshaven, unshowered, wearing slippers, boxers and his robe with a beer can in one hand. He'd skipped class all week, sweating into the couch. Empties cluttered the coffee table, some stacked up neatly, some on the floor at his feet. He kicked one under the coffee table and out into the middle of the room.

Nothing on television.

He flicked through from commercial break to soap opera to the music channel's lousy repeats of reality shows—having nothing to do with music. Outside the wide picture window, a red-chested robin landed on top of a bush. It perched precariously on the swaying branch and cocked its head sideways at him. Probably looking at his own reflection.

"What are you staring at?" he asked.

He changed the channel.

A car engine revved outside and barreled past the house, and the bird flew away. He rolled his eyes. Cars raced past his house all day long even though the road ended half a football field from his picture window. They sped the whole way down, just to turn around, running their tires up onto the lawn. He sipped his lukewarm beer with a snarl. He put it down and tuned in to the music channel's show about stupid kids living in a gorgeous house together. Amazing they still found things to bitch about. He leaned his head against the couch and his heavy eye-lids dropped for a moment.

"Dude!"

He woke up, and Pow stood over him.

"Hey," he said.

"Did you skip class again today?" Pow asked, taking off his backpack and dropping it onto the reclining arm chair.

"What time is it?" he asked, reaching for his beer.

"Four in the afternoon, homes."

"Wow. I must've dozed off for a while there." He sipped the piss-like liquid from the can. He smacked his mouth a bit. Terrible. No reason to waste a beer though. "Hey, Springer should be on. He's got under-age, transvestite sluts who think their mom's dress too sexy. Check it out," he said, fumbling with the remote.

"Dude, you're sad."

"No shit, I'm sad," he said, finally getting the channel changed. "Whoa, but not that sad," he said, pointing.

Pow turned and then gazed back at him. "You look like hell."

"Would you mind grabbing me a fresh beer, kid?" he asked, scratching his stubble. "Get yourself one, too."

Pow closed his eyes, slowly shook his head and smiled. "Nice try, Diffin."

"Oh, come on," he said. "Have a beer with me this one time. I won't tell anybody. You can still claim to be all straight-edge and shit."

Pow yanked him by the arm. Rather than resist, he

stood up and let Pow lead him down the hall. In the bathroom, Jim sat on the toilet and rested his head against the wall while Pow turned on the shower. Steam soon erupted from behind the curtain. Pow grabbed him by the front of his robe and pushed him into the shower. He barely had time to shed the robe as he stumbled past Pow and into the scalding hot spray. Screaming, he fell to the bottom of the tub and crawled against the wall under the water.

"Don't forget to scrub your ass," Pow said as he pulled the curtain closed.

Jim fumbled with the knob, spinning it. He sat in the steam with soaked slippers and boxers, waiting for the water to cool.

"Want coffee or something?" Pow asked from behind the curtain.

"No," he said. "I don't even have a coffee maker."

"Tea then?" Pow asked, his voice faded as if he were halfway out of the room already.

"Sure, put the kettle on. Two sugars and a splash of milk," he said, slowly rising into the warm water. "Throw a nip of Bushmills in, too."

Pow laughed and closed the door.

He scrubbed himself and had to admit that it did make him feel better. He threw his robe back on and found Pow sipping tea at the kitchen table in his grandfather's old seat. A cup of tea waited for him, too.

"How was your shower?" Pow asked, putting his steamy cup down.

"Fine," he said, sitting. "I feel a bit better."

"I was sitting here wondering," Pow said. "What strange discomforts will we miss when we die?"

"What are you talking about?" Jim asked, sipping tentatively from his tea. His face brightened. "You put the whiskey in?"

Pow smiled and cocked his head to one side in feigned resignation. Jim carefully sipped more.

"While you were showering," Pow continued, undeterred. "I burned the roof of my mouth on the tea."

Jim put his cup down. "You should be more careful."

"Now I got a bit of skin dangling. Shit's uncomfortable. You just got out of the shower. Don't you feel really cold between shutting off the water and getting your towel?"

"What are you getting at, Pow?"

"When we die, if heaven is as perfect as we were brought up to believe, what happens if we miss burning our mouths on hot tea or feeling chilly after the shower water goes off?" Pow reached two fingers into his mouth as if to pull the loose flesh away.

Out the window behind Pow's head, Jim saw Yeats's car pull up. He sipped more tea and said, "Sounds like that song by the Talking Heads." Pow looked perplexed. *"Ya know, Heaven... Heaven is a place... A place where nothing... Nothing ever happens..."* Jim sang softly.

Yeats burst in with Troy, each of them carrying a thirty-rack. Troy ripped open his cardboard case and stocked the bare fridge. Yeats put his down and bounded into the kitchen.

"Aw, atta-boy!" Yeats said, coming over to rub Jim's hair like he was ten. "You showered, ya fuckin' bum! Pow, you got him to shower. Good job, man," he said, shaking Pow's hand. "Now all you gotta do is shave that scruff off your face."

Jim rubbed the itchy hair. "I don't know if I feel like it."

"If you do, I'll tell you about a party tonight," Pow said.

He thought about it a moment, not a bad bargain, but

then again. "Aw, fuck it. You probably came here to tell me about a party tonight anyway, ya bastard," he said.

"But now that I'm here, and you're such a mess, I don't have to tell you."

Jim shrugged. He might as well shave. It didn't really matter to him either way and it was getting annoying. He finished his tea while Yeats and Troy cracked open their post-five o'clock beers, then he went into the bathroom and locked the door. The steam had dissipated, and he stared at his grubby-looking face in the mirror. Digging under the sink, he retrieved his pair of electric clippers. Taking a blade to a week's-worth of hairs could really hurt and take too long; instead, he'd give his face a once over with the clippers. After buzzing his face and neck, he ran his fingers through his hair once, then a second time, stopping to hold his hair down. He examined his head in the mirror.

A few minutes later, someone knocked at the door. "Hey, Diffin, what the hell's takin' you so long in there?" Troy asked.

"Nothing. Leave me alone," he said buzzing the last few strands of hair from his head.

"Some of us gotta piss."

"Use the other bathroom for fuck's sake," he said, running the hot water.

"Oh, right," Troy muttered.

He took the shaving cream and lathered his cheeks, his chin, his neck, his scalp and underneath his nose. With quick determination and short, steady swipes from his blade, he shaved every bit of hair from his face and head. He wasn't sure why he did it. It was a whim, a way of saying fuck it all and who cares about anything anyway. The back of his head stung all over from trying to shave by feel. No more stubble clung back there but the stinging and the spots of blood on his hand confirmed that he had shaved a bit too close. He rinsed the head of the bald man in the mirror and opened the door. The guys sat in the living room, and in a few strides, they'd seen him.

"Holy fuckin' shit!" Yeats yelled. Pow and Troy said nothing, apparently speechless. Yeats smacked his fleshy scalp gently, but repeatedly.

"Why'd you do that?" Troy asked.

He told them he didn't know, and they laughed at him, calling him cue ball. After rubbing his head and making fun for a while, they took him to a party, where he met a girl who liked bald guys. Maybe his luck was changing.

გა

Later that week, he and Yeats sat on the pool deck at work watching three or four geriatric swimmers bob their way from one end to the other at the downtown YMCA. Fortunately, Gräbe heard about Jim losing his job and hired him, giving him plenty of hours, too.

Gräbe came bounding into the pool area from the weight room, pulled up a chair and sat between Yeats and Jim.

"Guys, I need you to do me a huge favor."

Jim raised his eyebrow behind Gräbe's back at Yeats who's face also showed suspicion. "So long as you don't want us to wack anybody," Yeats said.

"Or do anything else illegal," Jim added.

"No, nothing like that. Well..." Gräbe paused. "I'm not actually sure it's legal, but if it's not, then it's probably no big deal."

Jim laughed and shook his head. Since taking the job for Gräbe, he'd gotten to talk to him a lot more than he ever did in the summertime. Back then, he thought his boss was a male chauvinist, a total weasel douchebag. But now that he worked for him again, and in a setting, which allowed Gräbe the freedom to come and hang out while they lifeguarded, he knew that Gräbe was a total weasel douchebag—though he was something more. He was hilarious.

The last time Gräbe had come in to talk to them, he wanted to know if either of them had ever done horse tranquilizers. It was never clear exactly what made him think of anything on any particular day, but that day he had regaled them with a long tripped-out tale involving this horse pill he had somehow purchased one drunken night at U.R.I. but hadn't been brave enough to take.

Later, of course the semester wore on, and, coming down from some other substance, he popped the horse pill. The story itself wasn't really that funny or entertaining, especially since he claimed not to know what happened for a span of about a week after popping the horse tranquilizer.

It was more in the telling. Most of his stories required him to stand up at some point. Gräbe had an amazing histrionic capacity. At U.R.I. he had gotten degrees in psychology and drama; he hoped one day to be an actor in Hollywood and if that failed to be "shrink to the stars." It sounded good, but how he was going to get from YMCA aquatics director in Providence, R.I. to Hollywood personality wasn't exactly clear. The end of the horse pill story had been: "If you guys ever get a chance to take a horse pill, don't do it. Cat tranquilizer—ya know, K—is way better." Then after sitting for a moment as if allowing that advice to sink in, he added, "But if you do come across a horse pill, buy it and call me immediately."

But today Gräbe sat calmly. "You guys can really

hook me up here. I'll even pay you if you want, or score you some extra dope Georgia Homeboy. I made the best batch yesterday," he rambled.

"Get to the point," Yeats said.

The point was that Gräbe had been in Riverside, visiting his parents the other day. On his way back to Providence, he drove past a certain girl's house and saw her car in the driveway. He had always been infatuated with this girl and a year after high school, he managed to sleep with her. The problem had been that he was way too wasted, and he never got completely hard. The one chance he had to rock this girl's world had been squandered by whiskey dick. Too embarrassed to face her, he never called her again. But driving by her house the other day had got him thinking that maybe he could face her now and if he could get her to sleep with him one more time, he was sure he could make a better impression.

How this affected Jim and Yeats was simple. The girl's house was less than a quarter mile from Ginglow's End. "I want to find out if she's single right now or not. All I'm asking you to do is go by her house on trash day and steal her garbage."

"What?" Yeats yelled.

"Shh. No big deal, right? I'm not even asking you to look through it. I'll do that," Gräbe explained straight-faced.

"No shit you'll do that," Jim said.

"So, you'll do it?" Gräbe asked.

"We'll have to think about it," Yeats said.

"But I don't think so," Jim said.

Gräbe squinted his beady eyes and worked his muzzle-like jaw in thought. "Can you at least check out her house when you drive by. See what kind of cars are parked there?" Yeats and he agreed that they could try to remember to do that.

⁊❧

A few days later as he pulled into Ginglow's End, he noticed a strange car in the driveway. He pulled alongside it and wondered who could be home. The spare key was still under the loose brick where it belonged. Maybe whoever used it had put it back there. Inside, the house was quiet and nothing seemed out of place. He stalked quietly through the kitchen, listening—no television on. Walking through the dining room, he peered around the corner and into the living room. Nobody there either. Nobody in the bathroom and nobody in Yeats's room. He sighed and dropped his backpack. Somebody must've come over, met up with Yeats, who drove them both wherever. Too bad, he kind of felt like having a friend over. Deciding to check his email, he meandered down the hallway. He opened his bedroom door and stepped toward his computer.

"Whoa!" a voice shouted. Jim turned around in time to be tackled to the floor.

"Holy shit!" he yelled, trying to wriggle free.

Gräbe, laughing with one hand over his mouth and the other bracing his abdomen, climbed off Jim.

"Fucker," he said.

Gräbe rubbed Jim's bald head. "Dude, your house is wicked easy to break in to, ya know."

"What do you mean, 'break in to'?" Jim pushed to his feet. "Didn't you use the hidden key?"

"Oh, that's right," he said falling into the doorjamb, one hand on his forehead. "You did tell me about a key."

Gräbe showed him how he had come over and, finding

no doors open, he had cased out the back windows. Sure enough, Jim had never taken the air conditioner out of the window in his grandmother's bedroom. Getting in had been a simple matter of jimmying the air conditioner out of the window and boosting himself up and in. Jim didn't know what to say. He was annoyed, but it wasn't like Gräbe was a thief; he was simply a harmless weirdo. Jim asked Gräbe to go outside and get the air conditioner. They put it in the bedroom and closed the window.

Gräbe had come over to ask him if he wanted to go clubbing with DeGawain and him that night. Jim didn't think twice; he could use a good club night, and they cracked open a few of the beers Gräbe had brought over.

They waited until ten o'clock at night for Yeats to come home, but when he didn't, they drove off in Gräbe's new car and met DeGawain downtown. They strolled through the narrow downtown streets toward the old jewelry district, filled with centuries old brick buildings. What was once the center of the State's thriving jewelry trade was now a few strips of nightclubs and restaurants closely grouped around I-195.

Gräbe's favorite club, The Complex, was the largest and most successful of the jewelry district clubs. The Complex housed four clubs in one: a piano bar; Polly Esta's, a 70s themed dance club; Algiers, a hip-hop club and a fourth club which seemed to change every two to three years. It had most recently been Desperado's—a cheesy western-themed dance hall—but with renewed interest in swing music, that fourth club had lamely converted to Swingers.

In line outside, DeGawain and Gräbe talked about a girl named Candy who was supposed to meet them. She had been in Gräbe's graduating class at U.R.I. and had also majored in Drama. She was a petite red-head with a tight little ass, perky B-cup breasts—which looked huge on her—and deep brown eyes. Apparently, she was very flirtatious and Gräbe wanted to go home with her, but he was concerned. His girlfriend's friends hung out at The Complex, and he didn't think it would be safe for him, at least not that night. Jim didn't bother to mention to Gräbe that he was already trying to employ him to stalk yet another girl.

Once in the club, they—Gräbe with his 21+ bracelet, Jim and DeGawain without—headed toward the bar. On the way a bubbly girl, who Jim assumed must be Candy, leaped in front of them. Candy hugged Gräbe and shook DeGawain's hand. She was hot—everything the guys had described—but struck Jim as a bimbo. He shook her hand and noticed her 21+ bracelet.

He pulled her close and leaned toward her ear. "Hi, I'm Jim. Why haven't you bought me a drink yet?" Attempting to be rude, he waited for a slap. Dating anyone new still lacked any real appeal. Diana might come back, and he definitely didn't want DeGawain seeing him flirt.

Candy smiled. She took him by the arm and led him to the bar. "What's your drink?"

Still wondering where his slap was, he asked for a chilled vodka shot. Something he could throw back left-handed before bouncers could notice he'd done anything wrong.

The wall near the bar in Polly Esta's was painted like a cityscape, and on the side of a brick building, graffiti read, "make love not war." Candy told him he had a nicely shaped head, handed him his shot, clinked her shot glass to his and threw her vodka back with him. She whisked him around The Complex all night, she kissed him upstairs by the piano bar, downstairs they danced to "Disco Inferno," and they swing danced—badly—in Swingers. All night Candy bought him vodka shots and together they threw them back.

Before he left with his friends, he took Candy's number and promised to call.

25

Jim rang the doorbell, then Yeats did, too. Their foggy breaths mixed in the chilly, night air. Behind them cars whizzed up and down Westminister Street. Someone had been shot three nights ago a block further down.

Gräbe flung the door open and stood a moment in the threshold, swimming goggles over his eyes, yellow dish gloves on his hands and a floral-print shower cap covering his hair. He leaned out over the stoop and looked both ways before waving dramatically, bidding them—Igor-like—with his upper body to enter his building.

"What's with the get-up," Jim asked as they climbed the creaking wood stairs.

"Oh this..." Gräbe said, looking at his gloves. "The chemicals used to create the G are really toxic and hazardous, so while I mix them up, I take every precaution."

"Toxic?" he asked.

Yeats paused on the landing. "Hazardous?"

"To be honest it's more the chemical reaction which

creates the stuff that's dangerous. Which, by the way, you are right in time to witness." Gräbe strode toward his apartment door. "Come check this out."

They followed Gräbe into the kitchen where some glass Pyrex measuring containers held murky liquids. Gräbe raised one cup, "This shit alone would kill you. Sip that stuff there," pointing to the larger bowl, "and you'd probably go blind. But... Stand back now..." Gräbe poured one liquid into the larger bowl. The two liquids battled, boiling ferociously, exorcised the noxious elements as the steam steadily escaped from the mix.

When it settled down, the liquid was perfectly clear, like water. "Is that it?" Yeats asked. "It's done?"

Gräbe yanked the goggles from his face and tore off the shower cap. "That's it," he said. "I mean, there were a few steps before you came, but that reaction right there; that's where the magic happens, why it's called Galactic Homebrew, and why I was wearing this shit." He stretched the yellow gloves from his hairy knuckles.

"So, can we throw back a few caps of that now?" Jim asked.

Gräbe covered the bowl with plastic wrap and lifted it from the counter. "Naw, this shit needs to cool. You pop this stuff back now, and your throat will be singed bad. And I ain't in the mood to take you to the emergency room."

"So, where's our stuff?" Yeats asked.

"Relax. It's in the fridge... Ya mind?" Gräbe stood by the refrigerator, holding the brimming bowl. Yeats opened the refrigerator for him. After placing the new mix in to cool, he emerged with two spring-water pint bottles of Gamma Hydroxybuterate.

The three sat on Gräbe's musty couches under dim lighting, smoked weed and popped a few capfuls to Pink

Floyd. Gräbe brought up his high school crush again. This time he told them there was a car for sale out front and thought they might go check it out for him. Pretend to be interested in the car as an excuse to somehow get inside the house. That way, they wouldn't need to steal her garbage. Jim and Yeats laughed.

Gräbe's live-in girlfriend came home, upset again. She was pushing thirty and expected Gräbe to marry her and find them a home in the suburbs. Her presence always created a strange tension. Why she thought she could take a drug-dealer with bachelor's degrees in psychology and drama and make him into a respectable husband, Jim would never understand. After a few moments of her storming around, they made their exit.

26

The next day at Ginglow's End, Jim wrapped the vacuum cord around the prongs, and as he clipped the end of the plug-in place, Yeats cruised in.

Yeats turned around, finally noticing the newly cleaned house. "Did you fuckin' vacuum?" He scratched his head, dropping his backpack in the middle of the room.

Jim nodded.

"Looks good, man. Thanks." Yeats pulled out a CD and turned on the stereo. "Did you return the keg, too?" he asked, referring to the keg they'd bought for their house warming party months before.

The low vocal tones of Cake's first song on their Fashion Nugget album kicked in, *"reluctantly crouched on the starting line..."* Jim walked past him with the vacuum. "Yup," he said.

Yeats plopped onto the couch and thumbed through his auto-repair manual that Jim had neatly placed on the coffee table. "What's the occasion?" he asked. "Ya mom comin' over? Do I gotta clean my room? Stay sober? Anything special?"

"Nope," he said. After putting the vacuum away, he told Yeats, "I'm going out with Candy tonight, and the extra ten bucks from the keg deposit got me started cleaning."

"Which one was she?" He knew Yeats wasn't being a jerk, but that he really wanted to know.

He dropped into the armchair by the hallway. "The girl from The Complex. Older girl, actress chick," he said.

"Oh, the girl Gräbe wanted to fuck."

"Gräbe wants to fuck every girl," he said rocking the chair.

"So, wait," Yeats said, tossing the book on the floor. "You're not bringing her back here, are you? Is that why you cleaned up?"

He shrugged and smiled. "It's only a first date, Yeats. But you never know what might happen, where things might lead. You know: 'Be Prepared' and all that."

Yeats nodded knowingly, then repeated the Boy Scout motto, "Be Prepared. Abso-freakin-lutely."

He picked up Candy from her parents' West Warwick home at eight that night. While he checked her out, her mother chatted him up about R.I.C., being an alumna herself. Candy was even prettier than he remembered; club lighting can often be overly flattering, leading to the strobe-light-honey effect, which the Black Sheep had lamented back in the day. A beauty in the club becomes a beast on the ride home or on the first date. Fortunately, this was definitely not the case.

The chain restaurant he chose for dinner had a short wait and conversation seemed to go easily, like at the club. The raven-haired hostess called their name, and he allowed Candy to follow ahead of him. Sometimes being a gentleman had extra perks. The hostess really knew how to move her hips; she worked it and her ass had a perfect roundness. Like Diana's, he wanted to bite it. Candy walked stiffly, in an affected blue-blooded uptightness, and her ass, while nice, simply didn't excite him as much.

Dinner conversation focused mostly on Candy's acting aspirations, but unlike Gräbe she actually had a plan. She belonged to a theater company that had put on performances at Trinity Rep downtown and South County's Theatre by the Sea. Her ambitions were large and involved lots of money, nice cars, huge houses and world travel. She came from one of Rhode Island's founding families. He told her he didn't have any monetary ambitions; his life goals involved happiness, perhaps a life of academia.

Many of the waitresses swooping by would be drop dead gorgeous if they didn't have to wear men's shirts and aprons. At least the pants they wore didn't restrict a good view of their asses.

After dinner, Candy directed him to some docks on Narragansett Bay. They sat at the water's edge and kissed. She tasted like the salmon she'd eaten. It even overpowered the chocolate cake dessert. She put herself in his lap and put her slender hand down his pants. He unbuttoned her blouse halfway and gained access to her B-cup breasts. They were a little bigger than Diana's, but not quite as firm. He put one in his mouth.

"Wanna come back to my place?" he asked.

"Not tonight," she said. This seemed to remind her that they might have done enough already. He took her home after a few more kisses. When he dropped her off, they promised to see each other soon.

27

Piles of clouds roiled and romped across the afternoon sun as he stumbled down the street behind Troy and Yeats. They headed to the house where the girl of Gräbe's high school dreams still lived in Riverside.

When he'd woken up earlier in the day, the guys sat around watching television. After his breakfast of corn flakes and Sam Adams—beer on the side, milk in the bowl—somebody had suggested they pop some G. Not long after a few caps had been thrown back, since it was a rather mild fall evening, they got the idea to go for a walk.

Now they traipsed down Willet Avenue on their way to the girl's house because Yeats had told Troy about Gräbe's latest stalking request. The one where Jim and Yeats would go and pretend to be interested in the car. To get into the house, they decided to pretend to need the bathroom, or maybe the phone, to call a parent about the details of the impending sale. Gräbe suggested that there were probably hundreds of excuses they could use to get inside. The idea had excited Troy to no end.

"Hey," Jim said as Yeats grabbed Troy by the collar to keep him from falling into the street. "Have we figured out who's buying the car or how we're planning on getting inside the house?"

The guys paused, turning toward him. He urged them to keep moving. Three guys standing on the side of the street in conference looked too suspicious, though that impression probably came from the drugs since it was barely three o'clock in the afternoon. They walked and talked, weighing options, stories, tactics and before they realized it, they stood before the old green Pinto with a big, fluorescent pink "FOR SALE" sign on the windshield.

He stepped up to the car and bent down to look for body rot around the fenders. On the other side, Yeats peered through cupped hands at the dash-board. Troy kicked the tire nearest Jim, and a chunk of caked mud splattered onto Jim's lip. He leapt up, wiping his mouth and shoved Troy who stumbled. He and Yeats laughed as Troy tripped across the front lawn.

"Is he all right?" A short, stocky woman, perhaps in her forties, seemed to have appeared by the car's rear bumper. She flashed a welcoming smile.

The Georgia Homeboy submerged any inhibitions. Jim's head felt light, and it seemed like he was watching an episode of slap-stick comedy. He cleared his throat. "Yes, ma'am. He's kind of an oaf." He chuckled at Troy's hurt expression. "My friend here," he said, thumbing toward Yeats, "is interested in the car, but I was hoping it'd be okay if I used your bathroom real quick?" He wondered if he'd come off as too insistent, if he'd slurred any of his words or if his tottering balance was as visible as he felt it must be.

With her hands on her wide hips, she looked them over for a moment. "No problem, hon," she said. "Follow me and," she looked at Yeats over her shoulder, "I'll be right back to talk about the car."

Inside, the house's close, warm air smelled like cat food. He followed the woman through a dining room separated from the kitchen by a long counter and down a dark hallway.

"Second door on the right," she said, pointing.

He closed the door to the bathroom and realized he wasn't even sure what he was looking for. A pink shower curtain draped into a white, claw-foot tub. Matching towels hung in a row beside the wide, two-sink vanity. He forced himself to piss into the white porcelain—at least he wouldn't be totally deceitful. Lacy, white curtains framed the tiny window which looked out into the backyard. How was he supposed to figure out if this girl was seeing anyone or not? Would she really have evidence of a boyfriend at home with her mother? This was the stupidest idea Gräbe had concocted yet. And there he stood, dribbling piss into a stranger's toilet, following through with it.

He shrugged and figured he'd at least check the medicine cabinet while he waited for the tap water to get hot. Behind the mirror, on the little shelves, sat rows and rows of toiletries and sundries: pink disposable razors, moisturizing soaps, girly deodorants, tampons, q-tips, combs, brushes, toothpaste, alka-seltzer, aspirin, lip-hair bleach, a home waxing kit and dental floss. No sign of testosterone, but what did that prove? He picked up the soap and lathered his hands, leaving the cabinet open.

As he was about to rinse his hands, a gray ball flashed onto the countertop. He threw his hands up, tossing the soap and smacking the shelves before him.

Medicines, hygiene products and other bottles, boxes and containers tumbled into the sink. A cat meowed innocently between the sinks. It dropped from the counter as he frantically plucked products from the sink, before he thought to shut off the water. He plucked up dripping items, shook them dry and tried to rearrange the cabinet.

A knock on the door stopped him. "Are you all right in there?" a woman's voice asked.

"Uh," he said, fumbling the top shelf back into place with soapy hands. "Yeah, the cat startled me is all."

"Okay," she said, doubtfully. He heard her moving away from the door. Her voice faded. "But it sounded like you were destroying my bathroom."

He got everything out of the sink, rinsed his hands, dried them and arranged the items on the shelves however they'd fit. No way could he remember how they'd been. He examined himself in the mirror, wondering if G affected the pupils like other drugs. The closer he stared, the less he could be sure. He rubbed his face with chilly fingers and left the bathroom. He passed a hottie in the kitchen, nodding shyly. Probably the girl Gräbe wanted them to find out about.

Outside, Yeats bullshitted about horse-power, gas mileage and other car crap. Jim tried to signal for Yeats and Troy to make their exits. The door opened behind him.

"Hey," the girl called from behind him. "You!" she shouted. "Mom!"

He took off across the lawn, figuring Yeats and Troy could fend for themselves.

The last thing he heard as he ran down Willet Avenue in the fading winter light was, "That bastard screwed with all our shit!"

He ran and didn't stop; he couldn't breathe after

three blocks, but kept going until he rounded the curve with the Riverside Kitchen on it. He sat on the cement slab, the base for the pharmacy sign, trying to catch his breath. Billowing clouds still sputtered from his burning lungs when Troy and then Yeats came puffing and panting over.

With the sun completely dropped below the horizon and the temperature sinking, they stumbled up the street, heading back to Ginglow's End. As they passed Chimney Corners, a block from Ginglow Street, a siren whooped, and lights blared. An East Providence Police car stopped beside them. Oh, fuck that. They called the cops, because he fucked up their cabinet? What the hell.

The door opened and Officer James stepped out. Oh, great. "Hey, boys," he said, adjusting his belt.

Jim decided to pretend innocent. "Good evening, Officer James," he said.

"What are you doing walking around the good streets of Riverside tonight?" the officer asked. It seemed Jim was off the hook for his snooping.

"Out for a walk, Officer James," Yeats said, falling into Troy.

"Well," Officer James said, marching toward them, "We get lots of calls about Bianese this time of year. I'd hate to have to bring you in for questioning because you tend to wander the streets at night."

What the fuck was a Bianese? Where the hell was Bian? What kind of racist bullshit was that? A lot of Bianese this time of year? And why couldn't they walk the streets at night? When had Riverside become a police state?

Jim placed a hand on Troy's shoulder to keep from falling and asked, "What's a Bianese, Officer James?"

Officer James rubbed his flat-top hair. "B and E's," he

said. "Breaking and entering." He pulled out his black flashlight and pointed its bright beam into Jim's eyes. "You guys have ID on you?" he asked.

Officer James knew him, grew up a street over; why did he need ID? He was about to give the pig a hard time when Troy pulled out his wallet. Yeats did the same, so Jim figured he'd go along, too. Officer James's light beam flashed from one to the next of them so quickly, Jim got a little dizzier.

He fumbled with his wallet, and then his driver's license fell and smacked the sidewalk. It sat there, face down on the concrete, miles away. Officer James flashed his light onto it, and the card seemed to grow even further away. He sensed the cop waiting for him to bend over and pick it up. How could his license be so far away? It was between his feet, after all. Knowing he was about to fall into Officer James's legs, he started to bend at the waist when Troy squatted and came up with the identification for him.

How the hell was Troy capable of doing that, when he wasn't? He looked at Troy and mouthed a thank you as Officer James checked the ID. "This still says you live on Becker Avenue, Mr. Diffin," he said.

"I know," Jim said, taking the license back from the officer's outstretched hand.

Officer James straightened his posture and put his light back on his belt. "You need to go down to the D.M.V. and update that."

"Yes, sir," Jim said.

Without another word, Officer James retreated to his car and ducked inside. The cruiser peeled away from the curb and sped off without its lights on.

28

The next day he drank tea with his mother. "She never answers my calls, ma," he said. "She never returns them either. Her mom must be lying to me when she says she's not there. Don't you think?"

"Probably," she said, sipping her tea. "My mother used to lie to boys all the time for me. Tell them I wasn't home when I was in my room."

He shifted in his seat. "That's messed up."

"Jim, if she wants you back, she'll call," his mom said. "Don't worry about it."

"But she doesn't like to call anyone about anything," he said, sighing. "That's why I keep thinking I need to call her."

"The heart wants what the heart wants," she said from her never-ending well of clichés. "If she wants you, she'd do more than pick up the phone, even if she hates it."

He shook his head. "I guess."

"No," she said, putting a cold hand on his arm. "I'm serious. Look at me. I've humiliated myself trying to get your father back. Following him around like a crazed woman." She scowled. "I trailed him to that woman's house. I drove my car up on that woman's front lawn and screamed like a shanty Irishwoman," she said, rubbing his arm.

"No?" he said, trying to picture his mother, waving an arm and screaming like a truck driver, her tire tracks across a pristine residential lawn.

She nodded slowly. "If I didn't love your father more than life itself, I never would've abased myself like that."

She cupped her tea in both hands to warm them.

"No, James," she said, squinting up at him. "Diana knows you're calling. She knows you want her back. If she wants you back, she'll do what she needs to do. For now, you can't worry your head about it."

"All right, ma," he said, sipping his scalding tea. The stereo randomizer switched the track from one CD to the next, The Pogues' "A FairyTale of New York" came lilting out. "I'm sorry. I must seem pretty stupid sitting here bitching to you about me and Diana, considering what you're going through." Slowly, he twisted his tea mug. "How is it going between you and dad anyway?"

"I'm not sure, James. I think he might be coming home. I didn't want to say anything because I wasn't sure."

"That's good, right?" He wasn't sure himself. Why would she want his lousy dad back? Would he ever be able to look him in the eye again? If his mother was strong enough to forgive him, then Jim guessed he'd have to try.

His mom stared off and nodded slowly before facing him again. "I want nothing more in my life than to have your father and my old life back."

29

One afternoon, Jim had driven to Pow's house where Pow had been hanging out with his Warwick friends, Dean and Nick. Now, Jim rode in the backseat of Dean's Beretta with Nick. Pow sat up front with Dean, switching through the stations. He didn't know exactly what they'd planned. When they'd still been in Pow's basement bedroom, Nick said something about picking at Garden City, whatever that meant. Jim thought that picking meant garbage picking, as in hauling couches and other perfectly good things off the curb on trash day. But Garden City was a strip mall.

Not long after they pulled into Garden City's parking lot and pulled behind one of the stores, he finally figured it out. A large, green dumpster sat beside a concrete wall. Pow climbed in first, followed by Dean and Nick. Jim found that by leaving the lot and climbing the road, he could get atop the wall which rose a few feet over the dumpster. Sitting down in the comparatively balmy fall night air, he wished he had a beer.

"Come on, Diffin," Dean shouted, tearing through some styrofoam.

"Yo, Diffin," Pow yelled over his shoulder. "Did I ever tell you Brian found a perfectly good VCR in this very dumpster?"

"Really?" he asked without getting up.

Nick stopped rummaging to stare at Jim for a moment before his face lit up and he hopped out of the dumpster. "Diffin gave me an idea!"

Nick left the lot and ran around to the top of the wall beside Jim and, without pause, flipped into the air, landing between Dean and Pow on a pile of styrofoam, packing peanuts and broken-down boxes. Once Dean and Pow saw this, they scrambled up and tried it, too.

Pow pulled himself free from a box. "Why don't you give it a go, homes?" he asked, looking up at Jim.

He rubbed the stubby hair on his scalp and stood. It seemed like these straight-edge adventures with Pow were crazier than his drunken ones. But he jumped off the wall anyway. He didn't try to flip, but dove into a stack of styrofoam next to Pow. After that, being inside a dumpster didn't seem so bad. There wasn't any rotten food or anything gross like he imagined. Other than the packing stuff, everything had once been for sale in a department store, but wound up in there because of some defect or broken part. Since nothing perfectly good had been thrown inside, they made a few more leaps before moving on to a fancy home furnishing store's dumpster. But it didn't have much in it, either.

"Man, slow night," Pow said, plucking a candelabra from beneath some broken cast-iron. Jim couldn't find anything, so they headed to the candle store's dumpster for Pow's fancy candle holder.

Jim jumped in first. "This is the first dumpster that ever smelled good," he said, digging through papers in search of broken candles. That dumpster was filled with dented, chipped, cracked or snapped candles of every size, color and scent. They found some that would fit Pow's candelabra and each took a few extra for themselves.

Pow dropped his candles beside his home furnishing find in Dean's trunk. "Let's check one more, homes."

On their way over to one of the other anchor stores, a cop car rolled up and followed them. Dean drove straight out of the lot. Jim asked why they didn't go to the next dumpster, and they told him that the cops harassed them for dumpster diving. Apparently, it wasn't legal.

Pow turned the radio down. "And I can't get into any trouble right now," he said.

Jim asked why, and they told him about Pow's recent arrest. Pow'd been hanging out the passenger window of Dean's car, cruising down Airport Road in Warwick with a paint-ball gun. They were having fun, messing with people they knew around Hoxy Four Corners, when they got pulled over, and Pow was arrested for brandishing a firearm. His court date was still upcoming.

"A firearm? A paint-ball gun?" Jim asked, chuckling.

"Yeah, no shit, right?" Nick said.

They laughed as Dean drove around. When the cop turned down a side street, they headed back for one last dumpster. This last one was tall, wide and full. He stood inside, elbow to elbow with Pow and chucked industrial-size garbage bags around, searching for anything eye-catching. Pow pulled open a garbage bag and dug through it. Jim shook his head; no way was he ready for that level of commitment.

"Whoa," Pow shouted. "Check this out, homes." He held up something shiny and cylindrical. Jim asked what it was, and Pow held up about two thirds of a once shrink-wrapped package of one hundred blank CDs.

Nick held up a set of dangly, plastic earrings. "Anybody want some jewelry?" he asked, pretending to model the set on his ear.

"Actually," Jim said. "I'll take those."

Nick and Dean squinted skeptically, but Jim strode over a few bags and snatched the earrings.

"Never know when a random gift'll be needed," he said, shrugging. He'd been thinking about getting Diana something for Christmas, maybe mailing her a gift, but he hadn't had motivation to go shopping. Earrings from a dumpster would be a start, something to make him go out and buy her more.

On the car ride back, Pow wound up in the back with Jim. Pow leaned over to nudge him. "You're not giving those to any of the girls you've been dating lately are you?" Pow asked.

Jim shrugged and looked out the window.

Pow handed him the stack of blank CDs. "Here," he said. "Your dad probably has a burner on his computer. I can't use these fucking things myself."

Jim thanked him and promised to burn him a bunch of his CDs.

"No sweat," Pow said. "But, homes, happiness doesn't come from trying to hold on to happiness."

Somehow Pow knew he was going to give the earrings to Diana and probably burn her a mixed CD, too; maybe Pow even guessed that he'd give her more still. Jim didn't really want to acknowledge it, though.

Instead, he decided to be a smart ass. "What does happiness come from then, my master?"

Pow laughed. "Nothing," he said.

PART IV

SPRING

"Everything changes, everything passes, things appearing, things disappearing. But when all is over—everything having appeared and having disappeared, being and extinction both transcended—still the basic emptiness and silence abides, and that is blissful peace."

— From Sanskrit Sources

30

Fragrant air swirled through the kitchen at Ginglow's End for the first time in months. Jim's hair had grown back; he needed a trim. Buds sprouted on trees in the backyard; birds flitted on branches again, and the grass reclaimed some of its green. A half-full bottle of Bacardi Limon waited on the counter. Jim packed a blender with ice, dumped in the rum, added sour mix and strawberries. As the machine revved up, it bucked and kicked the ice around a few times before biting in and chopping up the cubes.

A month ago, in February, he'd come home to his answering-machine light blinking. When he played it, Diana spoke, tentative and low. She didn't say a lot, except that she thought they needed to talk. Two months after the Christmas gifts he'd mailed her—the earrings, a mixed CD and polka-dot panties—he wondered what she could want. Her voice hadn't graced his ears since that day when she stormed out of the house, leaving her key behind. All the same, he didn't call her immediately. He hoped she wanted him back, but the prospect made him anxious.

Now he shut off the blender and tasted the daiquiri. It needed more strawberries, so he plucked the stems off of a half-dozen more and dropped them in, restarting the blades. The liquefied ice twisted into a whirlpool and sucked the red berries down one by one. He tasted it again, and this time it needed more sour mix.

As it turned out, he didn't need to call Diana. One day while his car was in the shop and Yeats was in class, he sat at home, doing school work, when he heard a car in the driveway. Peeking out the living room window, he saw a brown LeBaron and couldn't move. He waited in the kitchen for her knock at the door. Finally, he grew impatient and, biting his nails, he stepped outside.

Bent over on the far side of the garage, Diana had the loose flagstone on the ground and was picking up the hidden key. Her hair was darker, not bleached blonde any longer, more light brown. She hadn't seen him yet.

"Can I help you?" he asked, trying to hide his excitement.

Diana screamed and fell backward. "Holy shit, Jim," she said. "You scared the crap out of me." She wrung her hands. "I didn't think you were home since the driveway was empty."

"Car's in the shop," he said. "I put that key there, so my friends could make themselves at home if I was out." He liked feeling like he had her on the ropes for once, so he pushed it a little.

Diana picked up a small bag that she'd set down next to the brick wall. "I'm sorry, Jim," she said. "I wanted to leave this inside for you. Didn't think you'd mind if I let myself in so long as I..."

He couldn't resist any longer. She was still so

beautiful. He wanted to hold her close. "It's good to see you."

She smiled. "I missed you, Jim." She sauntered toward him. "I didn't think I would since you were such a cheating hornball." She laughed. "But we had fun, ya know?"

She gave him the bag, a rather belated Valentine's Day gift—a card and a Chieftains CD. He reminded her that they'd met on Valentine's, which she didn't realize. They hopped in the LeBaron with the top down and went for a drive, the cool March air singing in his ears and making Diana's hair dance behind her. After cruising the parkway, they sailed through the city, where clinking glasses and laughter poured from bars and restaurants and pedestrian traffic nonchalantly clogged Thayer Street. They sipped coffee at The Cable Car on South Main Street and talked. She'd liked the Christmas gifts, but it took her some time to admit that she missed him.

A few weeks after that day in the driveway, she asked if he'd like to go with her to a high school dance. After that, things seemed to go back to normal.

She busted his balls about being a cheater every once in a while; they still didn't have sex, but fooled around. He'd given her key away to Troy, but they went to a hardware store and made her a new copy. He went to her dance and, despite the lack of booze and being the oldest guy there, he had a good time.

Now, testing the daiquiri again, it was perfect, so he filled two glasses. In the living-room Diana sat on the couch, wearing a short, white skirt and a pink tank-top with her light-brown hair pulled into a ponytail. She'd kicked off her sandals and had her smooth legs up on the coffee table. He handed her the chilly cocktail, and before he sat down, they clinked glasses.

"To us," he said.

"To us."

She sipped her drink, smiling up at him, and he smiled down on her.

31

Boiling corned beef scented the kitchen, and the steam from the large pot filled the room with a thick, warm humidity. Jim dropped peeled potatoes into the water as Yeats left with Pow to buy more booze. Diana hadn't shown up yet. She hadn't even called. Whenever the phone rang, he ran at it, sure it would be her. This happened at least ten times, and every call brought with it only another confirmation from a friend.

A week earlier, he'd been to visit his grandmother at the nursing home. The walls, the floor, the curtains, everything white and lifeless—the place smelled shut up, stifled, leaking bodies mixed with medicines and generic, scentless air-deodorizers. Sitting beside his grandmother's bed depressed him more and more every time. The home seemed to break her spirit, wear down her mind, and often she called him William or Marty or even Henry (because Yeats visited her often). Even as her body wasted away, her skin hanging thinner and lower on each visit, she'd been his staunchest defender while he turned her old house into what his mother called a den of iniquity.

His grandmother's old neighbors on Ginglow Street had called her at the home before calling the police on him. She'd told them to leave her James alone. But after a few more parties, her lucidity waning, and his mother's siblings exerting pressure, Jim agreed not to have any more parties.

But St. Patrick's Day needed to be observed, so he decided to have a small dinner party—no more than a dozen people.

He cut the first head of cabbage, trying not to think of Diana. His shaking hands pushed the dull knife through the stem, forcing it all the way through to the wooden cutting board. He halved one side and a thought occurred to him. Maybe she'd emailed him. He dashed through the den and down the hall to his bedroom.

As he'd hoped, one new message in the mailbox from GODDESS339. He stared at the name for a moment, hesitant. As he read the brief letter, he breathed harder, faster.

Jim, I'm sorry, but I won't be able to make it. I couldn't get out of helping Mrs. Thorpe with the play. I know I promised, but other kids had to cancel plans, too, after she guilted us into staying. I know you're probably mad at me right now, but I didn't think it would be fair to let everybody here down.

~Diana

"What about letting me down?" He gritted his teeth. His heart rate rose. He balled his fists and paced the room. He wanted to smash something, to scream in her face, to beg, to plead, to ask why she tortured him.

How could she be so inconsiderate? Didn't she know

this holiday meant something? How could she not care? If she could've called. He could've asked her some things, maybe understood better, but this email bullshit struck him as disrespectful and mean.

His pacing took him on a tour of the house until the uncut cabbage stole his attention. Maybe a task would give him focus. His breathing came in shallow gasps, and his cutting became unsteady from the heaving. The knife slid clumsily through the second head of cabbage, and the room seemed to darken. A lightness took hold and he stumbled back. The knife's long blade glinted in the dying light. A falling sensation came over him, and his last thoughts were of that blade's shiny length.

Shining, gleaming in the sun, half-buried in sand, a huge bell, he needed to toll it. The hammer in his hand struck down, but the bell answered with a dull thud which would not do. Who would bury a bell in sand?

Next thing he knew, Pow and Yeats stood over him, and he felt like he'd been slapped. Yeats slapped him across the face. He swatted Yeats away. The knife lay across his chest.

"You all right?" Pow asked.

"I guess," he said, plucking the knife off his chest and sitting up.

Yeats pulled two six packs of Guinness extra stout from the brown liquor store bag. "What happened?" he asked.

He stood up, wondering the same thing. "I don't know. I was cutting the cabbage and hyperventilating over Diana..."

Pow eased himself into his grandfather's old place at the table. "Why?" he asked. "What's up with Diana, homes?"

Jim gripped the knife handle tighter, forgetting about his dream, or vision, or whatever. "She isn't coming."

Yeats took out a bottle of Skyy Vodka from the big brown bag. "She call just now?"

"Hell no," he said. "Evil bitch sent me a fucking email."

"That's cold," Yeats said.

He wondered if Yeats meant calling Diana an evil bitch was cold or if he meant her sending the email had been cold.

Pow pinched a braid from his forehead and twisted it. "Guess you passed out, homes," he said. "Good thing you fell back and not forward with that knife in your hand and all."

"Yeah," he said, wiping sweat from his face. "Whew. I gotta finish cutting."

Yeats snatched two shot glasses from the cupboard and cracked open the vodka. "Dude, no sweat," he said. "Calm down, have a fucking drink and forget about your women troubles. It's spring break!"

He placed the knife next to the halved and quartered cabbage heads. Holding the warm shot of vodka up to clink with Yeats, he paused. "Pow, you do one with us?" He added an encouraging nod, raising his glass.

"Nah, homes," Pow said, waving him away. "You know me."

"I had to ask."

"I know."

Yeats took over after that, holding up his glass. "To J.F.K."

"...And a dozen more besides!" Jim said, finishing the Pogues lyric. They downed their shots.

He set to work with renewed vigor, shooting warm vodka, cursing women and cooking dinner. He burnt himself dropping the cabbage into the steaming froth, but laughed and prescribed himself a hearty dosage of more vodka. By the time dinner guests arrived, he was sloshed. The rest of the night whirled past in a frenzy of eating, tentative food fights, an occasional boiled potato dunked, for no explicable reason, into a pint of Guinness and plenty of shots tossed back in the name of John Fitzgerald Kennedy.

The booze ran out; Yeats and Troy took him to a pub where Gräbe had introduced them to the owner, so they didn't get carded. They pounded car bombs, shots of whiskey, played darts, shot pool, cursed, sang and pushed each other around. Jim seemed to have forgotten Diana until the ride home. He sat alone in the back seat of Troy's car, Yeats riding shot-gun. The radio playing Big Bad Voodoo Daddy's "You and Me and the Bottle Makes Three Tonight," the buzz burning in his brain and the memory of Diana's email swirled together, sapping his spirits. His lower lip tightened and his eyes welled up. Before they got back to Ginglow's End, Jim degenerated into a blubbering emotional mess.

A few days later, recovered from St. Patrick's Day, he sat with Pow, Troy and Yeats in the living room watching reruns of *The Dukes of Hazzard*. Boss Hogg had Uncle Jesse locked up on some falsified charges, and the Duke boys were coming up with the perfect jailbreak scheme, when Yeats blurted out, "Canada."

Troy took a pull off a bottle of Bud. "What?"

Jim turned in his seat. "I don't think any of the Duke's are going to Canada, kid."

"Yeah, no shit, asshole. I'm saying we..." Yeats paused, erratically waving his hand back and forth as if to reinforce what he was saying. "We, all of us, go to Canada."

"Canada?" Pow asked as if Yeats had said, Mars. In Rhode Island nobody ever liked to drive very far. The state's tiny size, or maybe the proximity of things in New England might've been the reason, but in that region trips to the beach or the mountains—both mere hours away—were often made into vacations. People living in Providence rented beach houses an hour away in Charlestown. A day trip to the beach required a packed lunch and provisions, even if the beach was no farther than a half-hour drive. So, when Yeats suggested a trip to Canada, nobody considered the idea very seriously.

Yeats stood up to address the doubtful silence, when Jim interrupted. "Okay, Yeats," he said, sipping a beer. "Where the hell in your sick brain did this idea come from? The Dukes?"

"Yeah!" he said, his face lighting up. "Well, kinda. Hear me out here, all right? Diffin, you always want to throw theme parties, but nobody ever gets down with it, right?" Jim nodded and Yeats continued, "So, I'm sitting here thinking, 'wouldn't a *Dukes of Hazzard* theme party be phat.' But then I think maybe nobody'll be down with that and I think about a theme road trip!"

"A *Dukes of Hazzard* 'theme road trip' to Canada?" Jim asked, saying the words theme, road and trip extra slow.

"Oh hell, no. That would be wack," Yeats said waving away the idea.

Troy shifted forward in his seat. "Now you're making sense," he said. "But if not the Dukes, then what would the theme be?"

Yeats rubbed his elbow. "I was thinking of something less rated PG," he said. "And more..."

"Rated fuckin' X!" Pow shouted, laughing and pointing his finger for emphasis.

"Well, Pow," Yeats said with a slow nod. "I was going to say corrupted, but sure parts could be rated X."

"So?" Troy asked.

"Fear and Loathing in Canada," Yeats said, as if he'd proposed the perfect cure for cancer.

Ideas flew around the room, new ways of debauching themselves and all within the context of a foreign country had excitement dripping off everyone. Almost everyone, anyhow. Pow remained characteristically uninterested in pumping substances into his body. "I don't know about this whole theme road trip business, but I'm down with rockin' a new town on my break."

"Okay. How about this," Troy said. "How about Yeats, Diffin and I go up ahead of you."

"And while we're up there, we push the limits—Hunter S. Thompson style," Yeats said. "We'll figure out a place for you to meet up with us later and go from there,"

Suddenly, Pow jumped from his seat. "Yo, Troy," he said. "Shelby still at Lyndonville State?"

Yeats threw Jim a curious look, and he didn't know what to say. Eventually Troy and Pow explained that their friend Shelby went to school at Lyndonville State, a small state school in New Hampshire which was basically the last stop before Canada. Since the town was so lame, the students drove the few hours up to Montreal all the time. They'd ask Shelby about a good place for Pow and anyone else to meet with Yeats, Troy and him after they'd rocked the town Hunter S. Thompson style.

They agreed to make the trip happen. But first, they finished watching the Dukes.

32

Heat clogged the air in the car, and the radio played oldies at a reasonable volume. Outside, pollen circulated through the cool March air. His father drove with his eyes never straying from the road. After half an hour of driving on state and country highways, the car pulled into an apartment complex and parked to the left of the lot's entrance.

His father finally looked at him. "You feeling strong today?" he asked.

Jim nodded and they climbed from the car and walked toward the long, low apartment building. His father led him to a blue door facing the main road. Inside the apartment, nothing hung on the walls, no mirrors, no pictures, no art or decorations of any kind. The place looked and smelled clean with three boxes lined neatly by the hallway, a few empty soda cans stacked on the glass kitchen table, a television in the living room with no couch or any other chairs and beside it a computer on a plain wooden table.

Earlier that day he'd visited his mother, and she'd

asked him for a favor. His dad was coming back home and needed help moving some of his stuff. Jim hadn't been sure he could do that; it'd be so uncomfortable, but for the sake of his mother and his family, he agreed. When his father stepped through the door, all he said was, "James, want to go for a ride?"

Jim understood that his father would never explicitly ask him for help. That was why his mother asked. Nobody in the family liked to talk about unpleasant things. Instead, they always used his mother as the go-between.

Wiping his glasses with a handkerchief, his father looked around. "I'll take down the computer if you'll bring the boxes out to the car," he said, handing Jim the keys.

All three boxes were rather light and fit easily in the trunk of his father's suped-up Celica. The television was large and awkward to carry. His father thought Jim would drop it and stood up to help; it fit perfectly in the back seat. After that, the computer was ready to be taken out; piece by piece he carried it to the car, the monitor, the central processing unit, the printer, the cords, the speakers, all of it. His father took out the empty soda cans.

As they climbed into the car and closed the doors, his father yelled at him for closing the door too hard. Jim stared out the window. It seemed his father's mid-life fling with destruction hadn't changed his temperament.

Somewhere in the middle of the long drive home, without taking his eyes off the road, his father said, "That wasn't so bad was it." And before Jim could respond he added, "I'll need you to help me unload the car, too."

Back home, after unloading the car, lugging the boxes down to the basement, the television to his parents' room, the computer to his brother's room, his father looked at him and said, "Thanks, Jim. I really couldn't have done it without you."

Jim wondered if he meant more than carrying the boxes. Did he know how many times Jim's mother had cried on his shoulder? Did he know how much or how soon Jim knew about any of this? At least he'd thanked him.

His mother insisted that he stay for dinner. She cleared and cleaned the table and prepared dinner: roast beef, gravy, baked potatoes and broccoli. At dinnertime, his father lurched from his beer and television-induced stupor, then pulled up his regular chair at the table. Once all three of them sat down, his mother crossed herself and offered an uncharacteristic preamble prayer to grace. She thanked God for having her family together with a special blessing for the absent William whom she hoped God watched over, then she rambled into the usual: Bless-us-oh-Lord-for-these-thy-gifts-which-we-are-about-to-receive-from-thy-bounty-through-Christ-our-Lord. Amen.

They ate a quiet meal beneath the ceiling fan, and when his father finished, he left his plate on the table, excusing himself to sit before the television again. How long would his father's return last? Would his mother wonder why she ever wanted him back, or could things eventually change? After he ate, Jim helped clear the table and rinsed the dishes before putting on the kettle.

He and his mother drank their tea in the living room, so his father wouldn't get paranoid thinking they were talking about him, which meant they didn't talk at all. His father drank beer while, in an awkward silence, they watched news about the President's infidelity.

Before Jim left, he ducked into the basement to bring up some laundry. His mother's arthritic knees were acting up, again. He pulled balled-up whites from the long-cooled drier and, as he was searching the dark recesses to make sure he hadn't lost any wayward socks, he heard someone at the foot of the steps.

His father steadied himself with the railing in one hand and a beer in the other. Jim tried to sound casual. "Hey, dad. What's up?"

His father careened over to stop beside the drier, placing his beer down amid the stray lint and spare change. "I know we haven't always gotten along," he slurred, drops of spit landing on Jim's face.

Jim shrugged, dropping a sock into the laundry basket.

No, they'd never gotten along. Even when he was young, Jim remembered grating under his father's ideas of discipline. He'd always been too wild and energetic a kid to deal with the old notions of "children should be seen and not heard," which his father firmly believed in.

"Jim, I think I know why, too," he said, resting a hand on Jim's shoulder.

He wanted to say, because you're a hard-assed, selfish jerk. Instead, he stood still, wondering what his dad had in mind.

Leaning in closer, spitting and slurring with a smile, he said, "It's because we're so alike, Jim. Too alike really."

Oh, hell no. People had been saying how he and his father were the same since he was a kid, wearing thick-lensed glasses like his dad's. So because they both had bad eyes, it seemed that people thought they were the same. Their noses were different, his small, his father's large and pointy; their eyes were different, his green, his father's blue; and Jim could never be as uptight as his dad. Now he stood in the musty, cobweb-laden basement with his buzzed father whose theory about their disagreements hinged on this assumption that they were the same. If his father had influenced him at all, it was as an example of how not to be. Of course, he couldn't say anything like that. His father swayed gently before him, one hand still resting on Jim's shoulder.

"I know, dad," he said, not knowing what else to say.

His father hugged him and Jim squeezed back, feeling his dad's warm, bony spine under his palms. Jim started to pull back to get it over with, but his father didn't let go right away. When his father finally released him, Jim's scruffy cheek brushed against his father's scruffy cheek. Once his father climbed the steps, he searched in the drier one more time for lost socks.

33

At the Canadian border, an officer leaned into the Eclipse. "Are you boys carrying anything in your vehicle today other than your clothes?"

Jim hadn't slept the night before and after almost falling asleep at the wheel in Northern New Hampshire, he'd let Troy drive. After that, Troy gave him some vicadens to pop.

Jim's-doped up mind reeled through an inventory of random oddities. He stared at his glove box thinking: napkins in there, maybe some empty wrappers, my owner's manual, some gum perhaps... He glanced down, unsure of what might be hidden beneath his sweatshirt or under the car seat for that matter. Then he remembered all the drugs and alcohol, the Canadian money in his pocket, the empty fast food cups and straws in back, the spare tire—in a matter of moments, Jim inventoried everything in the car and couldn't figure how to answer the officer's question.

The border guard, probably looking to break up his routine, gave up his creative line of questioning and went back to the more traditional line. "Are you boys carrying any illegal drugs, alcohol or weapons of any kind?"

"No, sir," Troy answered from behind the steering wheel. Jim and Yeats shook their heads.

"No brass knuckles, no air rifles, no switch blades, nunchucks, or any sort of clubs?"

Again, they shook their heads. The gate lifted and they were in.

A few miles down the road, Yeats leaned forward to tap Jim's shoulder. "Dude, I was real stuck on that first question."

Jim laughed. "Yeah, me too!"

"I know with all the illegal crap we have!" Troy said.

"Nah," Yeats mumbled. "I was thinking about the candy in my pocket and my keys and my wallet or maybe even my toothbrush."

A few hours later, they arrived in Montreal. They settled into the hotel on St. Catherine Street and consulted the concierge about dinner options. Following his advice for cheap food, they hiked around the corner and ate sandwiches and drank Molson pitchers. On the way home, Yeats asked how they planned on eating the 'shrooms. They'd been in Yeats's book bag for weeks, then smuggled across the border inside Jim's shoe and now resembled pencil shavings. Trying to eat them might do nothing more than gunk up their teeth.

Troy suggested they eat them in something. When Yeats asked what they could put them in, Jim, unable to form a sentence, simply shouted, "soup." With the same excitement, Yeats blurted out how he loved soup at Chinese places. Troy started to ask where they'd ever find a Chinese restaurant in Montreal, when Jim laughed hysterically.

Pointing two doors down, Jim shouted, "There's one now!"

They stumbled and careened down the sidewalk, entering the restaurant like crazed lunatics. Inside, immaculate white tablecloths draped over rows and rows of tables set with shiny silverware and origami cloth napkins. Since it was between the lunch and dinner rushes, people ate at only two or three tables. A chandelier dominated the ceiling.

"Can I help you?" asked a quickly advancing, Chinese woman. Jim got the distinct impression this woman not only intended to provide prompt service, but hoped to bar their entrance and expedite their exit.

"Soup!" Jim said a little too loudly. The woman handed them each clean, fine menus, not paper copies. They pored over the selections and bought bowls of soup to go.

Back in Jim's room, on the high, white ceiling, pipes snaked in every direction, and a ceiling fan nestled in the midst of them. One solitary, twin bed rested in the middle, and opposite that, pushed to the wall, was a bureau, where Jim dumped out the mushrooms There was no television, and the bathroom was down the hall.

While Yeats pulled out his license and divided the crumbs into three equal piles, Troy rattled off a list of their Fear and Loathing in Canada stash: half a bottle of vicodin, several two-inch long marijuana buds, a pint of G.H.B., a plastic jug of vodka, the 'shrooms and the twelve pack they'd bought from the liquor store downstairs. Nothing to raise a Gonzo journalist's eyebrows, but it would do for them.

Yeats finished separating the 'shrooms, and they added the fungal ingredient to their soups, scarfing down the concoction after some quick mixing swirls.

"Now what?" Troy asked.

"We wait," Yeats said.

The three of them wandered into the hallway where the hotel staff had placed a couch on the wide landing, creating the sense of a communal living room for the floor. They made themselves comfortable on the couch and waited. Sitting on the end closest to his room, Jim felt gripped by nausea. Maybe he'd eaten too much, or too fast, maybe he hadn't slept enough, or drank too much. Whatever it was, he didn't like it.

He tilted his head toward Yeats and Troy. "I don't feel well."

"What?" Yeats asked. "You can't bail out now. The night is about to get going!"

"I know." He tried to shake off his dizziness. "Maybe I need to lie down for a little bit. Then I'll be ready to rock."

"I don't know if that's a good idea," Yeats said, putting his feet up on the dark wood coffee table.

"Come wake me up when the drugs hit you."

He shuffled to his room. Inside, he lay face down with the light out and listened to the ceiling fan. It whirled with a buzzing sound, a wzz, wzz, wzz, wzz, and he could almost see it from its sound, its vibration; it spun with intense energy. The spinning vibration of the fan affected him so much that he became the fan. He hovered above the room, spinning and buzzing and humming with vigor and gusto. Happiness filled him at the thought of being a fan. In the distance a riotous sound echoed, maybe from the hallway, but he barely registered these sounds as belonging to anything he knew, or to anything he felt important. Ceiling fans don't care about noises in hallways.

Then an explosion blasted open and through the door. Light and noise filled the room. A weight crashed upon him, dragging him from the ceiling and driving him into the bed. In a whirlwind, Troy and Yeats ran about the cramped room. Jim sat up and, before he could help himself, he flew about the room in the same whipped-up frenzy. No longer a fan, he was a tornado; they were a tornado.

Then it was over; Jim slumped at the open window, hanging halfway outside. Hotel towels hung from the pipes, from the mirror, lay under the bureau and all over the hardwood floor. Bed sheets were torn back and crumpled together. Troy lay next to the bureau, somehow wrapped around a pole with a fan mounted on it, the fan half-broken. In a corner, Yeats sat with a towel on his head.

Yeats glanced around, dazed. "What the fuck!" he said, yanking the towel from his face. "What are we Lynryd fucking Skynyrd or something?"

"I don't know," Jim said. "But we gotta get outta here before we spend our first night in Montreal tripping balls in a hotel room,"

"Yeah," Yeats said, struggling to his feet. "I was afraid of that when I brought them."

Bounding down the stairs like children, they were soon outside where night had fallen. They meandered up the street, heading to the city's center. "Don't worry, Jim" Yeats said. "When mushrooms first hit, it's a total rush, like jumping into a freezing pool or the pond on a cold morning. When you first plunge into the water, your body's shocked, the system's jolted." A homeless man with a thick Quebecois accent asked them for money, but not having any cash on him, Jim couldn't do more than shrug. Yeats continued, "Simply moving can be hard, but the best way to warm up and get used to the water is to move around."

Jim nodded, feeling tingly all over despite the cold night air.

Yeats slung an arm on Jim's shoulder. "In a few minutes, the initial shock ends," Yeats explained, stretching his other arm out. "And then you can enjoy your new environment, explore, swim—delve deep toward the bottom, moving through the water in directions not normally allowed because of gravity."

As the first jolt passed, Jim felt ready to explore. The jeweled neon lights of St. Catherine Street assaulted his new senses, each bright color feeling like conflicting emotions. Saint Catherine, herself, rolled in her grave every day and night because such a dirty, dirty, sexed-up, boozed-out, sinful, sinful street had been named after her. Strip clubs, dance halls, sex shops, packed pubs, pimps and their girls graced the *rue* as it ran through downtown.

The first challenge of crossing the street eventually overcome, they tweaked and twitched their way into the center of town. Passing a movie theater, Jim tripped over his feet and fell. He rolled on the ground and lay flat on his back, looking up at the bottom of a mirrored marquee.

"Hey," he said, not moving. "Check this out."

Looking up at the mirror, they didn't seem to understand, so Jim convinced them to lay down beside him. It looked like Yeats and Troy stood on either side of him.

"So what?" Troy said.

Jim tried to explain but no words came. At first, it seemed like more of a feeling he'd hoped they'd get. But then Pow came to his mind. "It reminds me of the kind of shit Pow's always babbling about."

They still didn't understand, so he tried to explain. "Emptiness. He said something about being mirrors to each other, or to the world, not leaving any traces for prejudices, or something. Like this mirror is blank, but everything in the world finds a place inside it. By being empty, it becomes filled."

Yeats rolled to his feet. "Your fucking head is empty, Diffin."

Troy rose, too, and they both stalked off. Jim lay, lingering under the mirror. His body shook and jerked; clouds of steam surrounded his head, and a dull pain tore through his limbs. Yeats walked back into the mirror and helped him to his feet.

"Sit still too long and you're going to freeze to death, Diffin."

The maitre'd of Club Super Sexe towered over them, wearing a flashy black suit with a little red rose on his lapel. He raised an inquiring, blond eyebrow—even though he had brown hair—at Jim and his friends. "Party of three?"

Yeats spoke up, "Yes, please."

As the man turned, his other eye-brow came into view. It matched the hair on his head.

"Did you guys see that dude's eyebrows?" Jim asked once they were seated.

"Yeah, that was fuckin' freaky," Yeats laughed. "I thought my eyes were messing with me."

A waitress swooped in and told them about the club's one-drink-minimum. He tried to communicate with his friends through facial gestures, eyebrows lowered, raised, lips curling and flattening, eyes darting in a frenzy. Did they want alcohol or not?

When he thought they'd reached a silent consensus, he straightened his face. "Coke, please," Jim and Yeats said in unison.

Troy nodded.

The waitress stormed off and brought them their non-alcoholic drinks.

Shifting, flashing lights of every color danced around

the room and across the ceiling. For a moment, he danced with the lights, warm and pleasant, before realizing how truly cozy he was. A leggy, busty, brunette undulated down on the stage, slowly unclasping her top.

"Hey, guys," Jim blurted. "You know what's cool about this. We were about to freeze to death outside and now we're warming up in a strip club filled with sexy naked ladies." Jim pinched his drink's swizzle stick, then slid it into his mouth. A strange impulse to gnaw seized him.

"Damn straight," Troy said, his face oozing toward the stage.

Yeats rolled his eyes. "Why is that so cool?"

He pulled the stick from his mouth and waved it vaguely. "Well, it's... can't you feel the Eros in the room. It's as if the warmth in here is bringing us farther from the death of the dirty, freezing street, and the reproductive energies saturating this room parallel our recovery."

"Yeah, that's a good point," Yeats said, nodding. "Here we've got bouncing titties and plenty of warmth."

"Yeah," Troy said. "And there's all these flashy lights, too."

Jim twisted the stirrer between his teeth and frowned at Yeats who grimaced back.

He couldn't tell whether Troy was ogling the dancer or following the lights around the room. Jim, himself, concentrated on the lights. He was conscious of the dancer on the stage and vaguely of her nudity, but that interested him far less than the light show.

Finally, inside a strip club, and he didn't even care for the dancing girl. All he wanted to watch were the lights and the other patrons. Old business men, still in business suits, yuppies, geriatric couples, middle-aged couples, couples of every age, young men like Jim and his friends and people of every class filled the club.

Not that he completely ignored the naked woman. Her sultry routine genuinely impressed him with its fluidity and acrobatic deftness.

Troy went to the bathroom, and Jim leaned over the table. "Dude, do you get the feeling that Troy isn't really with us on this trip?" Jim asked, before jabbing the swizzle stick back into his mouth.

Yeats rolled a straw between his fingers. "Yeah," he said. "Like he's kinda following us rather than having his own trip."

Jim sighed. "I don't think I really like him so much tonight. Maybe I never really liked him, but I didn't notice 'til now. Like it took the drugs to exaggerate his personality enough for me to notice."

Yeats leaned away from Jim. "Ya think?"

"I don't know," he said. "It's like all people are either suns or moons. Like you and I have our own thing going. We don't follow society or even each other really, but people like Troy are moons."

"Moons, huh?"

Down on the stage the girl used her cartoonishly swollen breasts to pick up two-dollar coins from men's mouths.

"Yeah, they don't have light of their own to shed. So, they reflect the light of those around them or of the default light, the light from the dark sun of society."

The dancer rubbed her naked crotch in some businessman's face. Was that even legal?

"Huh. I get it. So, you and I are suns with our own light, our own style to project and Troy is a moon?" The music seemed to get louder. Yeats leaned closer. "So, what's Diana?"

Sun. Of course, right? What made her a sun though?

He couldn't think straight; what if he'd been following a moon around all this time? Blinded by her smile and strength. Before Jim could respond, Troy sat back down.

"What're you guys talking about," Troy asked, a goofy grin on his face. Jim didn't really want to discuss his crazy, unflattering theory with Troy.

"Nothing," Yeats said, sipping his watered-down soda. "An idea The Diff came up with,"

Jim's eyes opened wide as Troy waited to hear it. He explained tentatively. Once Jim ran through it again, Yeats scratched his head. "Are we born one way or another?"

Jim pointed with the swizzle stick. "Maybe. But I think I was born a sun who tried to be a moon. I think that's why I had such a hard time fitting in as a kid. I didn't know I had my own light to shed. But as it turns out, a sun isn't very good at reflecting light and a true sun can't change its own light to match that of anyone else." Was Diana reflecting Helen? Or was Helen trying to reflect Diana? No. Helen clearly revolved around the dark sun, society.

"So, a moon, or someone acting as a moon can become a sun. But can a sun become a moon?" Yeats asked, finishing his soda.

Jim needed to contemplate that one. His molars ground down on the stick. "I don't think so," he said, finally. "Maybe some personal tragedy could put a sun into a shock deep enough that it'd change. But I can't imagine such a thing happening."

Yeats nodded silently. "What do you think of Diffin's theory?"

"I don't know, man," Troy said, arms across his chest. "I don't really like it. I mean, I see where you're coming from, but it needs work."

Jim nodded. "Well," he said. "Just a drug-induced

idea." He thought Troy knew deep down that he was a moon, perhaps the moon they were talking about.

Another girl slinked on stage, kissing the other one. Then they tumbled in tandem, wrestled, writhing, giving each other oral sex on the stage from sitting and standing positions. It never occurred to Jim this stuff ever happened in strip clubs. Strangely, probably from the drugs, it didn't arouse him. Finally, one girl clung to the middle of the pole, extending her body at a rigid right angle, presenting her crotch to the other. It did impress him, though. Who knew this stuff was even possible?

Somehow Jim and Yeats started communicating on some sub-linguistic level, using nothing but proxemics, gestures and facial expressions. So, when the waitress came by insisting they had stayed too long and needed to buy another drink, they silently decided to take off. Troy followed.

They wandered St. Catherine Street, first heading for another strip club, but as Troy neared the threshold, they made eye-contact and changed their minds. Nearing Peel Pub where the line snaked around the block, they shared another glance and veered off course again, briefly leaving Troy alone in line.

After a minute, Troy dashed ahead and jogged backward wanting to know where they were going. Jim shrugged. They seemed to be wandering aimlessly. Some kids shouted something behind them. Expecting a fight, Jim turned to see a bunch of guys break into song outside a pub. None of them sang in time, so he couldn't make out what they sang.

When he turned around, Troy had disappeared. Looking at Yeats, he learned that Yeats hadn't seen Troy split either.

The closest storefront was a cafe, so they popped

inside. One man sat at the counter, leaning over a cup of coffee. His thin gray hair flowed long and draped over his collar. He had a scruffy beard and wore a red flannel jacket and blue jeans. He looked up from his coffee, nodded at them and asked in a thick French-Canadian accent, "Mushrooms?"

Jim and Yeats stood shoulder to shoulder, their mouths hanging open, considering the impossibly intuitive man. The old man, thinking they hadn't heard him, spoke again, "Mushrooms?"

"Wha... What?" Jim whispered.

He and Yeats snapped into a huddle. "Did you hear that?" he asked with his face.

"He said mushrooms!" Yeats said aloud. "How the hell does he know?"

They turned back to the now very puzzled Quebecois without saying anything. The old man patiently repeated himself, "Mushrooms, you friend. He in da rushroom?"

"Oh," Jim realized. "Yes, our friend. We're waiting for him to come out of the restroom."

No sooner had Troy emerged, than they stepped back into the street, once more in silent hunting mode. A few blocks off the main drag, they realized what they'd been looking for. Murphy's Irish Pub stared them in the face with a neon shamrock glowing green in the window, and dark, polished wood interiors invited them to sit and drink, to come down from their trip in a comfortable atmosphere.

After eight perfect pints of stout, Jim could no longer ignore his bladder's call for the bathroom. But once he descended the stairs and passed the phone, his bowels sent a clear message, demanding attention, too. The air inside the grimy stall vibrated with the sounds of chairs moving above, someone slamming a paper-towel dispenser nearby and an ambient humming.

The air embraced every inch of his flesh, the same air, he considered, surrounding the stall door. By extension, he actually touched the stall door and the sinks beyond, the stairwell, too, even his friends and all the people and things of the world. Everything connected; emptiness was actually full; up was raised by down; left defined by right. Nothing existed outside of now. Clearly, he hadn't come all the way down from the mushrooms.

He went upstairs, and they closed out the pub. They stumbled back toward the hotel, stopping for hot-dogs, cheese fries and water. Jim didn't actually remember going to bed.

The next morning, he showered, changed and woke up Troy and Yeats. They spent the afternoon drinking an entire case of warm beer and smoking Cubans. Afterwards, they went out to meet up with Pow, Shelby and anyone else who'd traveled with them. He couldn't wait to see what Pow would make of the strip clubs. By the time they arrived at Super Sexe, it was five-thirty p.m. They weren't supposed to meet up with Pow until ten. So, they decided to check out a smaller strip joint they'd passed up the night before. They paid, got their hands stamped and this time ordered alcoholic drinks, watched the strippers and even had a few lap dances.

At nine, they arrived at Super Sexe, and the host gave them decent seats. They scanned the crowd for Pow, in case he came early, too, but they didn't see him. Jim, totally trashed, decided after a while to get a better look at the second stage where the girls teased each other with a purple dildo. After standing, gaping at the girls until his legs grew tired, he stumbled back through the thick throng toward his friends. On his way, a thin, red-headed stripper leaned over a booth-table, trying to sell lap-dances. Weaving through the packed crowd, Jim tried to reach behind him, between people and cop a feel of the girl's exposed butt-cheek. He didn't think she'd ever know who'd done it.

No sooner had he touched her warm flesh, than something pushed him. Turning around, boobs bounced left to right, and the red-head screamed at him. Still stumbling, he looked over his shoulder to avoid tripping on a chair; he still thought he could avoid an embarrassing scene. When he looked around at the stripper to claim innocence, a fist greeted him. He staggered back, again trying not to trip. Raising his head, bare breasts danced before him, and then another punch drove into his face. By now, two six and a half foot tall men in suits had arrived.

Taken out back, beaten to a pulp, left for dead in a freezing cold Montreal alley—instead, the bouncers gently guided him by the arms. It seemed as if they thought being beaten up by a stripper in front of everyone was punishment enough. He tried to tell them that he needed to grab his friends, but they didn't listen. He waved toward his friends, shouting over the music, but they seemed not to see or hear him.

Jim stood alone on the cold street, wondering what to do next. It was nine-thirty. He really wanted to talk to Pow about his trip from the night before; now, it didn't seem like he'd see Pow in Canada. He could freeze to death if he waited outside the club for Pow to show up. Especially since Pow was often late. Jim sat on the curb and weighed his options.

Eventually, Troy and Yeats came up from behind him. Apparently, they witnessed the entire fiasco, but needed to decide whether or not to leave the club because of Jim. Jim thanked them for not abandoning him, and when they remembered the stamps on their hands, they returned to the club from earlier in the night

Once inside, they bought more lap dances, and Troy tried to humiliate Jim by telling a stripper what he'd done at Super Sexe. The slender girl with short, dark hair smiled. She grasped Jim's hand, put it on her ass and jiggled it. She laughed, saying she couldn't understand why a girl would be upset by Jim touching her anywhere. Then she took him to the V.I.P. room and gave him a free lap dance. She wouldn't go back to the hotel room with him, though.

The next morning, they finished their spring break by cleaning seven inches of snow from the Eclipse before hitting the road. On the way home, Troy drove again while Yeats snapped pictures of the New Hampshire crags, including the Old Man in the Mountain. Jim jotted down some of his impressions of the weekend. He wasn't so sure the astrological theory of personalities made sense anymore, but he wrote it out anyway to think about later. What really interested him was his experience in the pub bathroom. For a moment he thought he'd understood Pow's stupid nonsense, even the shit with the whistle and the swans. But when he tried to put it into words, his pen failed.

34

The week before Easter, Jim sat in the pews on the left side of the church with his brother William and his cousins from the Cape. The priest stood before the altar and talked about going to heaven while his grandmother lay in her casket up front. She'd died a few days before, his mother by her side. His grandmother had been sick for so long that nothing about her death shocked him. He felt guilty that he wasn't sadder. But more than anything, he felt relieved she no longer suffered. He'd miss her, but at least he'd spent plenty of time with her over the years. As a kid, if none of his friends were home, he'd pedal his bike the half-mile to visit her.

Now, as the priest droned on about the afterlife, tears welled in Jim's eyes, then streamed down his face. He'd planned on being stoic. All around the church, most people attending the funeral service appeared as if this were a regular mass. He wiped his tears on his sport-coat sleeve.

Jim, William and their cousins were pallbearers, and

when the mass ended, they took up the coffin. He marched in front and held his head high, but couldn't stop more tears from streaking his face. It upset him that friends and family—even his father standing beside his mother—probably pitied him.

Afterwards, the family went back to Ginglow's End, but now the house had been decorated the way it had been before Jim moved in. Family Jim never saw poked around, mingling with more familiar relatives, sitting in arm-chairs, snacking on chips and dip and drinking beer and wine. The place ceased being Ginglow's End and again became his grandmother's house, a social hub one last time. Somehow this resurrection seemed strange now that his grandmother was dead. His bedroom and Yeats's remained the same, but his mother, aunt and uncle had made clear that Yeats would move out as soon as he could find a place to live. Jim, on the other hand, could stay on while they sold the house, the real estate agent having told them that lived-in houses were easier to sell than empty ones.

The reception remained tame, people rarely chuckling over a story. Though most of the tales were about his grandfather, or about his grandparents together. Yeats was the one friend of his who came. Not that his family would've wanted to see Pow and his braids, or any of Jim's other friends, but it would've been nice if Diana had shown up. Since Jim came home from Canada, she hadn't returned any of his calls—Diana being Diana, not using the phone. She didn't even know that his grandmother had died.

Weeks later, Jim sat alone in his grandmother's kitchen, studying for upcoming finals. Yeats had moved into an apartment with Troy on the East Side of Providence, off North Main Street. He'd talked to Diana once since the funeral. She said she was sorry about his grandmother and felt bad she hadn't been there for him. But he still hadn't seen her. She always seemed too busy driving Nina around, working extra hours at the pizza place, or taking care of her horse.

Thinking about this made it hard to study. He tried to concentrate, but kept watching the clock's hands, waiting for them to come around when Diana got out of school. He needed to talk to her. When the time finally came, he took a deep breath and picked up the phone from his grandfather's mahogany desk. Tentatively, he pushed the seven digits. His sweaty hands trembled and the phone rang.

"Hello?" It was Nina.

He asked her if Diana was home, and she said she thought so. The phone got slimy under his grip. What did he want to say exactly? He meandered into the living room with the phone and sat down.

"Hello?" Diana said.

"Diana. It's Jim," he said, wiping his palm on his shirt.

"I know," she said, letting out a chuckle. "What's up?"

Jim tugged on his eyebrow, rubbed his forehead and sighed. "I feel like this isn't really working out," he said. "I'm way more interested in you than you'll ever be in me despite what you say."

A pause, no response.

He pushed on. "It hurts too much." Unable to sit still any longer, he stood up and paced in front of the big desk. "I think we should call it off. I hope we can still be friends," he said. Did he care to be friends with her? Wouldn't it hurt to see her and not kiss her, not hug her, or to know she was seeing someone else?

"Everything's been so good, Jim," she said. "Why end it now, after everything?"

Good question. But she couldn't shake his resolve. He wished he could say something mean. "Call me when you can love me," he said and hung up.

Waiting by the phone for a minute or two, he hoped she'd call back and say she loved him. The phone didn't ring and he knew it never would.

He wandered into the kitchen and mechanically lit the burner under his kettle. He busied himself with clearing the kitchen table of dirty silverware and motley papers, then with getting the sugar bowl ready, putting the teabag in his usual mug and trying to reread an old essay he'd written, waiting to be revised for the semester's final portfolio.

The kettle finally whistled; he tossed the paper on a nearby chair and poured his tea. He let it steep, put in the sugar, the milk... There was no milk.

Sighing, he closed the refrigerator door.

Outside the fresh air of early spring, not quite choked off by the ominous clouds above, struck him with wonderful promise for another beautiful summer at Camp Waetabee. He pulled his hand out of his pocket, letting go of his car keys. He walked down the driveway and headed on foot for the corner store.

Moments later, he passed loitering high school kids, hanging out, perhaps waiting for the junior high bus to drop off their younger buddies or siblings. Jim bought his whole milk and took his change from the paunchy Indian man behind the counter. As the door closed behind him, a thunder clap crackled and it poured.

Jim smiled as the high school kids ran toward him, seeking the shelter of the store's awning. The birds lining the power lines scattered, diving for cover. As he crossed the small lot, the school bus rolled up. Little boys and girls holding books or umbrella's over their heads scurried in all directions. A few ran to the awning.

Jim kept smiling, kept strolling through the chilly downpour. He held the plastic bag with the milk in his right hand, tilted his head back and imagined the shower cleansing him of the slight sweat he'd worked up.

Shivering children bolted past, heading for the dry warmth of their homes. He shivered a bit, too, but relished it in a way. A warm summer lay ahead with polleny perfumes and lush green leaves swaying. This dark, rainy day would make the June sky brighter; the warmth, warmer; the trees, the fields and all life much greener. The drowning, life-giving rain sheeted down and streamed along the curb and gushed into gutters where it tugged at twigs and swept away dust, detritus and car exhaust.

He laughed amid it all.

ACKNOWLEDGEMENTS

Special thanks to Joanne Meschery for all her guidance and clear incisive advice on writing in general and this book in particular. I also want to thank Dr. Sherry Little for her care, attention and praise of the earliest drafts of this book, and to Dr. Howard Mueller for his insight and wisdom. To all my friends and family who believed in me, I'm especially grateful. And to everyone who encouraged me and enabled me to keep the dream alive like Brendan, Sunshine, Byron, Ryan C., Jack G & Jack S., P.J., John L., Jon S., Amy, Amanda O., Abbie, my brother Pete, and so many more. And to Jess G. And an especially hearty thanks to Miette Gillette and Whiskey Tit for seeing the art and soul I poured into this book and allowing me to share it.

ABOUT THE AUTHOR

Mathew Michael Hodges lives and writes in Providence, RI. His fiction has been published by a variety of literary journals from academically affiliated to independent arts publications, both online and in print. He earned his MFA from San Diego State University and has taught writing and Literature at Dean College, The Community College of Rhode Island, Bristol Community College, and Roger Williams University.

ABOUT THE PUBLISHER

Whisk(e)y Tit is committed to restoring degradation and degeneracy to the literary arts. We work with authors who are unwilling to sacrifice intellectual rigor, unrelenting playfulness, and visual beauty in our literary pursuits, often leading to texts that would otherwise be abandoned in today's largely homogenized literary landscape. In a world governed by idiocy, our commitment to these principles is an act of civil service and civil disobedience alike.